Robert Williams Buchanan, Roden Noel

Poems of the Honorable Roden Noel

A Selection

Robert Williams Buchanan, Roden Noel

Poems of the Honorable Roden Noel
A Selection

ISBN/EAN: 9783337407001

Printed in Europe, USA, Canada, Australia, Japan

Cover: Foto ©Andreas Hilbeck / pixelio.de

More available books at **www.hansebooks.com**

The Canterbury Poets.

EDITED BY WILLIAM SHARP.

POEMS OF

THE HON. RODEN NOEL.

₊₊ FOR FULL LIST OF THE VOLUMES IN THIS SERIES. SEE CATALOGUE AT END OF BOOK.

WORKS BY THE HON. RODEN NOEL.

Crown 8vo, Price 6s.

SONGS OF THE HEIGHTS AND DEEPS.

Small Crown 8vo, Cloth, 3s. 6d.

A LITTLE CHILD'S MONUMENT.

Small Crown 8vo, 6s.

THE HOUSE OF RAVENSBURG.

Foolscap 8vo, Cloth, 7s.

BEATRICE, AND OTHER POEMS.

Small 8vo, Cloth, 6s.

THE RED FLAG, AND OTHER POEMS.

Demy 8vo, Cloth, 5s.

ESSAYS ON POETRY AND POETS.

London : WALTER SCOTT, LIMITED, 24 Warwick Lane.

POEMS OF THE HON. RODEN NOEL. A SELECTION. WITH AN INTRODUCTION BY ROBERT BUCHANAN.

LONDON:

WALTER SCOTT, LIMITED,

24 WARWICK LANE.

NEW YORK: 3 EAST FOURTEENTH STREET.

CONTENTS.

Lyrics.

CONTENTS.

Mystical Poems of Nature.

Poems of the People.

Poems of Human Beauty.

𝔑arrative, 𝔇ramatic, and 𝔇escriptive.

𝔑eflective, 𝔓hilosophical, and 𝔄llegory.

CONTENTS.

Elegiac.

PREFATORY NOTICE.

————•●•————

IT is something, in this age of disillusion, when the Poet
is a well-bred gentleman on easy terms of relationship
with his publisher and his banker, to have come across
one who wears, in good Hellenic fashion, the loose singing robes of Apollo, who sings for singing's sake, and
who is comparatively indifferent to the praise or blame of
coterie critics and literary cicerones. Out of the portals of
a Temple of white marble, glimmering through the fogs and
clouds of contemporary literature, Roden Noel stept like
a young god, with a message from the old Greek world
which is ever new. The joy of earth was with him, the
sunlight of a lost Divinity clung around him, and so light
was his footstep that he seemed to walk on air. Even
so I saw him approaching, many years ago, and my heart
went out to meet him, in the full certainty that he could
speak to me of the hidden things of Hellas, of the
vanished Wonderland where gods were born. This he
surely did, so that for me, as for Sainte-Beuve, *Ganymede*,
Pan, and the *Water-nymph* lived again. Even then,
however, there was something foreign, even uncouth, in
his accent and expression, as if he were struggling with
the idioms of an alien tongue. He had forgotten his
native Greek, in which he could have expressed himself

*a**

so perfectly, and was stumbling through the intricacies of our savage English. This was a minor trouble; the greater and supreme trouble came when this young god, or poet of godlike breed, found himself out in the world and confronted with the carven Christs of the altar and the roadside. How could a poet sing the joy of earth with those piteous eyes upon him ! How could the lover of the mountains and the sea pass on merrily, singing of youth and godhead, when the spectres of Calvary gathered around him ! That he *did* continue to sing, that he still preserved much of the old swinging movement of human happiness, was little short of miraculous. Many a year has passed since then, and the poet, still living, exhibits both in life and song this striking incongruity,—the happy impulse and fervid animalism of ancient Greece mingled with the doubt, the mystery, the introspection of modern England.

What will first strike a reader unfamiliar with these poems is the point to which I have already alluded,—the frequent inefficacy and barbarity of the expression. If the reader is one who assumes that in verse a spade must be called a spade, or that musical singsong is essential, he will doubtless turn elsewhere, to his own great subsequent loss; but if, on the contrary, he is an idealist, seeking for the very soul of poetry and disdaining all mere tricks of popular patter, he will soon discover in Roden Noel one of those divine messengers whom the gods send now and then to "brighten the sunshine." Three qualities distinguish this poet from most, if not from all, of his contemporaries :—(1) a subtlety of sensuousness and of sensuous perception only to be found among pre-Christian singers ; (2) an ever-present mood of moral exaltation ; and (3) a phenomenal power of sympathising with and interpreting the most secret moods of Nature. And first, as to the quality of sensuousness

and sensuous perception.   In the majority of these poems
it is tempered and chastened by the *Welt-Schmertz* of
modern thought; but in some, as in *Ganymede*, it is
frankly and fearlessly pagan,—interpenetrated, that is to
say, with the joy and glory of mere life, with that sense
of living beauty which is primitive and instinctive.   Take
this passage, opening the poem so loved by Sainte-Beuve,
to which I have twice alluded :—

GANYMEDE.

Azure the heaven, with rare a feathery cloud;
Azure the sea, far-scintillating light,
Soft, rich, like velvet yielding to the eye;
Horizons haunted with soft dreamlike sails;
A temple hypæthral open to sweet air
Nigh, on the height, columned with solid flame,
Of flutings and acanthus-work instinct
With lithe green lizards and the shadows sharp
Slant, barring golden floor and inner wall.

A locust-tree condensing all the light
On glossy leaves, and flaky spilling some
Sparkling among cool umbrage underneath;
There magically sobered, mellow, soft,
At unaware beholding gently laid
A youth barelimbed, the loveliest in the world,
Gloatingly falling on his lily side,
Smoothing one rounded arm and dainty hand,
Whereon his head, conscious and conquering,
All chestnut-curled, rests listless and superb;
Near him, and leaning on the chequered bole,
Sits his companions gazing on him fond,
A goat-herd, whose rough hand on bulky knee
Holds a rude hollow reeden pipe of Pan,
Tanned, clad with goatskin, rudely moulded, huge;
While yonder, browsing in the rosemary
And cytisus, you hear a bearded goat,
Hear a fly humming, with a droning bee
In yon wild thyme and in the myrtles low,
That breathe in every feebly-blowing air;
Whose foamy bloom fair Ganymede anon
Plucks with a royal motion and an aim

> Towards his comrade's tolerant fond face.
> Far off cicada shrills among the pine,
> And one may hear low tinkling where a stream
> Yonder in planes and willows, from the beam
> Of day coy hiding, runs with many a pool,
> Where the twain bathe how often in the cool!

The expression is archaic, awkward even, but when we brush aside the mannerism, as one puts aside overhanging branches, what a picture comes before the vision, and what instances of verbal felicity, such as the magical line,

> " Horizons *haunted* with soft dreamlike sails!"

Here, and throughout the poem, the very atmosphere is loaded with Greek sunlight. Then, for supreme sensuousness, take the description of the beautiful boy in the eagle's grasp :—

> "So lightly lovingly those eagle talons
> Lock the soft yielding flesh of either flank,
> His back so tender, thigh and shoulder pillowed
> *How warmly, whitely, in the tawny down*
> *Of that imperial eagle amorous !"*

We should have to search for a long time, out of Keats, for effects so close akin to those of pictorial Art. But in the inevitable nature of things the golden boy was to be left far behind,* while the poet, haunted still by the beauty of all the gods, full still of the old sunlight of the old landscape, came face to face with the Man of Sorrows who is not yet dumb. I do not know, I have not cared to inquire, to what extent and in what measure Roden Noel accepts the popular religion (to my thinking a poet's opinions are of little consequence, so long as they do not imply belief in baseness), but it is from popular religion

---

* *Ganymede* is one of the author's early poems, and I have quoted from the poem as originally published.

that he derives his second great quality as a poet, that of moral exaltation. No singer of our time is so eager to perceive, so quick to apprehend, the problem of Evil ; in poem after poem he shows himself alive, not merely to personal sorrow, but to the pain of Humanity at large ; yet no singer of our time, of equal gifts, is so stirred to exalted utterance by a spiritual message. Let it be noted that the poet's religious mood is as childlike and primitive, as direct and simple, as his former mood of pagan sensuousness. Nowhere in our language is personal sorrow more supremely expressed than in the noble series of poems called with touching tenderness *A Little Child's Monument.* This is a book for all loving souls, above all for the bereaven, and I am glad to know that its popularity with the great public has been in proportion to its merits as poetry. It is not only with his own suffering as an individual, however, that the poet has to deal. His personal sorrow is merely a key to the great heart of humanity. Just as surely as he felt the joy and sunlight of the pagan world, does he feel the storm and stress of the post-Christian. The same vivid keenness of perception, of insight, is brought to bear here as there—

> "On massy bridge, on broad-built quay,
> Tumultuous tides of hurrying wealth
> Sweep the marred sons of misery
> (Who thrid by sufferance, by stealth,
> Their faint way ; near the parapet
> Cower, dull aware of fume and fret,)
> Sweep them to where they may forget !
> For riverward wan eyes are bowed ;
> Beside whom roars the traffic loud,
> And the many-nationed crowd."

Everywhere in the poem from which these lines are quoted, *Poor People's Christmas*, there is the same haunting sense of the details of misery, the same picturesqueness of *chiaroscuro*. And the eyes of the Christ look out upon us from the printed page.

"The poor are Mine, that I may heal!"

says the voice from the Cross. Roden Noel's so-called spiritual poems have, moreover, one great merit to distinguish them from the latter-day poetry of Christian apology; they are seldom or never rectangular and argumentative, like, *e.g.*, many of the poems of Browning. The poet approaches the truth in the frank, free spirit of the lost paganism, eager to see all, to learn all, to suffer and sympathise with all, and he finds his answer to the problem of Evil in his own heartbeats, by becoming (according to the precept) even as a little child.

But it is when we turn to this writer's third great quality as a poet, his power of sympathising with and interpreting the most secret moods of Nature, that we realise to what extent and how wonderfully, in his genius, the pagan and the Christian blend. I have no hesitation in saying that no living poet whatsoever equals Roden Noel in wealth and variety, power and profundity, of natural description. It is quite true, of course, that no living poet has *attempted* so much in this direction. Beautiful transcripts of Nature abound in modern verse, —they are our inheritance from Wordsworth and Byron, and to some extent from Shelley; but seldom or never are they charged with the informing spirit of human passion, and still less seldom do they exhibit vital elemental sympathy as distinguished from merely curious observation. As *observer*s of Nature, Virgil and Tennyson are unsurpassed, but both these fine poets view it as spectators, as artists, rather than as sharers of its elemental joy. With the poet of *Thalatta* and *Suspiria*, it is altogether different. What a sea-swing and cadence there is in these mighty lines!

"**I bathe and wade in** the pools, rich-wrought with flowers of
  the ocean,
Or over the yellow sand run swift to meet the sea,
Dive under the walls of foam, or float on a *weariless motion*
Of the alive, clear wave, heaving undulant under me!"

The tautological sound and cadence—"heaving undulant
under me"—perfectly represent the monotonous movement of ocean-waves, and the newly-coined word "weariless" is curiously felicitous.   But it is not by verbal excellence that Mr. Noel's Nature-poems will win admirers.
Some of them, indeed, are far from admirable in style.   The
poet, wrestling with his vocabulary, tries to express too
much of what he feels and knows, and becomes inarticulate from pure emotion.   Yet in the main the Nature-
poems are wonderful for their knowledge, their insight,
and their natural passion.   Even when most rugged, they
are imposing and "elemental."

I have just glanced at the three great qualities of the
poet who came to me years ago full of youthful enthusiasm
and fresh from wanderings in the far East.   I was living,
in somewhat Bohemian fashion, in a village on the Sussex
coast, not far from Hastings; and thither, one summer
day, wended the author of *Beatrice.*   We were three
in number, a nest of young Radicals, and not much pre-
disposed to one who put "honourable" before his name,
and was an aristocrat by birth and education; but before
many days had passed the freemasonry of youth and
poetry had bound me close to a new friend.   It is a far
cry to that time now, to the time when we swam together
in the tumbling waters of the Channel, wandered in the
Sussex lanes, and talked of the old poets and the old gods.
I got one of my first lessons in toleration when I first met
and talked with the aged Earl of Gainborough, simple,
child-like, a Christian, and with that beautiful soul his
Countess, a peerless woman and a loving mother.   From

this good and gracious stock came Roden Noel, fortunate in an inheritance of sane and gentle blood. His early youth had been spent at his father's seat in Rutlandshire and at the Irish seat of his maternal grandfather, the Earl of Roden. At twenty he went to Cambridge, with a view of studying for the Church, but religious scruples intervened and he never took orders. Soon after taking his degree he spent two long years in the East, visiting Egypt and the Holy Land, Lebanon, Greece, Turkey, and Palmyra, and gathering in the course of many romantic adventures the materials for some of his finest poetry. His marriage took place during this pilgrimage, and was a little romance in itself. Struck down with fever at Beyrout, he was nursed back to life by Madame de Broë, wife of the director of the Ottoman Bank, and he married her eldest daughter Alice shortly after his recovery. That marriage, I think, was the crown of a fortunate life! It has kept this poet calm and happy, in times when most of us are troubled and storm-tossed; and it has given to him the consecration of a faithful and pure domestic love. While others have been fighting with windmills and struggling for bread, peace and rest have dwelt with the young wayfarer from Hellas; and if he has known, as all must know, the acute agonies of human sorrow, if his hearth has been darkened by the wings of the destroying Angel, the issue has still been holy, thanks to the faith that comes to us through Love alone. Often as his thoughts may wander back to Hellas, while the pagan stirs within his blood and he hears from afar the voices of the Dryad and the Naiad, the Satyr and Sylvanus, he has learnt by his own fire the one great modern lesson,—that the god of Humanity has conquered and subdued to his own likeness all the gods of the world that lies beneath his feet.

In making the above remarks I have not attempted to

conceal that the writer of the following poems has been for many years my personal friend. I have little or no faith, as my readers possibly know, in the wisdom or the honesty of contemporary criticism, and I am well aware, moreover, that those who roll most logs for their acquaintances will protest most loudly against an Ishmaelite like myself following their example. Yet I am writing after due deliberation, with the full knowledge that I shall be confronted with my own folly if I overstep the mark. As a rule, friends, honest friends, are tricksy critics, presuming on their intimacy with the subject to animadvert most strongly upon shortcomings; but after all, the best critics of literature are those who appreciate it, and my appreciation of the writer under review dates far back behind the time when I first was favoured with his companionship. In reality, the poems of Roden Noel required no introduction, and I need hardly say that any introduction from *me* would prejudice many readers against the subject. I shall nevertheless, in the present summary preface, as in all my writings to the public, say exactly what I think, without any sort of hesitation or apology.

That Roden Noel will ever become, in any broad sense of the word, a popular poet, I do not for a moment believe. There is little or nothing in his writings to appeal to those who regard a poet as a manufacturer of pretty verses, and their marked mannerism, their composite structure, their often barbaric expression, are certain to awaken polite antagonism. Moreover, they are too intensely speculative, too wistful, and too problem - haunted, for all who, like our Cockneys, measure their masterpieces by rule of thumb. We must cut the fruit right down the middle, right through the rough and husky rind, to get at the heart of this pomegranate! Having done this, and having

rejected everything that is merely outward and super-
ficial, we shall find here, what we miss in nearly all
contemporary products—the very fruit and essence of
original poetry.

Spiritual in the very highest sense are nearly all these
poems ; a few of them, like *Pan* and *Summer Clouds to a
Swan*, are perfect in form, while many, though somewhat
formless at first sight, have in reality a fine and masterly
coherence. If we turn for a moment from them to the
writer's efforts in simple prose, we shall be reminded that
he possesses, besides his gifts as a poet, those of a very
remarkable speculative philosopher ; so clearly is this the
case that it is certain he might, had he chosen, have
attained high rank as a metaphysician pure and simple.
His articles on philosophical themes, and notably his
masterly summary of the teachings of Schopenhauer,
fully establish this position. No poet of our time
surpasses him in extent of reasoning power on
abstract subjects. This power, exhibited from time to
time in prose, underlies all his poetry,—clouds and
troubles it indeed not unfrequently, and makes it difficult
reading. Fortunately, he never forgets for long that the
crowning beauty of all great verse is absolute directness
and simplicity. He never trifles with his art, or blows
bubbles for the mere sake of prettiness. A deep and
benign purpose, a fine if somewhat fitful inspiration,
animates all his work, both the worst and the best. He
is, in a word, as every real poet must be, a *Thinker*,
a man whose business it is to help us to fathom the
problems of life and thought. Fortunately for himself,
all the shafts of modern doubt have failed to penetrate
the white armour of his fully reasoned faith. He has
passed his forty days in the wilderness of moral despair,
only to return secure in insight and certain of his mission,
which is to offer the good tidings of Hope to all men.

He is, in other words, the poet of Christian *Thought*. Surely a strange sight is here; the young pagan, fresh from the woodlands of Pan, and from the dark, shadowy mountains of modern speculation, flinging himself down on his knees at the foot of the Cross!

If we miss this fact in Roden Noel's poetry, we shall miss its whole power and purpose. He is a Christian thinker, a Christian singer, or nothing. Not that I conceive for one moment that he accepts the whole impedimenta of Christian orthodoxy,—he is far too much of a pagan still ever to arrive at that. But he believes, as so many of us have sought in vain to believe, in the absolute logic of the Christian message : that logic which is to *me* a miracle of clear reasoning raised on false premises, and which to others is false premises and false reasoning all through. To me the historical Christ, the Christ of popular teaching, is a Phantom, the Christ-God a very Spectre of the Brocken, cast by the miserable pigmy Man on the cloudland surrounding and environing him. I conceive only the ideal Christ, as an Elder Brother who lived and suffered and died as I have done and must do ; and while I love him in so far as he is human and my fellow-creature, I shrink from him in so far as he claims to be Divine. With Roden Noel, as with so many other favoured souls, it is different. Where we can find little comfort and no solution, he finds both. He embraces in full affluence of sympathy and love that ghostly godhead, and credits *him* with all the mercy, all the knowledge, all the love and power, which we believe to be the common birthright of Humanity,—the accumulation of spiritual ideals from century after century. But where I and those who think with me are at one with Roden Noel is in the absolute moral certainty that, in the estimate of the Supreme Intelligence, what we *believe* counts for nothing, in so far as it merely represents what we *know*.

The atheist and the Christian, the believer and the unbeliever, meet on the same platform of a common beneficence. Faith in Love is all-sufficient, without faith in any supernatural or godlike *form* of Love.

There is nothing nebulous, however, about Roden Noel's religious belief. It is clear, direct, and logically reasoned out. He is, moreover, in the highest sense of the word, a spiritualist, as all true poets must be. The pessimism of Schopenhauer and Leopardi is as far away from his sympathy as the gross materialism of Holbach and Zola. Even disease transmutes itself, under his tender gaze, into images of loveliness and hope. At the present epoch of our progress, thinkers of this kind are sadly wanted. The history of our poetry for the last twenty years has been a melancholy record of mere artificiality and verbalism; and in spite of the splendid flashes of power shown by one or two of our prosperous poets, there has been little or no effort to touch the quick of human life. True, the miasmic cloud of Realism, which is darkening and destroying all literature by robbing it of sunshine and fresh air, has not yet reached our poetry; the majority of those who write in verse being neither realists nor idealists—only triflers, who imagine verse to be a schoolboy's exercise or an idle man's amusement. Hence the utter neglect of Verse, and the attitude of indifference towards verse-products, shown by the reading public; hence the decadence of original thought, and the preponderance of dilettante criticism. If Poetry is ever to resume again its old prophetic function, and to regain any influence over the lives and thoughts of men, it will be through the help of such writers as Mr. Noel,—men who believe with Novalis that Poetry is the only absolute Reality, the only living Truth, who sound in their verse the highest and solemnest notes of life and thought, and who reject with all their soul the fatal tricks and trivialities

of the poetaster, or mocking-bird.   Let it be said in this
connection that Mr. Noel's work, however variously it
may be estimated by various minds, is absolutely and
entirely his own.   The thought, the feeling, the style, the
merits and the blemishes, are invariably *sui generis*.
No living poet of equal power appears so free from the
influence of any school, past or present.   This in itself is
something, but taking cognisance of the intrinsic value of
the utterance, it is much.   In these poems we are offered
no mild Tennysonian infusion, no decoction of Browning
and commonplace, no dilution of Byron's strong tipple or
of Shelley's etherealised dillwater.

It was right that the task of making the following
selection should be assigned to the poet himself; he
alone was the judge of what should be submitted, as
samples of his quality, to the general public.   The result,
it appears to me, is a happy one, affording the most
occasional reader an opportunity of estimating, as far as
lies in his power, the extent and range of the poet's
accomplishment.   At the same time, it should be clearly
explained that much of the writer's work is injured,
rather than helped, by detachment from its context, since
it is by total strength and coherence, rather than by
occasional felicity, that such a poet as Mr. Noel should
be judged.   *A Little Child's Monument*, for example,
suffers greatly through being represented by detached
poems.   To be thoroughly enjoyed and appreciated, it
must be read in sequence, poem by poem; for although
it assumes no continuity in form, it is as homogeneous a
production as *In Memoriam*.   From the simplest
murmurs of natural hardly-articulate anguish, up to the
highest cadence of spiritual utterance, it passes musically
on.   The keynote of passionate pain and sympathy for all
weak created things is struck again and again, as in the
following lines of most child-like simplicity :—

"THAT THEY ALL MAY BE ONE."

Whene'er there comes a little child,
My darling comes with him ;
Whene'er I hear a birdie wild
Who sings his merry whim,
Mine sings with him :
If a low strain of music sails
Among melodious hills and dales,
When a white lamb or kitten leaps,
Or star, or vernal flower peeps,
When rainbow dews are pulsing joy,
Or sunny waves, or leaflets toy,
Then he who sleeps
Softly wakes within my heart ;
With a kiss from him I start ;
He lays his head upon my breast,
Tho' I may not see my guest,
Dear bosom-guest !
In all that's pure and fair and good,
I feel the spring-time of thy blood,
Hear thy whispered accents flow
To lighten woe,
Feel them blend,
Although I fail to comprehend.
And if one woundeth with harsh word,
Or deed, a child, or beast, or bird,
It seems to strike weak Innocence
Through him, who hath for his defence
Thunder of the All-loving Sire,
And mine, to whom He gave the fire.

But from mere pain and sympathy we rise again and
again to inspiration, and to insight. It is not until we
have read the entire book that we fully understand the
varied wisdom and wide catholicity of the writer. Fortunately for purposes of selection, however, Mr. Noel has
written few poems of any great length. *A Modern Faust*
is the longest, and even that is in reality a series of
poems linked together by an elastic theme, rather than a
single poem of one shape and form. If a fault is to be
found with the last-named poem, it is a little formless and

inchoate, exhibiting far more lyrical and emotional, than shaping and dramatic, faculty. *The House of Ravensburg*, with all its moral grandeur, shows conclusively that the poet's genius is not dramatic. His business is to phrase his own fine thoughts and intuitions, not than to express the moods and passions of other men. His sympathy with humanity is wide and far-reaching, but it is seldom or never specialised in the way of individual characterisation. He is no more a dramatist than Shelley, to whose genius that of Mr. Noel is in many respects closely akin.

My present purpose, however, is not to criticise the works I have enjoyed, but to draw attention to their general importance as contributions to literature. The office of literary cicerone, so eagerly filled by many in those days of ciceroneship, is distasteful to me, and I decline to imitate the performances of the many holders of the office, who glibly pass judgment on the rank of dead and living writers. It is enough, I think, to know that a man is a poet by natural sight and prerogative, without deciding how far he falls short of or excels predecessors or contemporaries. In the republic of Poetry, there is no aristocracy ; all the citizens are equal by right of a common gift ; and it is only those who have never learned what Poetry *is*, or what the poetic power and temperament mean, who presume to distinguish impertinently between poet and poet, and to throw around one the purple they deny to the other. That Roden Noel is a poet, no reader of these selections will doubt. That he is a very remarkable and original poet, I personally believe. My personal belief and bias, however, can be nothing whatever to those whose sympathies he may fail to touch, and who may prefer lighter styles and less difficult methods. The only true critic of all good literature is he who understands and enjoys it. With this preamble I must leave the reader to the perusal of the following selections, merely hoping that he may be able to share my own enjoyment of them. Whatever final judgment he may pass on individual merits, he will be certain to recognise several qualities not too common in English verse,—deep earnestness, ever-present sympathy, and fully reasoned-out faith in the divine destiny of Man.

ROBERT BUCHANAN.

LYRICS.

LYRICS.

TO A CHILD, WHO ASKED ME FOR
A POEM.

You ask me for a poem, dear,
You want from me a lay,
Who are a music blithe and clear
Sung sweetly day by day!
You, child, have songs within your heart
More pure than aught of mine;
For Life, my dear, is more than Art,
Who sings you is Divine.

EARLY APRIL.

Is it sweet to look into one another's faces
Over where the clear laughing water races,
Where the herbs are all like delicate laces ?
Are ye in love with one another's faces ?
    Flowers of the wildwood, tell me !

Virginal purity of pale primroses !
Petal on petal of a sister reposes,
And the shadow of either on either dozes ;
    Wildwood flowers, we hail you !

Many daintily-formed green leaves have met,
Strawberry leaf and violet,
'Tis a little too cold for the nightingale yet ;
    Philomel, he'll not fail you !

Fairy windflower, wood anemones,
Delicate company under the trees,
Snowflake ruffled by a merryfoot breeze,
Frolicsome singing aërial glees,
    Frail white stars of the wildwood !

EARLY APRIL

Every frail face looking a different way,
O'er you arriveth a silver ray ;
Bronze boughs embroider a pearly grey,
    Luminous air in the wildwood.

O white windflower with the purple dyes,
Your candour of innocence meets mine eyes,
And bids the bowed heart in me arise ;
You are kin to the little ones, humble and wise,
    Young, newly-born in the wildwood.

The joy of our Earth-mother thrills through the
       groves ;
A long cooing sound of woodland doves !
Feathered folk serenade the fair nest-lying loves,
    Call young flowers in the wildwood.

We are glad you are here again lovely and gay,
Dull was the winter when you were away ;
We never have had any heart to play,
    While you were afar from the wildwood ;
    And now we are off to the woodland !

Come along, little children ! blithe birds are
       singing,
Budding leaves with a magical melody ringing,
Flowers faint censers of odour swinging ;
    Come along, little loves, to the wildwood !
    We may find fairy forms in the woodland !

All the boughs are alive with a luminous green,
Leaflets uncurl fairy frills to the sheen,
Wings dip and dart over the woodland scene;
We listen and lighten, we know what they mean;
    Spring has arrived in the wildwood!
    Sing heigh! sing ho! for the woodland!

THE SECRET OF THE NIGHTINGALE.

THE ground I walked on felt like air,
Airs buoyant with the year's young mirth ;
Far, filmy, undulating fair,
The down lay, a long wave of earth ;
And a still green foam of woods rose high
Over the hill-line into the sky.
In meadowy pasture browse the kine,
Thin wheat-blades colour a brown plough-line ;
Fresh rapture of the year's young joy
Was in the unfolded luminous leaf,
And birds that shower as they toy
Melodious rain that knows not grief,
A song-maze where my heart in bliss
Lay folded, like a chrysalis.
They allured my feet far into the wood,
Down a winding glade with leaflets walled,
With an odorous dewy dark imbued ;
Rose, and maple, and hazel called
Me into the shadowy solitude ;
Wild blue germander eyes enthralled,

Made me free of the balmy bowers,
Where a wonderful garden-party of flowers,
Laughing sisterhood under the trees,
Dancing merrily, played with the bees;
Anemone, starwort, bands in white,
Like girls for a first communion dight,
And pale yellow primrose ere her flight,
Ushered me onward wondering
To a scene more fair than the court of a king.
Ah! they were very fair themselves,
Sweet maids of honour, woodland elves!
Frail flowers that arrive with the cuckoo,
Pale lilac, hyacinth purple of hue,
And the little pink geranium,
All smiled and nodded to see me come;
All gave me welcome; "No noise," they said,
"For we will show you the bridal bed,
Where Philomel, our queen, was wed;
Hush! move with a tender, reverent foot,
Like a shy light over bole and root;"
And they blew in the delicate air for flute.

Into the heart of the verdure stole
My feet, and a music enwound my soul;
Zephyr flew over a cool bare brow—
I am near, very near to the secret now!
For the rose-covers, all alive with song,
Flash with it, plain now low and long;

Sprinkle a holy water of notes ;
On clear air melody leans and floats ;
The blithe-winged minstrel merrily moves,
Dim bushes burn with mystical loves !

　　Lo ! I arrive ! immersed in green,
Where the wood divides, though barely seen,
A nest in one of the blue leaf-rifts !
There over the border a bird uplifts
Her downy head, billed, luminous-eyed ;
Behold the chosen one, the bride !
And the singer, he singeth by her side.
Leap, heart ! be aflame with them ! loud, not
　　dumb,
Give a voice to their epithalamium !
Whose raptures wax not pale nor dim
Beside the fires of seraphim.
These are glorious, glowing stairs,
In gradual ascent to theirs ;
With human loves acclaim and hail
The holy lore of the nightingale !

A SONG OF NEREIDS.

DING, dong, bell !
We breathe you a sea-spell !
While we leap into the blue,
Link hands with ours, dear mortal, do.
Away ! away ! away !
Our clear green waters are at play
With a wave-bewildered ray,
Where the billow-bathed shell-floor
Looks a fantasy unsure
Through the fluctuating billow,
Where will be your pillow !
Fish float there in opal mail ;
Ere your senses wholly fail,
We will tell you a wondrous tale,
We alone may truly tell
Of what befell
Before the mournful years began
For mind-beclouded, wildered man ;
With our rhythmic rise and fall
We will ring your funeral !
Cease the civil war of life ;
For the turmoil and the strife

Of a human heart and mind
Are more than toil of wave or wind !
You who lay in Love's white bosom
Shall find more fair our cool sea-blossom ;
Leander homing to his love,
And lipping the fond seas he clove,
We lured to our still coral grove,
Where years might ne'er deflower his youth,
Nor wither slowly with no ruth ;
While our kind fair Hylas took
From his lover's longing look.

    You who late could climb the rocks,
Where the tidal water shocks,
You who dared to breast the wave
That yields wild rapture to the brave,
Life at full, or glassy grave,
Come and sleep, and be at rest ;
We will lull you on our breast !
Never weep, nor strive, nor cry,
Nor wait till age shall strand you high
Afar from our sweet revelry,
And our wild, aërial glee !
But plunge into our gulfs, and cease,
Finding there a sweet release !

    Foam, like lace illumined, smiles
Round the feet of granite piles ;
O'er sunny sands for miles and miles,
Along the breezy briny bay,
Melodiously we plash and play ;
Our wild joy's tumultuous sound

Fills the air and all around ;
You are young, and you are old,
You are warm, and you are cold,
Never wearying we sing,
All our foamy bells we ring ;
    Away ! away ! away !
Link hands with ours in play,
While we leap into the blue,
Link hands with ours, dear mortal, do !
We are breathing a sea-spell ;
    Ding, dong, bell !

(Porthcurno.)

SEA SLUMBER-SONG.

SEA-BIRDS are asleep,
The world forgets to weep,
Sea murmurs her soft slumber-song
On the shadowy sand
Of this elfin land ;
"I, the Mother mild,
Hush thee, O my child,
Forget the voices wild !
Isles in elfin light
Dream, the rocks and caves,
Lulled by whispering waves,
Veil their marbles bright,
Foam glimmers faintly white
Upon the shelly sand
Of this elfin land ;
Sea-sound, like violins,
To slumber woos and wins,
I murmur my soft slumber-song,
Leave woes, and wails, and sins,
Ocean's shadowy might
Breathes good-night,
        Good-night !"

(*Kynance Cove.*)

O YEARS!

O YEARS, years, years !
Would ye were rolled away,
And I, 'mid April smiles and tears,
With my true love at play.
O years, years, years,
Who were all one May !
Ah ! the fragrant pine,
The fountain's pure, low bubble ;
Flowers fondle her feet and mine ;
Air-and-bird-wings trouble
Lightly light young leaves
Of our enchanted wood,
While the season weaves
Around our vernal mood
A beautiful silk sheath
Of sight and scent and sound,
Where we lie warm and breathe,
Softly folded round,
And our young pulses bound.

O years, years, years !
That have nor warmth nor sun,

O YEARS!

And little else that cheers,
We are drifting on
With other things that were
Rose-red once and fair.
O years, years, years!
Drooping bowed to earth
With sorrows, wrongs, and fears,
Radiant your birth,
All one morning-mirth!
Now feeble, faint, in tears,
Wings low trailed in dust,
On your mail the rust,
Years, years, years!

DYING.

THEY are waiting on the shore
For the bark to take them home ;
They will toil and grieve no more ;
The hour for release hath come.

All their long life lies behind,
Like a dimly blending dream ;
There is nothing left to bind
To the realms that only seem.

They are waiting for the boat,
There is nothing left to do ;
What was near them grows remote,
Happy silence falls like dew ;
Now the shadowy bark is come,
And the weary may go home.

By still water they would rest,
In the shadow of the tree ;
After battle sleep is best,
After noise tranquillity.

LOVE—TO A.

As of old the wildered dove,
Wandering over waters dark,
Finding neither fount nor grove,
Sought shelter in her home, the ark,

So my little one, my love,
Turns my restless heart to thee,
Weary, wheresoe'er she rove
O'er the inhospitable sea.

Time hath linked us heart to heart
With links of mutual memory,
Of gentle power if aught would part
To bind us close until we die.

If the world arise to sever,
Steals a tiny spirit-hand,
Glides to reunite us ever,
From the holy silent land.

Find the birthplace of sweet Love ;
All our fairest gifts may go,
Yet will He immortal prove,
Fairest of all gods we know !

Find his nest within the grove
Of mystic manifold delight,
Though all the summer leaves remove,
He will abide through winter's night ;
Unsearchable the ways of Love !
Though all the singing choirs be gone,
Love himself will linger on.

Discover hidden paths of love,
Explain the common miracle,
Dear abundant treasure-trove,
Celestial springs in earthly well,
In human vase Heaven's œnomel !

WAS IT WELL?

Was it well? was it well?
When at evening shadow fell
In the great cathedral square,
With a gable-roofing fair,
And the only glimmer there
Was a flutter of a dress,
Ever waning less and less,
As my gaze enamoured clung,
Till the moving masses wrung
It earthward and it fell;
Was it well? was it well?

Was it well? was it well?
Where a fragrant azure fume
Pervades a Gothic gloom,
And jewelled gleams illume,
With a melody of lights,
Marble slumber of the knights,
Till their stony bosoms bloom
Warm to flowers on the tomb:

There the morrow at a shrine
On thy kneeling form Divine
Mine eyes to worship fell:
Was it well? was it well?

Was it well? was it well?
Where a bubbling water fell
From the snakes in carven stone,
Grasses fine about them blown;
In the greenwood lying prone
At thy feet, a boy in love
Murmured idle rhymes he wove;
While we mingled flame of eyes,
In leaf-lattices the skies
With soft suffusion fell:
Was it well? was it well?

Was it well? was it well?
Now the holy glamour fell
Upon every living thing
From the spirit of the spring:
Birds in yielding sweetly sing:
Flowers have innocent confest
Soft allurements of the West;
Leaves and herbs benumbed in death
Feel and bless the living breath,
Gladden hill and dale and dell:
Was it well? was it well?

Was it well? was it well?
Only we defied the spell:
We were timid, we were wise,
Maimed the wings of Love that flies,
Putting out his dove-like eyes,
Tamed with prudence hearts that yearned,
Cooled with caution breasts that burned;
Bosoms dreams of love made tingle,
Limbs afever till they mingle,
Only they defied the spell:
Was it well? was it well?

Was it well? was it well?
Ask no more! I cannot tell.
Spring confused her lovers all,
Each obeyed the sacred call;
Only we refused to fall,
Sanely, calmly self-incurled
'Mid such sweet madness of the world!
O'er twain that trembled into one
Love's own sweet mouth hath vainly blown,
Futile his golden tide hath flown,
Henceforth for ever passing on,
And we are still apart, alone!
Might our clashing kindle Hell?
Ask no more, I cannot tell;
Was it well? was it well?

A SONG AT A WATERFALL.

Athwart the voice of a wild water,
   Falling for ever,
Do I hear some song of the foam's daughter
   Fairily quiver?
Is it song of a naïad, or bee,
Or a breeze from the tree,
Haunting the cave of the wild water?

For evermore leapeth the fall plashing
   Into a pool,
And nigh me, away from the foam flashing,
   Quiet and cool,
Lies a hyaline gulf olive-green,
Where ferns overlean,
And boughs embower the wave-washing.

In a clear hyaline, lo! the leaves waver,
   While, as a cloud,
Stones below melt in the pool-quaver:
   And with the loud

Shout of the waters blithe
Mingles, airy and lithe,
A tune, like a lingering flower-savour.

Fearless fronteth the sound-ocean,
　　Even as a bird
Breasting the resonant storm-motion,
　　Low is it heard,
Sundering soft the cold
Roar, like a gleam of gold,
Wandering warm with a mild motion ;

Visiting every flower-blossom,
　　A humming-bird ;
Floats and falls on the wind's bosom
　　Many a word.
'Tis ne'er a naïad who sings,
Nor aught with wings,
But a maiden fair as the foam blossom !

For now, disentangling the tree-cover,
　　Resteth she fair
On a stone, a mere child ; and her own lover,
　　All unaware
Of a heaven in her, laughs free ;
While blithe as a bee
Singing she roameth the world over.

Ah ! sweeter far than the fall roaring,
    Or any wild sound,
Is the carol of thy young life pouring
    Joyance around !
Yet a vanishing voice of the spring,
With a fleeting wing,
Is thine in the realm of the long roaring !

For the bee will go from the wild water,
    With blossom and breeze ;
And thou, more fair than the foam's daughter,
    Even as these,
Wilt fade with the hours away
From the weary play,
And the wildering roar of the wild water !

THE SWIMMER.

YONDER, lo ! the tide is flowing ;
Clamber, while the breeze is blowing,
Down to where a soft foam flusters
Dulse and fairy feathery clusters !
While it fills the shelly hollows,
A swift sister billow follows,
Leaps in hurrying with the tide,
Seems the lingering wave to chide ;
Both push on with eager life,
And a gurgling show of strife.
O the salt, refreshing air
Shrilly blowing in the hair !
A keen, healthful savour haunts
Sea-shell, sea-flower, and sea-plants.
Innocent billows on the strand
Leave a crystal over sand,
Whose thin ebbing soon is crossed
By a crystal foam-enmossed,
Variegating silver-grey
Shell-empetalled sand in play :
When from sand dries off the brine,
Vanishes swift shadow fine ;

But a wet sand is a glass
Where the plumy cloudlets pass,
Floating islands of the blue,
Tender, shining, fair, and true.

Who would linger idle,
Dallying would lie,
When wind and wave, a bridal
Celebrating, fly?
Let him plunge among them,
Who hath wooed enough,
Flirted with them, sung them,
In the salt sea-trough
He may win them, onward
On a buoyant crest,
Far to seaward, sunward,
Ocean-borne to rest !
Wild wind will sing over him,
And the free foam cover him,
Swimming seaward, sunward,
On a blithe sea-breast !
On a blithe sea-bosom
Swims another too,
Swims a live sea-blossom,
A grey-winged sea-mew !
Grape-green all the waves are,
By whose hurrying line
Half of ships and caves are
Buried under brine ;

Supple, shifting ranges
Lucent at the crest,
With pearly surface-changes
Never laid to rest :
Now a dipping gunwale
Momently he sees,
Now a fuming funnel,
Or red flag in the breeze ;
Arms flung open wide,
Lip the laughing sea ;
For playfellow, for bride,
Claim her impetuously !
Triumphantly exult with all the free,
Buoyant bounding splendour of the sea !
And if while on the billow
Wearily he lay,
His awful wild playfellow
Filled his mouth with spray,
Reft him of his breath,
To some far realms away
He would float with Death ;
Wild wind would sing over him,
And the free foam cover him,
Waft him sleeping onward,
Floating seaward, sunward,
All alone with Death ;
In a realm of wondrous dreams,
And shadow-haunted ocean gleams !

THE OLD PIANO.

In the twilight, in the twilight,
  Sounding softly, sounding low,
Float some cadences enchanted,
  Eerie songs of long ago.

In the gloaming, in the gloaming,
  Sits our child with lips apart
Near her mother who is singing,
  Near the woman of my heart.

O how thinly, O how feebly
  Rings the ancient instrument !
When it opened, slowly yielding,
  What a weird, unwonted scent !

Plaining wildered all forlornly,
  As it were surprised from death ;
On a plate of faded ivory
  Some lost name faint wavereth.

Wildered sorely, wildered sorely,
In oblivion mouldering,
To be challenged now for music
That the dead were wont to sing!

Are they rising, are they rising,
As I gaze through mist of tears,
In the savour, in the music,
Vanished visions of the years?

Stilly stealing, stilly stealing,
Glide the dead in companies;
Thinly flow their words and laughter,
Faintly radiant their eyes.

And they mingle, lo! they mingle,
With my living wife and child,
Seem to thrust them from their places
And confuse their presence mild.

See a maiden, a fair maiden,
Vestured in a garb of yore,
Singing yonder while her lover
Pleads with longing eyes for more!

Then a mother, a young mother,
With her child, in guise of eld,
She appears; full blown to woman
Now the maid whom I beheld.

Then a widow, a grey widow,
　　See her now ! before he died
Love lay withered—worn and faded,
　　Lo ! she plays where played the bride.

. . . In a moan of wind they vanish,
　　Dead and living ; I alone
Hear old Time insanely mumble
　　In the sea's low monotone !

ODE TO ENGLAND. *

ARM ! England, arm ! for all men point the finger
Toward thee with scorn they little care to veil :
" Doth not the mouldering hull of England linger
Upon her sea of gold, with idle sail ?
Once she was other ! once we shrank dismayed
Before the lightning of her baring blade ;
Once through the storm her ocean glory burst,
She, stormy petrel, she the ocean-nurst,
Upon her foes, who pale beheld the stream
Of her bright ensign, like Aurora, gleam
Over foam-billows bounding wild : hurrah !
England is drowsier than at Trafalgar ! "

Arm ! England, arm ! the halcyon hour must wait
When Love and Righteousness shall vanquish Hate.
Jesus of old was royal hailed in scorn :
Now the world crowns Him—still it is with thorn !
Nobles and kings go armèd to the teeth :
Lo ! where thy loving sister bleeds beneath

* Written at the time of the Franco-German War.

Their haughty feet: she calls thee to her side:
They clank their swords at thee with insolent pride.
"Old England, mumbling, paralysed, and cold,
Shrinks closer clutching at her hoards of gold!"
Why should the mailèd sons of tyranny taunt
Thee, champion of the free, with windy vaunt?
Arm! England, arm! they mouth at Liberty,
Who with a mother's impulse turns to thee!
Fair is our dream of universal peace;
But there be wolves, and lambs of tender fleece.
Tyranny summons all her swarms of slaves,
Horrent with weapons: daughter of the waves!
Is it a time for thee to loll and bask,
And murmur at the burden of thy casque?
Yea, thou art sedulous to nurse thy health,
Resentful of a menace to thy wealth:
But in the hour of thine extremity,
Look for no pitying tear to cloud one eye
Among the sister nations loitering by!
Now that thy faithful friend is in the dust,
Whose features fair may next inflame the lust
Of her inexorable conqueror,
Or of his mailed kinsman emperor?
If thou, the hope of Freedom, lie supine,
Indifferent beyond thy belt of brine,
While Freedom wrestles with a libertine,
Beware for thine!
Shall not God judge the race that cannot feel
Itself a member of one living commonweal?
That nation dies; elects to be alone;

Severed in sooth, dead lumber, shall be thrown
Among bare buried piles of bone !
Canst thou, then, fear to arm thy children free,
Who cradled lay upon the bosom of Liberty?
Whom from herself she nourished, whom with motion
And lullabies of the everlasting ocean
She soothed from earliest infancy,
While, in loud winds and waves careering, she
Sings to her mariners who rule the sea !

Arm all thy children ! not a caste of drones :
Then shalt thou see those anarchs on their thrones
Abase their domineering front—behold
Helvetia, splendid, blithe, and bold !
The sons who breathe her liberal mountain air,
The men who scale her precipice and dare
All dangers of her bleak eternal snows,
A race of hardy hunters, who repose
Fearless beneath her sparkling stars, nor blanch
To dream their bed may prove a thunderous avalanche,
Whose spirits with their native eagle soar,
Whose kindred souls dilating love the roar
Of icy cataracts, the Aar, the Rhine,
The Rhone that foams among the murmuring pine—
Are these not armed? Yea, every man will bleed
For the fair land of Arnold Winkelried !

France waved the banner of the free,
When it fell from the hands of Italy :

3

Alas ! she fails—but England, thou
Hast a Daughter of starry brow,
Whose arms receive thy setting sun ;
She, in a forest vast and lone,
With awful gladness hears intone
Niagara, and the Amazon !
Freedom before her mountain citadel
Placed you, two giants, each her wakeful sentinel !

"THE PITY OF IT."

If our love may fail, Lily,
If our love may fail,
What will mere life avail, Lily,
Mere life avail?

Seed that promised blossom,
Withered in the mould,
Pale petals overblowing,
Failing from the gold!

When the fervent fingers
Listlessly unclose,
May the life that lingers
Find repose, Lily,
Find repose!

Who may dream of all the music
Only a lover hears,
Hearkening to hearts triumphant
Bearing down the years?

Ah ! may eternal anthems dwindle
To a low sound of tears?

Room in all the ages
For our love to grow,
Prayers of both demanded
A little while ago:

And now a few poor moments,
Between life and death,
May be proven all too ample
For love's breath !

Seed that promised blossom,
Withered in the mould !
Pale petals overblowing,
Failing from the gold !

I well believe the fault lay
More with me than you,
But I feel the shadow closing
Cold about us two.

An hour may yet be yielded us,
Or a very little more—
Then a few tears, and silence
For evermore, Lily,
For evermore !

LOST ANGEL.

Lost angel of a holier youth,
O maiden fair beyond compare !
Young dream of joy, return for ruth,
Dawn, breathe around a holier air !
Evanished where?
Dear naïad, in a shadowy grot,
Fair nymph, who lave within the cave,
I yearn for you, and find you not,
O freshness of the early wave !
The river rolleth broad and strong,
Great vessels glide upon the tide,
High storied tower and temple throng
With human toil, and pain, and pride.
But where the purple light of morn,
And thou, fair queen of what hath been ?
Ah ! holy land where Hope was born,
Ah ! freshness of the early green !
O shrined within the lucent air,
Where Youth hath bath with morning mirth,
Clear-welling crystal blithe and fair,
Leaf-mirror from the loins of earth !

But I am drifting far away,
With many a stain, with many a pain,
I near the shadowy death of day,
And youth may never dawn again.
O grand cathedral where you prayed,
Divinely dight with jewelled light,
Soft woodland water where we played,
Low music in the summer night !
Melodiously flowing river !
Ah ! blithe sunshine upon the Rhine,
We would have leaned, and looked for ever,
Your eyes more luminous, lady mine !
Dark as a russet forest pool,
With many a dream within their gleam,
Now glancing mirth, now veiled and full ;
Were they, or did they only seem ? . . .
There is no grove like yonder grove,
No water clear as our mild mere,
No dawn is like the dawn of love,
Nor any later flower so dear
As are the earliest of the year. . . .
Evanished where ? . . .
Holds life, or death, immense and still,
Thee darkly fair beyond compare ?
May Love her silver orb fulfil
Unhindered there,
Where Honour may not fetter will,
Nor Love himself bid love despair ?
And you were one long vernal kiss,
Immingling glows of lovelit rose,

Perfume, rare amber, ambergris,
And all the fervid Orient knows !
Ah ! mellow-ripe-of-autumn hue,
Young, willowy, warm, impassioned form,
Tone gentler than the turtle-coo,
Brown eyes that took the heart by storm,
And lovelier inward grace that drew
My soul with all-compelling charm !

A CASUAL SONG.

SHE sang of lovers met to play
"Under the may bloom, under the may,"
But when I sought her face so fair,
I found the set face of Despair.

She sang of woodland leaves in spring,
And joy of young love dallying;
But her young eyes were all one moan,
And Death weighed on her heart like stone.

I could not ask, I know not now,
The story of that mournful brow;
It haunts me as it haunted then,
A flash from fire of hell-bound men.

THE MERRY-GO-ROUND.

THE merry-go-round, the merry-go-round, the merry-go-
round at Fowey !*
They whirl around, they gallop around, man, woman,
and girl, and boy ;
They circle on wooden horses, white, black, brown, and
bay,
To a loud monotonous tune that hath a trumpet bray.
All is dark where the circus stands on the narrow quay,
Save for its own yellow lamps, that illumine it brilliantly :
Painted purple and red, it pours a broad strong glow
Over an old-world house, with a pillared place below ;
For the floor of the building rests on bandy columns small,
And the bulging pile may, tottering, suddenly bury all.
But there upon wooden benches, hunched in the summer
night,
Sit wrinkled sires of the village arow, whose hair is white ;
They sit like the mummies of men, with a glare upon them
cast
From a rushing flame of the living, like their own mad
past ;

* Pronounce *Foy.*

They are watching the merry-make, and their face is very
    grave ;
Over all are the silent stars ! beyond, the cold grey wave.
And while I gaze on the galloping horses circling round,
The men caracoling up and down to a weird, mono-
    tonous sound,
I pass into a bewilderment, and marvel why they go ;
It seems the earth revolving, with our vain to and fro !
For the young may be glad and eager, but some ride
    listlessly,
And the old look on with a weary, dull, and lifeless eye ;
I know that in an hour the fair will all be gone,
Stars shining over a dreary void, the Deep have sound
    alone.
I gaze with orb suffused at human things that fly,
And I am lost in the wonder of our dim destiny. . . .
The merry-go-round, the merry-go-round, the merry-go-
    round at Fowey !
They whirl around, they gallop around, man, woman,
    and girl, and boy.

EARTH-AFFLICTED CHILDREN SINGING IN HEAVEN.*

THEN, with a fountain's delicate rain noises
(A silver moss leaps plashing where it poises),
I heard afar melodious young tones
Of children, warbling limpid antiphons,
Of singing children, sister answering brother,
And flying, flying after one another.

THE FOUNTAIN SONG.

First. 'Where is the rainbow?
Where may I find it?'
Second. 'In a fountain falling
With the sun behind it!'
First. 'Where the flying silver
Falls loose, dishevelled?'
Second. 'At an airier fountain
Your look be levelled!
Where gems enhancing
Aerial blue
Are glimmering, glancing,
A delicate dew!'

* From " A Modern Faust."

First.   'Come you, and show !
           I never shall find !'
Second. 'Wait till he blow !
           Ah ! whims of the wind !'
First.   'Silent in airy dew
           Playfully wafted,
           Rainbow, the fairy, flew
           Swift from the shafted
           Watery column !
           He will beguile
           Old over-solemn
           Faces to smile !'
Second. 'Here, over the leafage
           Glowing to golden,
           Not for a moment
           Will he be holden ;
           A glamour of glory
           Over the trees !
           Ever murmuring story,
           Low melodies !'
First.   'Now he is laving
           Clear in the pool !
           Wavelets are waving
           Delicate, cool !
           He is all azure,
           Purple and yellow,
           Following pleasure,
           Beautiful fellow !
           Awhile appearing,
           Now here, now there !

    Vanishing, veering
    A Glendoveer !
    Everywhere ! '
Second. ' A bird who is washing
    In a water-lily bath
    A very fine flashing
    Leaf-laver hath !
    The young jet of joyance,
    Clear with no colour,
    Will yield all her buoyance
    In a ruffling corolla,
    Fall, a resolving
    Soft silvery flower,
    Woven water involving
    Heaven-hues in a shower !
    Deliciously dying is
    Dear as the fleet
    Swift thrill of flying
    Morning to meet ! '

MY LITTLE ONES.

Ah! little ones! my little ones!
When will your sorrows end?
We deemed you daughters, deemed you sons
Of our Eternal Friend!
Yet ever tears of blood we bleed
Above your bitter mortal need!
I deem that it may be your part
To break, and melt the world's hard heart:
And when ye know, ye will rejoice;
In Heaven, will you give your voice
For earthly pain, your own free choice?
In the life that follows this,
Will you, with your forgiving kiss,
Pile the saving coals of fire
On cruel mother, cruel sire?
Little ones, my little ones,
Ah! when will be the end!
We deemed you daughters, deemed you sons
Of more than earthly Friend!
We want you fair, and hale, and strong,
Full of laughter, mirth, and song;

For when we hear you weep and moan.
Our Lord is shaken on His throne !
If later years be dull and sad,
Leave, O leave the children glad !
Little ones, my little ones,
However all may end,
Earth may fail, with moons and suns,
But never, Love, your friend !
For Jesus was a little child,
And God Himself is meek and mild.

MAD MOTHER.

AFTER moonrise in autumn,
By a wandering water,
When a half-muffled moon,
Dazed in a cloudland
Of wandering grey,
Looked pale from the cloud,
Dim branches uncoloured,
In a line with the moon,
Under, over the moon,
Faintly repeated,
A dark woven lacework
In the wan wave . . .
I heard a low singing,
Thin, shadowy singing,
Unwordable woe,
A wail from the ruin
Of a heart desolated,
A mind out of tune,
As a wail from the wind:
A thin faded form by the pale flying moon,
A face with the youth faded out from the eyes,
From the wan, weary eyes,

Save for her not a soul !
Save for her, and a child,
Whom she held by the hand,
In the shadowy silence ;
But she ceaseth her singing,
Low saith to the child—
" Come along, dear, with mammy
Under the water,
The soft flying water,
The sheltering water,
The kind, hiding water ;
You are going with me !"
Then they went from the shelving
Low shore together
Into the water :
And the child little knew
Where he was going,
Only clung to the mother,
Deeming her wise.
Was she not ever
Wise for her little one,
Love for her little one ?
Yea, Love is wise !
Ah ! she was true ;
But the woes of the world,
Driven home by the devil,
Had maddened her mind,
And the child little knew,
Knew not the mother
Herself little knew,

4

Even she, even she
Herself little knew!
So they went in together,
Mother and child,
Awaking the cloudland
In the wan water,
Awaking the moon.
"O mammy, how cold it is!"
" Yea, very cold, dear!
Only 'tis colder
Yonder on earth, love,
Yonder on land!"
A gurgle, a silence,
Low wind in the rushes,
Never note more of song now;
Nor mother, nor child knew;
Ah! none of us know!

"AH! LOVE YE ONE ANOTHER WELL!"

Ah ! love ye one another well,
For the hour will come
When one of you is lying dumb;
Ye would give worlds then for a word,
That never may be heard;
Ye would give worlds then for a glance,
That may be yours by ne'er a chance;
Ah ! love ye one another well !

For if ye wrung a tear,
Like molten iron it will sear;
The look that proved you were unkind
With hot remorse will be blind;
And though you pray to be forgiven,
How will ye know that ye are shriven?
Ah ! love ye one another well !

"THE CLOUD MAY SAIL THERE."

THE cloud may sail there,
Day flow and fail there,
And the eagle fly,
Haze overshadow
A smooth snow meadow,
And gleams of silver
Fleeting fly
From yon cloud-delver
Of gleaming eye !
The moon may tarry with
Her pale bow,
And moonrise marry with
Virgin snow,
Blue heavens abide,
Or solemn-eyed
Stars by night, who gaze and go :
Ah ! ne'er pollute
With a mortal foot
Yon realms of spirits aerial ;
All but the lute
Of air be mute
From rosy morn to evening fall,

While flowerets blue,
Fair with dew,
Laugh to the azure over all ;
Let a music mazy,
Born of the hazy
Play of a tender light and shade,
On hallowed ground
Dance with the sound
Fairy horns have faintly made ;
A cloud of snow
Softly blow
On the blue verge of the form so white,
Delicate curl
In a windy whirl ;
But man, be far from the holy height,
Soil no fair fields of frosty light !

ALPINE HUNTER'S SONG.

THE hunter sings, as he strides along :
   Halloo !
The paths are perilous and long ;
But a hunter's heart is light and strong :
He jodles, and the ice crags jodle too :
   Halloo ! halloo !

Hark to the clang of his iron heel !
   Halloo !
He grapples granite with grip of steel ;
The mountains echo to his merry peal ;
He splinters, and he mounts the ice wall blue :
   Halloo ! halloo !

Who spies a gem from the top of a bluff ?
   Halloo !
A shaft hath tumbled him sure enough ;
Though hunter's fare be scant and rough,
He quaffs for wine the air, the stream, the dew :
   Halloo ! halloo !

His seasoned frame is hard as a rock :
        Halloo !
He doth indomitable mock
Lauwine, red lightning, rolling block ;
He springeth over icy chasms blue :
        Halloo ! halloo !

He lies out under a cave by night :
        Halloo !
He communeth with still starlight,
And snow-peaks in their shrouds of white :
In far ravines hoar torrents roaring go :
        Halloo ! halloo !

The hunter peers from a stony jag :
        Halloo !
A Lammergeyer unfurls the flag
Of vans, that shadow all the crag !
He shouts ! death hovers ! hurls him down
    below !
        Halloo ! halloo !

And as he falls, falls in the deep :
        Halloo !
With him the rocks rebounding leap ;
Rouse all the demons out of their sleep,
Who laugh, as he lies cold in snow :
        Halloo ! halloo !

EARLY LOVE.

Our early love was only dream !
　　Still a dream too fair for earth,
Hallowed in a faint far gleam,
　　Where the fairest flowers have birth,
Let it rest ! no stain e'er trouble
Magic murmur, limpid bubble !

There two spirits in the calm
　　Of moonlight memory may go,
Finding pure refreshing balm,
　　When life traileth wounded, slow
Along dim ways of common dust,
As dull lives of mortals must.

Early love, fair fount of waters,
　　Ever by enchantment flowing,
Where two snakes, her innocent daughters,
　　Were wont to swim among the blowing,
Wilding flowers thou knowest well,
In the wood of our sweet spell !

Never Fear found out the place,
  Never eyes nor feet profane !
Of our innocent youth and grace
  Love was born ; if born to wane,
We will keep remembrance holy
From the soil of care and folly.

No weariness of life made wise,
  No canker in the youngling bud,
No lustre failing from our eyes,
  Nor ardour paling in the blood !
Neither ever seemed less fair
To the other playing there.

Still asleep, we drift asunder,
  Who met and loved but in a dream ;
Nor kissing closely, woke to wonder
  Why we are not what we seem !
Fairy bloom dies when we press
Wings young zephyr may caress.

Fare you well ! more might have been !
  Nay, we know more might not be !
A moment only I may lean
  On your bosom, ere you flee,
Ere the weary sultry day
Hide my morning and my May !

Yet a fairy fountain glistens
　　Under soft moon-lighted leaves,
And my wistful spirit listens
　　For a voice that glows and grieves,
Breathing, when my heart would fail,
Youth from yonder fairy vale,
Where sings a nightingale.

LOVE HIDING.

Love was playing hide-and-seek,
   And we deemed that he was gone,
Tears were on my withered cheek
   For the setting of our sun ;
Dark it was around, above,
But he came again, my love !

Chill and drear in wan November,
   We recall the happy spring,
While bewildered we remember
   When the woods began to sing,
   All alive with leaf and wing,
Leafless lay the silent grove ;
But he came again, my love !

And our melancholy frost
   Woke to radiance in his rays,
Who wore the look of one we lost
   In the far-away dim days ;
No prayer, we sighed, the dead may move,
Yet he came again, my love !

Love went to sleep, but not for ever,
    And we deemed that he was dead ;
Nay, shall aught avail to sever
    Hearts who once indeed were wed ?
Garlands for his grave we wove,
But he came again, my love !

FROM "THE WATER-NYMPH AND THE BOY.'

I FLUNG me round him,
I drew him under ;
I clung, I drowned him,
My own white wonder ! . . .

Father and mother,
Weeping and wild,
Came to the forest,
Calling the child,
Came from the palace,
Down to the pool,
Calling my darling,
My beautiful !

Under the water,
Cold and so pale !
Could it be love made
Beauty to fail ?

Ah ! me for mortals :
In a few moons,
If I had left him,
After some Junes

He would have faded,
Faded away,
He, the young monarch, whom
All would obey,
Fairer than day ;
Alien to springtime,
Joyless and grey,
He would have faded,
Faded away,
Moving a mockery,
Scorned of the day !
Now I have taken him
All in his prime,
Saved from slow poisoning
Pitiless Time,
Filled with his happiness,
One with the prime,
Saved from the cruel
Dishonour of Time,
Laid him, my beautiful,
Laid him to rest,
Loving, adorable,
Softly to rest,
Here in my crystalline,
Here in my breast !

MYSTICAL POEMS OF NATURE.

PAN.

" PAN is not dead, he lives for ever !
 Mere and mountain, forest, seas,
 Ocean, thunder, rippling river,
 All are living Presences ;
 Yea, though alien language sever,
 We hold communion with these !
 Hail ! ever young and fair Apollo !
 Large-hearted, earth-enrapturing Sun !
 Navigating night's blue hollow,
 Cynthia, Artemis, O Moon,
 Lady Earth you meekly follow,
 Till your radiant race be run;
     Pan is not dead !

" Earth, Cybele, the crowned with towers,
 Lion-haled, with many a breast,
 Mother-Earth, dispensing powers
 To every creature, doth invest

With life and strength, engendering showers
Health, wealth, beauty, or withholds;
Till at length she gently folds
Every child, and lays to rest !
   Pan is not dead !

" Hearken ! rhythmic ocean-thunder !
Wind, wild anthem in the pines !
When the lightning rends asunder
Heavens, to open gleaming mines,
Vasty tones with mountains under
Talk where ashy cloud inclines
Over hoar brows of the heights ;
Ware the swiftly flaming lights !
   Pan is not dead !

" Whence the ' innumerable laughter,'
All the dancing, all the glees
Of blithely buoyant billowed seas,
If it be not a sweet wafture
From joy of Oceanides ?
Whence the dancing and the glees,
In the boughs of woodland trees,
When they clap their hands together,
Hold up flowers in the warm weather ?
Gentle elfins of the fur,
Flowers, Venus' stomacher,
Grey doves who belong to her,

Singing birds, or peeping bud,
Lucid lives in limpid flood,
Fishes, shells, a rainbow brood,
   If Pan be dead?

" Naiads of the willowy water !
Sylvans in the warbling wood !
Oreads, many a mountain daughter
Of the shadowy solitude !
Whence the silence of green leaves,
Where young zephyr only heaves
Sighs in a luxurious mood,
Or a delicate whisper fell
From light lips of Ariel,
   If Pan be dead?

" Wave-illumined ocean palaces,
Musically waterpaven,
Whose are walls enchased like chalices,
Gemmed with living gems, a haven
For foamy, wandering emerald,
Where the waterlights are called
To mazy play upon the ceiling,
Thrills of some delicious feeling !
Sylph-like wonders here lie hid
In dim dome of Nereid ;
Tender tinted, richly hued,
Fair sea-flowers disclose their feelers

With a pearly morn imbued,
While to bather's open lid
Water fairies float, revealers
Of all the marvels in the flood,
    And Pan not dead !

" We are nourished upon science;
Will ye pay yourselves with words?
Gladly will we yield affiance
To what grand order she affords
For use, for wonder; yet she knows
No whit whence all the vision flows !
Ah ! sister, brother, poets, ye
Thrill to a low minstrelsy,
Never any worldling heard,
Ye who cherish the password,
Allowing you, with babes, to go
Within the Presence-chamber so
Familiarly to meet your queen;
For she is of your kith and kin !
Ye are like him of old who heard
In convent garden the white bird;
A hundred years flew over him
Unheeding ! All the world was dim;
At length, unknown, he homeward came
To brethren, now no more the same;
Then, at evening of that day,
Two white birds heavenward flew away;
    Pan is not dead !

" Spirit only talks with spirit,
   Converse with the ordered whole,
   However alien language blur it,
   May only be of soul with soul.
   In our image-moulding sense
   We order varied influence
   From the World-Intelligence;
   And if Nature feed our frame,
   She may nourish pride or shame,
   Holy, or unholy flame;
   Real forms the maniac sees,
   Whom he cherisheth, or flees;
   Real souls the sleeper kens
   In dreamland's eerie shadowed glens.
      Pan is not dead!

" Every star and every planet
   Feed the fire of Destiny;
   Or for good, or evil fan it,
   Herè, Hermes, Hecate;
   By ruling bias, and career,
   To all hath been assigned a sphere,
   In realms invisible and here,
   Obedience, administration
   For individual or nation.
   Ceres, Pluto, Proserpine
   Are the years' youth, and decline,
   Seasonable oil or wine,
   Phantasmagory yours or mine;

And if sense be fed by Nature,
With ne'er a show of usurpature
She may feed our spirit too,
And with hers our own imbue,
Ruling influence from her,
Tallied with our character;
Dionysus, Fauns may move
To revel, or the lower love,
Unrisen Ariel control,
Undine of yet unopened soul,
Fallen ghost invite to fall;
Or she, who is the heart of all,
Uranian Aphrodite, whom
The world laid in a Syrian tomb
Under the name of Jesus, She
May dominate victoriously,
    And Pan be dead!

"Whence are plague, fog, famine, fevers,
Blighting winds, and 'weather harms'?
Are sorceries malign the weavers,
Through inaudible ill charms?
Disease, confusion, haunting sadness,
Lust, delirium, murder, madness,
Cyclone, grim earthquake, accident,
In some witch-cauldron brewed and blent?
Now I see the open pit;
Abaddon flameth forth from it!

Like lurid smoke the fiends are hurled
Abroad now to confound the world!
Disordered minds
Howl, shriek, wail in the wailing winds!
    Pan is not dead!

"Whence the gentle thought unbidden,
    Resolve benign, heroic, just,
    Lovely image of one hidden,
    Higher cherished, lower chidden,
    Self down-trodden in the dust?
    Silent hand of consolation
    On the brows of our vexation,
    On the burning brows of sorrow?
    Much of all, be sure, we borrow
    For that Profound of ours within
    From our holy kith and kin!
        Pan is not dead!

"Warmth and light from shielding, sheeny
    Wings of angels, or Athene,
    Call the Guardian what you will,
    Impelling, or consoling still!
    While if to Christ, or Virgin mother,
    Hate, greed, offer prayer, no other
    Than Belial, Mammon, Ashtaroth
    Draw nigh to hear, and answer both:
    When lurid-eyed priest waves the cross

For slaughter, gain that is but loss
Demons contemptuously toss !
What though ye name the evil clan
Typhon, Satan, Ahriman,
　　Pan is not dead !

" Their bodies are the shows of nature,
　Their spirits far withdrawn from ours ;
We vary in our nomenclature
For the Demiurgic Powers,
To whom high duties are assigned
In our economy of mind,
As in our mortal order ; they
Lead souls upon their endless way ;
From whom the tender, sweet suggestion
Arrives uncalled, unheralded,
Illumination, haunting question,
Approval, blame from some one hid,
Perchance from one we count as dead ;
Our eyes are holden ; they are near,
Who oftenwhile may see and hear !
By the auroral gate of birth,
In the youthful morning mirth,
At the portal of dim death
Their guardianship continueth ;
　　Pan is not dead ! . . .

" Ah ! why then shrilled in the Egæan
The choral wail, the loud lament,

Confusion of the gods Idæan,
Dire defeat, and banishment?
When the lowly young Judæan
Dying head on cross had bent,
  'Great Pan is dead!'

"Sun, and Moon, and Earth, and Stars,
Serene behind our cloudy bars,
With the Magi from the East,
Yield glad homage to the Least,
Offer myrrh, and gold, and gem
Before the Babe of Bethlehem,
  Now Pan is dead!

"Yea, before the wondrous story
Of loving, self-surrendering Man
Paled the world's inferior glory,
Knelt the proud Olympian;
Then the darkness of the cross
Enthroned supreme Love's utter loss;
Then Ambition, Pride, and Lust
Into nether hell were thrust,
And Pan was dead!
The loveliness of Aphrodite
Waned before a lovelier far,
Fainting in the rays more mighty
Of the bright and Morning Star;
(Lovely will to give and bless

Maketh form and feature less)
Young-eyed Erôs will sustain
His triumph, following in His train;
Kings conquered by One more Divine
In the courts imperial shine,
Thralls owing fealty to Him,
Who dying left their glory dim;
Feudatories, ranged in splendour,
Sworn high services to render,
With lions, leopards, fawning mild,
And drawn swords round a Little Child!
    Pan, Pan is dead!

" For while the dawn expands, and heightens,
Greater gods arrive to reign,
Jupiter dethrones the Titans,
Osiris rules the world again,
But in a more majestic guise;
Sinai thunders not, nor lightens,
Eagle, sun-confronting eyes
Veils before mild mysteries!
Balder, Gautama, full-fain
Pay humble tribute while they wane;
All the earlier Beauty prone is
Before a lovelier than Adonis!
Till even the Person of our Lord,
In yonder daylight of the Spirit,
On all the people to be poured
By the dear influence of His merit,

Will fade in the full summer-shine
Of all grown Human, and Divine,
And every mode of worship fall,
Eternal God be all in all ;
   Pan lives, though dead ! "

THE SEA, AND THE LIVING CREATURES.

"Then I thought, in the bosom of Nature, whom I love so, who has revealed herself to me from a boy, will I forget now the misery caused by human sin, hardness, indifference, and mad cruelty — forget these confusions also of poor human understanding, vainly endeavouring to pierce the darkness of a night unassuageable by any star, troubled only, not illuminated, with sinister fires of wreckers along the shore, where human ravage lies tossing in the wild surge, ground to fragments on the iron rocks. And now I found myself by the sea."

THE cliffs resemble a roll of long reverberate thunder,
Dark solid-bodied form of some rock-crashing peal,
Long reverberate roll of a loud tumultuous peal ;
They are a rampart round the pylon rent asunder
From the mainland by the might of yonder waves that
    steal
Slowly and surely in from where they roar in the distance ;
I hasten over the sand that paves the lonely court,
Pass through the giant pylon, and with a swift insistence
Climb rocks in front of the cave that is the Sea's resort.
Only He for awhile hath left His grand Sea-palace,
And I may enter, daring for a moment to explore,
Until anon beneath the Titan arch He dallies,
Ere He arrive to play with the boulders on the floor ;

Arch He hath hewn for Himself in scorn of our rondure
of arches,
Tall, irregular, huge, in outline lightning forked,
While day and night He moved in four great moon-led
marches,
And mouths of the foaming surge with the hollow
mountain talked.
Was not the Architect Chaos? the storm's abraded edges,
Gloom-model after which He set Himself to mould,
Or the journeying billows' beetling, mountain-rupturing
ridges?
Old Chaos hath a genius primeval, vast and bold,
Who tints the windy walls with dim red rust and gold!
When the Main is here at home his lucid halls are paven
With a foamy-veined, and shifting shadowed emerald;
When he leaves, the ponderous purple boulders are
engraven
With fairy tales of the water by the mighty scald.
I bathe and wade in the pools, rich-wrought with flowers
of the ocean,
Or over the yellow sand run swift to meet the sea,
Dive under the falls of foam, or float on a weariless
motion
Of the alive, clear wave, heaving undulant under me!
The grey gull wails aloft; he floats on the breast of the
billow,
And a wet seal flounders flippered on a shelf of the cave;
He knows well I'll not hurt him, brother of mine, dear
fellow;
His mild brown eye beholds confidingly and suave.

Yonder the mouth of the dark long subterranean hollow,
Where with a light in my hat I drove the birds one day,
Who seeing the narrowing end, and a swimmer per-
    sistently follow,
Dived unexpectedly under, and rose up far away !
  But the cavern hath awful tones, dull crimson hues of
    the henbane,
Blood-red, as ancient Murder had been hiding here,
So old and unremembered, gory tints of the den wane ;
Nay, for a smell of slaughter haunts the antres drear !
I will not remember, I thought ! forget by the brine that
    I love so
All the terror of human sin that made me grieve !
Ah ! refreshed for a moment, how may I hope to
    remove so
From the wrongs of those, my brethren ? 'tis but a brief
    reprieve !
I deem some Horror hides in yonder gloom of the
    hollows,
The surge returns to glut them somewhere near my lair ;
And while the sullen sound my lone ear gloomily follows,
With some foreboding cold to gaze around I dare.
Oh ! what are these at my feet ? Ship-timbers, masts
    that are shattered,
In the howl of the hurricane, crunched on the iron of
    rocks—
And lo ! 'tis a corpse in the corner, swollen, sodden, and
    battered,
Nodding, and tossing its arms with the swirl against the
    blocks !

For the Sea hath returned already, He enters the outer-
  most portal ;
Let a man begone, or drown, by the crag-walled vestibule ;
Let him begone, or drown, by the echoing vestibule !
Ah ! 'tis the corpse of a boy there—hear the wail of a
  mortal
Who weeps by a fire in a far land, and waits for her
  beautiful !
The sea hath returned already ; He laughs in the outer-
  most portal ;
He washeth over the boulders, thundering to and fro !
Who are they that inhabit here aloof from the mortal ?
What awful Powers, indifferent to human joy or woe ?
Of Demiurgic Powers, afar from the man and the woman,
Are these dim echoing chambers the mystical veiled
  thought,
Indifferent, aloof, or enemy to the human ? . . .
How, then, are they a haven for minds and hearts o'er-
  wrought ?
Ah ! many and many an hour in your sublime communion
I pass, O gods unknown, of ocean, wind, and cloud ;
I find profound repose, refreshment flow from the
  union . . .
Yet, O my soul, divorce no sufferers in the crowd !
Nay, for I hear in the air that pestilence of the voices—
And it is not all the gale, nor cry of the wild sea-mew !
" Say what sinister joy, not man's this time, rejoices,
The loud, shipwrecking, murderous tempest-whirl to
  brew ?"

THE CALL OF THE CAVES.

"WE allure you, lo ! we call
Into our storm-moulded hall,
Where the emerald water-pulse
Moves the laver and the dulse,
Where swim cloud-white living gems
Of dream-born form ; jade, amber stems
Bud living flowers ; we liberal fling
Live jewels o'er drowned queen and king,
While the haughty heads of them
With some consuming diadem
Of clinging life we crown ; white limbs
Our oozy robe corroding dims ;
Ship timbers jammed between great stones
Are mixed with fish-peeled human bones ;
Grotesque mailed creatures sidle athwart
From some dark cranny of their fort.
Here the yellow sands are silting
Over lips how lately lilting,
Here the shadowy waters moving
Over hearts how lately loving !
Our lilac and our purple dye,

Our shelly incrustations vie
With gold embossed, rich broidery,
Fair spoil washed here from precious freight
Of that fair ship which bore the state
Of royal pilgrim, guard and priest,
Journeying to a marriage feast,
And here by winds and billows broken,
When the fatal word was spoken ;
Where now in lordly isolation
Our waters, after devastation,
Wander with their wild, free voice,
Causing wild hearts to rejoice,
Wander through the lordly halls
Echoing their lone foot-falls,
Singing songs that charm and cheer,
Warbled for no mortal ear ;
Yet if one surprise their scope,
He will be blessed beyond all hope.

Beyond the demon-guarded portal,
Fashioned by no hands of mortal,
Where towering monsters still as stone
Hear old ocean's monotone
Sound and resound for evermore,
Watch the restless entrance-floor
By rude purple rock roofed o'er,
Whose rippled surface-hues invoke
Memories of woodland smoke—
Beyond where twilit water reaches,

There be dim mysterious beaches,
Whence should put forth some elfin bark
To ferry pilgrims toward the dark
Under a storm-wrought architecture,
That fills the soul with strange conjecture,
Where a courage-conquering sound
Travels from the gulf profound,
Like muffled thunder murmureth,
As though some sea-god threatened death,
Drowsy-souled, with bated breath,
To whosoever dared intrude
Upon his awful solitude !
Here unhuman consciousnesses
Inhabit green sea-drowned recesses,
Clothed in a fantastic form,
Native to the realms of storm,
And ocean calm, the mystic deep,
Where many thrilling secrets sleep.
Come and swim, or wade, or float,
Bring the light, oar-dripping boat !
Here's rare fretwork, hued like wine,
More richly gemmed than storied shrine,
Or monstrance ; clear piscina pool
With fairy lives made beautiful,
Finely frilled, and delicate tinted,
Or shyer beauties only hinted ;
Here landwater ceaseth not
Dropping from the groined grot,
Whose tender fresh green ferns above
Look like a dream of virgin love.

We allure you, lo ! we call
Into our storm-moulded hall ;
Where the shadowy wave is still,
If you who are so weary will,
Crooning, we will rock to rest
In the twilight of our breast ;
In sleep we would all ills disperse,
Crooning like some ancient nurse,
And dissolve the ancestral curse !

Yet there is one private gate,
Consecrate to royal state
Of ocean billows ; there they dance
Buoyant under the sun's glance,
Clear-green, hilarious, in and out,
Foam-laughing, ever-fluctuant rout ;
Fair traces of their blithe swift feet
In heaved long floating lines you meet,
Long loose lines of silver foam
Round high rock-ramparts of their home ;
O'er these faint shadows of the clouds
Slowly mount, like welcome shrouds ;
Within the surges hold high revel,
All unaware of good or evil,
But what they do in that dim court
Is known to them who there resort,
And to none other ; the rude arch,
Sacred to their sounding march,

So hewn as though the forked levin
Had been the norm for walls uneven,
Leans back upon the sheer grey crag,
Loud haunt of sea-bird, mer, and shag,
Or gulls that gleam in poised flight
About the grey cathedral height.
A herb-sown pentroof crowns the pile,
That doth the soaring eyes beguile
Aloft o'er what seems window vast,
Which Time, the old Iconoclast,
While the centuries rolled by,
Slow-fashioned there in irony
Of Gothic minster, Gothic creed,
Human worship, human need ;
For there the wind sings all the psalms,
With the wave in storms and calms,
Whose congregations pouring in
Know nor penitence, nor sin ;
There unseen they hold high revel,
No thralls to righteousness or evil.
Rich traceries on the cliff were wrought
By subtle hands with tempest fraught,
O'er that great Eastern front rust-red,
Grey or golden, high and dread,
Shagged with byssus like a beard,
Where the wild bird broods are reared,
Ere they assay their glorious flight
Round the blue-imbathed hoar height.
But that rude mimicry of fanes
The mocking mountain ill sustains,

With his huge protending flanks,
And the maned sea-surge in ranks
Chafing round his iron feet;
For such a part he's all unmeet!
Bastion, buttress, battered, bruised,
Spire with pinnacle confused
Were ne'er for human worship used;
Rough-hewn battlements and towers
Bewray the Elemental Powers!
Lawless, abrupt, their lines have nought
Of human; but the Genii wrought
Jamb, soffit, frieze, and architrave,
For giant porches of the wave.
The huge pile leans to view the sky,
And all his mighty lines awry
Reveal the mountain-irony;
So some huge Pagan, masked as priest
At a solemn Christian feast,
Might leer, and reel, disguise let fall;
Stand revealed a Bacchanal!

. . . Here a boy who sought a nest
Was laid by reverent hands to rest;
In winter he was prisoned here,
Away from all who held him dear,
By ravening waves the loud winds churn;
To humble home they barred return.
Though he and his with longing eye
One another could descry

Beyond the maniac revelry,
Of cold and drought they saw him die.
Surge batteries had availed to sever
By long, implacable endeavour
'This arid isle from the mainland,
Save for one causeway; none might stand
There when it was tempest-swept,
And the wild billows o'er it leapt.

Still they allure me, still they call
Into their storm-moulded hall!

THE SPIRIT OF STORM.

HAIL, royal ocean ! in thy presence-chamber
Arrived, I feel thy deep abounding life
Transfused into my blood, replenishing
My dwindling store ; alone, and at thy feet,
Dear as are human hearts, I am at home !
　Sheltered within a cleft of the tall crag,
Granite of many delicate tints, I hear
The wind's vast voice make chorus with the sea's,
Broken upon grim, dark rock-teeth below,
Ruins of the mainland ; neighbouring which the shoals
Are green as beryl, wine-stained with the weed
Of stone submerged ; one wrinkled indigo
Watery wastes aloof from shore, inlaid
With devious lines, like branching mercury.
The groundswell, sullen heaving, shows the sea
Perturbed by rumours of far water-war.
Atlantic reigns immeasurable, alone,
Far as the weary wandering eyes can range,
Save for one ghostlike, mist-enshrouded isle
There in the offing, and more nigh at hand,
Yon brown sail of the bark that brought me hither,
And bears dear comrades, great-limbed fishermen,
Whose grave reserve derives from the stern sea.

But westward from my lair the crags are shattered
Into the semblance of a palace-fort,
Or temple hypæthral, tower and battlement,
Pinnacle, buttress, gurgoyled arch and spire.
Chasms yawn between twin walls; one longs to know
Where, and how far, into the mountain heart
They labyrinthine wander; one would fain
Ask of the restless surge, or the wild bird,
Who are made free of them, who wander ever
Unchallenged in and out the sombre halls,
And corridors roofed over with wan cloud,
Ceiled with the storm-drift!—Hurrying vapours
    gleam
Anon with slant pale shafts from the veiled sun,
Watery rays, that faintly fitful pour
A ruffled silver lustre on the deep,
Irradiating the white wings of mews,
That hover o'er the abysses; but more bright
And warm this ardent beam from forth my heart,
That blesseth and illumineth with love,
Beloved birds! your multitudinous cry,
Music I dearly cherish; far inland
Erewhile I heard the wail of one of you
Imprisoned; mine eyes melted; for there flashed,
As though revealed in a dark night by lightning,
Flashed unaware upon my sense within,
The vision of the glory of the sea!
    Ye weave delightful motions in the air,
Passing, repassing; call to one another,
And cherish in the abysses your brown young.

Now one alights upon the bounding wave
A moment ; now he cleaves the darkling air.
How the unfettered sweep of his poised pinion
Vies in majestic freedom with the fall
Of a blown billow in mid-ocean, driven,
Fierce-hounded by the blast ! the roller bows
With large, deliberate, imperial bend
Of haughty crest, and massy-muscled neck,
Neck clothed with thunder, as the Roman fell,
Who in the Curia, at the feet of Pompey,
By treachery struck, fell, royal-robed, a king.
So swings, so falls, the Atlantic wave to ruin,
Smitten by immense vans of the strong south-west ;
For all is noble and grand about the sea.

O hymn sublime, confounded, infinite
Of Tempest, how the chaos in my soul
Responds to your appeal, and drifts with cloud !
I too am worn with many moods at war,
Wind thwarting tide ; stern duty, passion, love,
Wrestle while, unresolved to harmony,
They urge me blindly, violent, confused.
The old-world order passeth, and the new
Delaying dawns, one crimson, loud with voices
We know not, with wild wars in earth and heaven ;
The fountains of the great Deep are broken up,
Threatening deluge ; our firm earth goes under ;
Even as well-beloved familiar stars
Beneath the dusk horizon disappear
For him who journeys over alien seas,
So the ideals of our childhood change ;

And as for such lone wanderers there rise
Clear constellations all unknown, for us
Ideas undivined of common weal ;
New duties are the children of new needs,
And wider wants ; yet in the onward way
Stand venerable godlike forms opposed,
Reverend from usage and dear memory.
Young-faced ideals, rosy like the dawn,
Beckoning promise joy, then eagerly
We hurtle old familiars, while we wound
Hearts well beloved, responsive to their call,
And full-mouthed ardours of their warm embrace.
Then Conscience bleeds, for Virtue shocks with
    Virtue
And sweet Affection, on the embattled plain,
While Passion raving more embroils the strife.
And what is duty, what is only pleasure,
In the uncertain glimmer who can tell ?
Tumultuous conflicts in the elements
Have counterparts more terrible within ;
Those rend the body, these lay waste the soul.

One sees his brethren crushed to earth and maimed,
Tortured, and slowly ground to powder, starved,
Harried by hard Vicissitude, or Man
More cruel ; then he questions, doubts, denies
The omnipotent God of justice and of love,
To whom he lifted childish hands in prayer,
Taught by a sainted mother ; whom she trusted
Through a long life, and, dying, leaned upon.
We may not find the wholly excellent

In frail mortality ; we vainly seek
Or in ourselves, or others for the type,
Which hides within the Heart of the Most High,--
Foundation-stone of this inferior sphere.

   More loudly roars the tempest in my soul !
For all the creeds make shipwreck on grim reefs
Of iron Fact before mine eyes ; no charts
Of olden time have laid them down ; discovered
But yesterday, the ravening surge for prey
Claims the pale crews, who have embarked their all
On such frail planks, firm Faith, aspiring Hope,
High confidence that all will yet be well.

   Sheltered a little in the rude cliff-cleft,
I sit and hear the turmoil of the storm,
Where strange small fissures in the lofty crag
Suggest dwarf homes of some weird troglodyte,
Or dim cave-tombs of a long buried race ;
While round white boulders near high-water mark
Lie under ; rain flings full athwart the stone.

   I send my spirit adrift upon the storm,
Careering along the triumph of the blast,
Exultant ! well I know the living God,
God the creator, for destroyer too ;
Who purifies by hurricane, evolves
From birth-throes of rebellion, fraught with fear,
Perplexity and pain, the common weal,
Raised to a higher excellence: wise measures,
With blind experiment, crude theory
Of men who deem that they initiate,
Yea, feel in them the mystical free-will,

Though whirled in broad winds of æonian motion,
Wheeled in predestined orbits round their sun,
All issue in the nobler type of Man.
Lo! the World-Soul commandeth to emerge
From dead, resolved, more simple forms the higher
Through pain, defect, death, folly, sorrow, sin,
Compelleth all to be themselves, through all.
　From thee, O mystic Mother, deeply dark,
From thee, O mother Nature, impulse floweth,
Urging mankind to launch, like wintering bird,
Upon the unknown dim airs, by faith to find
Fair undiscovered realms beyond the dawn!
From thee the whisper, never disobeyed,
"Advance a pace into the Infinite;
Claim young dominions from the formless Deep!"
For Man is child of Nature; on her breast
He lieth; she feeds him; body feeds and mind
From her more large, her all-involving soul.
Change wells from dark unfathomable Founts
Of Love and Wisdom other, more than ours;
Ours a poor rill from these; and therefore we
Must fail to comprehend them; yet we know
Wisdom and Love are by the Antagonist,
Absorbed, assimilated in far worlds
Beyond our knowledge; though we travel thither.
　But who of us that loved would murder one
Child by slow torture? worse the Highest doth
Through Man, through Nature! or say that he
　　permits,
Who could prevent! nay, freely choose your horn!

Yet Reason proves Intelligence supreme ;
Not Force ; nor Chance ; unfathomable then
That all-wise Will, that moral character
By the plumb-line of our intelligence.

I fling my heart abroad on waves of pleasure,
For pleasure is a very friend of man ;
And yet would moderate, would guide my course,
A calm, strong swimmer ; with a modern mind
Float in the turbulence of revolution,
Challenge outworn, intolerable Wrong,
That may have been for olden times fair Right,
And still, amid the clash of swords and sounds,
Forehear, enraptured, heavenly harmonies ;
In tattered, streaming banners of the cloud,
Marching to battle, would divine, foreknow
The vision of the firmly founded State,
The calm, eternal City of the Lord. . . .
  . . . Huge purple phantoms, ash-pale wings, wan,
      wide,
Are marshalled as for conflict ; and they move
Momently changing their weird outline ; deep
Growls a far thunder ; lo ! a sudden glare
Within them tells of angers ; while the main
Reflects pearl, Tyrian dyes, chalcedony,
And opal, from the interspaces, clear
A moment, shining, delicately veiled.

The peoples now begin to reach warm hands
Of fellowship athwart the estranging bounds
Of sea and land, for mutual defence
Against the common tyrant, who can crush

Them jealous, disunited, one by one.
For mutual service are the countries linked
By thrilling nerves electric; how they flash
With human feeling, swift intelligence!
While great fire-breathing vessels, throbbing trains,
Hurry the many-languaged throngs from home,
With bales of produce for exchange, fair wrought
By whirling-limbed machines; thus arteries
Are highways for the transport of supplies
To every several organ; and the frame
Yields to imaginative informing thought,
That moulds a many-functioned manifold
Into one body from an embryo.
Confusion reigns for eyes that only view
Cells moving blindly through a tiny tract
Of tissue, seeming at cross-purposes;
And so the Race, through varying minds and wills,
And clashing ends of personality,
Grows to one Body, after that fair Type,
In the eternal mind of the Most High.

For me, I would be faithful, point the way
To heights communing with ethereal worlds,
Though I myself should stumble on the spurs
Far under; yet in face of all their clamour
Would save the Good uninjured; but the Ark
Is God's, not mine; the whole wide world His own,
How should He lose one single creature in it?
All are in Him, and He abides in all.

Will not the Soul, in Her immortal flight
Along the ages, change Her loss to gain?
But Virtue pushes from Her sepal-sheath,
Proving a prison, though it sheltered well;
And in Her alien habit of the flower
Men may mistake Her for Her fallen fair sister.

I, when I dared presumptuous to ascend
The perilous heights of contemplation, left
Void windows of the outer sense; but now
Keen glances filled them; gazing, I beheld
The Empyrean wholly clear of cloud,
All azure, save for what appeared the wing
Of a great Angel, guardian over all,
Plumy, and soft, and full-irradiate,
Reaching athwart wide heaven; until it grew
To some celestial armour, like chain-mail;
Only the links were tender down, with blue
Between the interstices; mild ocean under
Mirrored blue air, and alabaster cloud;
It seemed as calm indeed as when of old
One stilled the angry waves on Galilee!
And all the storm was hushed within my heart.

SUSPIRIA.

Lines addressed to II. F. B.

Do you remember the billowy roar of tumultuous ocean,
  Darkling, emerald, eager under vaults of the cave,
Shattered to simmer of foam on a boulder of delicate
    lilac,
  Disenchantless youth of the clear, immortal wave?
Labyrinths begemmed with fairy lives of the water,
  Sea-sounding palace halls far statelier than a King's,
Seethe of illumined floor with a never-wearying motion,
  Oozy enchased live walls, where a sea-music rings?

Do you remember the battle our brown-winged
      arrowy vessel
Waged with wind and tide, a foaming billowy night,
To a sound as of minute guns, when gloomy hearts of
    the hollows
  With sullen pride rebuffed invading Ocean's might?
Do you remember the Altarlet towers that front the
    cathedral,
  Dark and scarred sheer crag, flashed o'er by the wild
    sea-mews?

How they wheel aloft lamenting, souls of the ululant
    tempest !
And the lightning billows clash in the welter Odin
    brews !

    A sinister livid glare from under brows of the
        Storm-Sun !
Brows of piled-up cloud, threatening grim Brechou,
Bleaching to ghastly pale the turbulent trouble of water,
    While the ineffable burden of grey world o'er me
      grew !
Yea, all the weary waste of cloud confused with the
    ocean
    Fell full-charged with Doom on a foundering human
      heart :
Our souls were moved asunder, away to an infinite
    distance,
    While all the love that warmed me waned, and will
      depart.
Fiends of the whirlwind howl for a wild carousal of
    slaughter
    Of all that is holy and fair, so shrills the demon wail ;
Ruin of love and youth, with all we have deemed
    immortal !
    My child lies dead in the dark, and I begin to fail !
Wonderful visions wane, tall towers of phantasy tumble ;
    I shrink from the frown without me, there is no smile
      within ;
I cower by the fireless hearth of an uninhabited chamber,
    Alone with Desolation, and the dumb ghost of my sin.

7

I have conversed with the aged; once their
  souls were a furnace;
Now they are gleams in mouldered vaults of the
  memory :
All the long sound of the Human wanes to wails of a
  shipwreck,
  Drowned in the terrible roar of violent sons of the sea !
  In the immense storm-chaunt of winds and waves of
  the sea !
And if we have won some way in our weary toil to the
  summit,
  Do we not slidder ever back to the mouth of the pit?
When I behold the random doom that engulfs the
  creature,
  I wonder, is the irony of God perchance in it ?
'Tis a hideous spectacle to shake the sides of fiends with
  laughter,
  Where in the amphitheatre of our red world they sit !
Yea, and the rosiest Love in a songful heart of a lover,
  Child of Affinity, Joy, Occasion, beautiful May,
May sour to a wrinkled Hate, may wear and wane to
  Indifference,
  Ah ! Love an' thou be mortal, all will soon go grey !
O when our all on earth is wrecked on reefs of disaster,
  May the loud Night that whelms be found indeed
  God's Day !

  Our aims but half our own, we are drifted
    hither and thither ;
  The quarry so fiercely hunted rests unheeded now ;

And if we seized our bauble, it is fallen to ashes,
  But a fresh illusion haunts the ever-aching brow.
Is the world a welter of dream, with ne'er an end, nor an
    issue,
  Or doth One weave Dark Night, with Morning's
    golden strand,
  To a Harmony with sure hand?
Ah! for a vision of God! for a mighty grasp of the real,
  Feet firm based on granite in place of crumbling sand!
O to be face to face, and heart to heart with our dearest,
  Lost in mortal mists of the unrevealing land!
Oh! were we disenthralled from casual moods of the
    outward,
  Slaves to the smile or frown of tyrant, mutable Time!
Might we abide unmoved in central deeps of the Spirit,
  Where the mystic jewel Calm glows evermore sublime!
The dizzying shows of the world, that fall and tumble to
    chaos,
  Dwell irradiate there in everlasting prime.
But the innermost spirit of man, who is one with the
    Universal,
  Yearns to exhaust, to prove, the Immense of Ex-
    perience,
Explores, recedes, makes way, distils a food from a
    poison,
  From strife with Death wrings power, and seasoned
    confidence.
O'er the awakening infant, drowsing eld, and the mind-
    less,
  Their individual Spirit glows enthroned in Heaven,

Albeit at dawn, or even, or from confusion of cloudland,
  Earth of their full radiance may remain bereaven:
  Yea, under God's grand eyes all souls lie pure and
    shriven.

        Nay! friend beloved! remember purple robes
          of the cavern,
And all the wonderful dyes in dusky halls of the sea,
When a lucid lapse of the water lent thrills of exquisite
  pleasure,
  A tangle of living lights all over us tenderly,
When our stilly bark lay floating, or we were lipping the
  water,
  Breast to breast with the glowing, ardent heart of the
    deep!
That was a lovelier hour, whispering hope to the spirit,
  Breathing a halcyon calm, that lulled despair to sleep;
Fairy flowers of the ocean, opening innermost wonder,
  Kindle a rosy morn impearled in the waterways,
A myriad tiny diamond founts arise in the coralline,
  Anemones love to be laved in the life of the chrysoprase:
The happy heart of the water in many unknown recesses
  Childly babbled, and freely to glad companions:
We will be patient, friend, through all the moods of the
  terror,
  Waiting in solemn hope resurrection of our suns!

      Cherish loves that are left, pathetic stars in the
        gloaming;
      Howe'er they may wax and wane, they are with us to
        the end;

The Past is all secure, the happy hours and the mournful
  Involved i' the very truth of God Himself, my friend !
It is well to wait in the darkness for the Deliverer's
    moment,
  With a hand in the hand of God, strong Sire of the
    universe;
It is well to work our work, with cheering tones for a
    brother,
  Whose poor bowed soul, like ours, the horrible gulfs
    immerse;
Then dare all gods to the battle ! Who of them all may
    shame us?
  The very shows of the world have fleeting form from
    thee :
Discover but thy task, embrace it firm with a purpose;
  Find, and hold by Love, for Love is Eternity.

    O to be sure for ever ! weary of hopes and guesses,
  I would the film might fall that veils our orbs in night!
At eve grey phantom armies guard the mighty mountain,
  Denying free approach to wistful wondering sight:
A Presence dim divined through blind impalpable motion,
  An awful formless Form, i' the core of change unmoved,
No more was ours, until the grand invincible Angel,
  The clear-eyed North blew bare Heaven's azure heights,
    and proved
Hope's heavenliest flight weak-winged; his breath with
    clangorous challenge
  Dissolved the cloud-battalions, withering shamed away:
Behold, in sunrise dyed, a wondrous vision of high crag,

Spires of leaping flame arrested in mid-play;
Peak, rock-tower, and dome; huge peals of an ocean of
　　　thunder
Assumed a bodily form in yonder wild array!
And the long continuous roll of cloudy storm subsiding
　　Was tranced to awful slopes of smooth grey precipice,
While over all up-soared, retiring into the heavens,
　　Ever higher and higher, snows and gleaming ice!
Plain beyond plain, the strophes of a glorious poem,
　　Voyaging stately and calm to heights of the argu-
　　　ment . . . .
How to be sure for ever? deepening all our being,
　　And emptying self of self, with Truth we shall be blent.

　　　　Yon hierarchy sublime of calm ethereal mountain
　　Was born of earth's fierce passion, world-confounding
　　　throes,
Fire, and battle, and gloom; the livid demon of lightning
　　Flashed his zigzag blaze to be a norm for those;
Birth and death, monotonous toil in deeps of the ocean,
　　Co-operant blind to fashion a far-off repose.
Whose brief earth-hour may taste ripe future fruit of the
　　ages?
　　Gauge with a life's one pace the march of the armies of
　　　God?
Forestall results of time, flash all the sun from a dew-
　　drop?
　　But where the Sire hath willed, there every footstep
　　trod.

'Tis only a little we know; but ah! the Saviour
    knoweth;
I will lay the head of a passionate child on His gentle
    breast,
I poured out with the wave, He founded firm with the
    mountain;
    In the calm of His infinite eyes I have sought and
    found my rest.
O to be still on the heart of the God we know in the
    Saviour,
    Feeling Him more than all the noblest gifts He gave!
To·be is more than to know; we near the Holy of
    Holies
    In coming home to Love; we shall know beyond the
    grave.

    Ah! the peace of the beautiful realm, like dew,
        sinks into my spirit;
True and tender friend, I love to be here with thee.
The pines, tall fragrant columns of a magnificent temple,
    Are ranged before the ethereal mountain majesty:
While a dove-coloured lapse of the water merrily murmurs
    a confidence
    Into a quiet ear of twilit beautiful bowers;
Sweet breath of the pyrola woos us, white waxen elf of
    the woodland,
    And two tired hearts may play awhile with the
    innocent flowers.

                  (*Sark and San Marino.*)

MONTE ROSA.

Rosa ! thy battlement of beaming ice
Burns, like the battlement of Paradise !
One block of long white light unsulliable
Glows in deep azure, Heaven's cathedral wall,
Gleams, a pure loveliness of angel thought,
With Heaven's inviolable ardour fraught.
A myriad flowers play fearless at thy feet,
And many a flying fairy sips their sweet,
While with the Sun of souls, the Paraclete,
Thou communest up yonder, rapt from earth,
Robed in the evening-gold, or morning-mirth.
One cloudy surge from thy tremendous steep
Recoils, and hangs a warder o'er thy sleep,
Whose awful spirit in deep reverie
Above the world abides eternally :
While seraphs roam around thy silver slope,
Nestle in thy hollows, and with fair-flying hope
Temper the intolerable severity
Of holiest Purpose ; many a floweret blows
In the unearthly Honour of thy snows,
Like innocent loves in souls erect, sublime,
Who breathe above the tainted air of time :

While many a falling water kisses
Tinkling emerald abysses
Of shadowy cavern with cool rain,
Clear gliding rills in polished porcelain
Channels descending o'er a crystal plain
From the Frost-Spirit's palace bowers
Of sea green pinnacles, and toppling towers,
And grim white bastion defiled
With rocky ruin of the wild:
While over all thy luminous pure ice
Rears the stupendous radiant precipice,
High terraces the seraphim have trod,
Stairs dwindling fainter, as they near the abode,
Where in light unimaginable dwells God.

But now around thee sullen, murmuring Storm
Flings his dark mantle; such around the form
Of awful Samuel, summoned from the tomb,
At Endor rose: then all is rayless gloom
About thy Presence for a little while ;
Until God draws in His cathedral aisle
The folding shroud from thy dread countenance.
Behold! above the storm, as in a trance,
Thy grand, pale Face abides, regarding us,
As from Death's realm afar, like risen Lazarus!

Isled in dusk blue, one star thrills faintly shining
Over thy crest in mournful day's declining:

Far away glens deep solitary blanch
With snow fresh fallen of the avalanche;
Forested prowls the haggard wolf, the craven,
While o'er me croaking weirdly wheels the raven;
Yonder in twilight, fretted with fierce fire,
Lower vast vans of hungering lammergeyer !
Dark vassal crags, who guard thine awful throne,
Wearing dim forests for a sounding zone,
Divide to let thy torrent coursers flee
With thunderous embassage to the great Sea.

Behold ! on grand long summits bowed
A huge ghost-cataract of cloud !
Niagara motionless, unvoiced,
In dim rapt air portentous poised !
But ruffled plumes of Tempest lower
Where the giant cliffs uptower,
While their impregnable fort frowns
Defiant, and their haughty crowns
Their vapoury veils,
Livid ice-ribs, and wolf-fanged teeth
Threaten implacable with death
Rash mortal who assails !
Beneath them the heart fails.
One rayless wilderness of stone
Upreared, they warn from their bleak throne ;
Ruined halls of lonely storms,
Whose are weird dishevelled forms,

Dark as eerie crags that loom,
Brooding haggard in the gloom,
Assuming semblance of rent thunder,
While they wait expectant under.

Lo ! one wide ocean of tumultuous sound
Terrific bursts ! flooding Heaven's profound,
Shatters the concave ! hark ! how, one by one,
Each monarch mountain on his far white throne,
Shocked, buffeted by that infernal word,
His own portentous utterance hath roared,
Tearing night, startled with flame-sweep of sword,
And bellowing fierce frantic wrath
Into the steam of that hell-broth
Around: white fires flash swift unfurled
Over dim ruin of a watery world !
Hark ! huge war-standards ponderous unrolling
Over wild surges of tempestuous blast !
While storm-stifled bells are tolling
For souls of pilgrims who have passed
Home at last !
But here amid earthquaking shocks,
Whirlwinds rave around the rocks:
Great pines, agonising horrent
O'er the white terror of the torrent,
In wild lightning-fits leap out
From death's womb, a ghostly rout,
And all wild demon-chariots roll,
Hurtling, chaotic, blind, reft from control;

Until the elemental rage subsides;
Ebbs the fell fury of ethereal tides;
Atlantic billows of slow sullen sound
Subsiding wander o'er the immeasurable Profound.

. . . . Rosa! the Moon soothes thine unearthly
    rest,
And Peace pervades the snows upon thy breast!

                 (*Macugnaga.*)

IN THE CORSICAN HIGHLANDS.

CLOUD-CHAOS surges o'er a crest sublime,
That seems forked lightning spell-bound into stone ;
Abruptly steep flame-pointed precipices,
Dark as the night, dissolve to opaline
In phantom foldings of circumfluent sea.
Their natures blend confused ; the mists assume
A semblance of impenetrable rock ;
Stern rock relents to luminous faint cloud.

Their banners rent as in uproarious war,
Behold ! the vaporous battalions
Unclose, dispelled and routed of loud winds,
That drive them scared, and scattered ; so Jehovah
Clove that astounded sea for Israel.
Yonder beneath me, the enormous crag
Reveals, between grey ghostly robes of them,
Solid, and rude, and perpendicular,
A mighty front of Titans grandly piled,
Umber, and gory red, and pallid green,
Reared in some alien world beyond the cloud,
Stronghold stupendous of immortal gods.

The rude, immense, straight pillars of grey pine
Scale heaven, sustaining tempest-writhen roofs
Of scant, green, level umbrage ; they are built
Athwart yon vaporous and vasty walls
Of far-off mountain : over them arise
Ruinous tower, fantastic pinnacle,
And icy spire in a blue burning air.
They overhang deep, forest-filled ravines
Wandering seawards ; whose dim serpentine
Night ever hears a solemn utterance
Of torrents, with deep monotone attuned
To these wind-oracles of ancient pine.
Yonder a gaunt trunk-Skeleton upbraids
With blasted arms the Bolt that shattered it.
Tusky black monsters reign within the gloom
Of forest, and dead waters desolate :
Dim mists drive blindly through portentous trees
While a weird Sun blinks dwarfed within the drift :
Legions of shadowy shaggy ilex climb
Yon narrow-cloven hollows of the crag.

Now evening falls : an aromatic breath
Of amber oozing from a dun-red bark,
And mountain herb, and many a mountain flower
Pervades the air slow clearing from the cloud :
A vaselike cleft between two snowy peaks
Glowingly fills with a pale violet ;
Beneath appears fair Ocean's purple line,
Far away from far portals of the pass.

Lower, a surge of huge dun purple rock,
Tumultuously contorted, rolls a rude
And shadowy chaos interposed between
Dark peaks and me : Night's ever-deepening gloom
Engulfs the gorges : all is mighty Music,
Phantasmal symphony of ghostly Form,
A visionary Chorus with no sound !

Stern-visaged Isle ! upon thy rocky breast
Two sons were nurtured, heritors of fame.
The one drew pride and ruin from thy veins,
Towering portentous, terrible, alone,
A scourge of God ; Napoleon drew power
To desolate the world ; while Paoli
Drank from dark fountains of thy resolute blood
The patriot's unshamed integrity.

Behold ! I stand within a place of graves,
Low wooden crosses o'er the lonely dead.
Within the wondrous amphitheatre
Of mountains overshadowing they rest ;
Watched, warded, in those awful arms they lie.
Ah ! Nature here hath roused herself to robe
Her oft unheeded royalty in robes
Of godlike splendour, that our eyes may see ;
Hath sounded, as with trumpet-blast of doom,
That our dull ears may slumber not, but hear !
Brands with fierce fire upon the heedless heart
Her names of wonder ! yea, I know ye now :

I bow my head in worship : yea, I feel
Your majesty of godlike Presences ;
Stand here abashed, with mortal head bowed low
Before you, Angels, Demons of the Lord !

Yet with no rapture of strong youth's acclaim
I hail you, as a lowlier brother may
Hail a liege lord, a hero, or a king.
But I have come into your awful courts,
A poor blind broken pilgrim from afar,
Who faltering chances upon some august
Assembly of dread princes, and bows low,
Yet only craves to learn if haply he,
Who used to lead his poor blind footsteps on
With such clear-seeing love, a little child,
Who has been lost to him, alas ! for long,
And whom he vainly seeks about the world,
About the dreary, barren world, be here ?
But meeting no response to his demand,
He can but idly weep a moment, ere
He grope his weary way abroad again.

These are but void and ruined courts to me
Of faded splendour, unremembered Power !
I cannot see aright, I cannot feel.
And while men prate of knowing all the laws,
The mortal cold possessing human hearts
Weighs down their eyes in deep sepulchral gloom.
But if some Angel's sword from forth the night,

With vasty voice of Doom, by human tongues
Called thunder, leapt, and smote me out of all
These evil dreams named living, might I find
My little child, and with him find the Lord?

  We journey ever higher, through a grove
Of moonlit chestnut, where a babbling stream,
At intervals, in open forest glades,
Flashes with ruffled, wandering, pale flame.
The air is richly laden with sweet spoil
From fragrant flower, and foliage faint-green;
Shadowy-folded hills and dells involved
Whisper of verdure lush, luxuriant,
Known to fair elves, or rills who tinkling glide,
Telling sweet secrets, haunted of shy beams,
Whene'er the whims of leafy Ariels,
And cloudy gossamer, aloft allow
Their gentle wandering; tall asphodel,
And flowery fennel, either side our way,
Often we dim discern; but where the woods
No longer in their colonnades of gloom
Involve our path, beyond the precipice,
Behold! how all the regions of the north,
Height, depth, and breadth, are held, filled, domi-
    nated
By one supreme pale presence, Monte d'Oro!
His spirit-robes far floating, a dim grey,
Sombre with forest, pallid with the moon,
His kingly crest snow-gleaming to the stars.

Pan is not dead !   He lives !   He lives for ever !
These awful Demiurgic Powers named Nature
Nourish, involve a half-alive, blind soul,
A human soul, who fondly deems them dead.
Surely the Lord is making us alive !
Mine aching wound shall heal ; for I shall find
My lost, for whom I long ; from thee, my friend,
The weary burden of thy doubt shall pass.
Sorrow and Wrong are pangs of a new birth :
All we who suffer bleed for one another ;
No life may live alone, but all in all ;
We lie within the tomb of our dead selves,
Waiting till One command us to arise.

A SOUTHERN SPRING CAROL.

O Spring ! O Spring ! O Southern Spring !
What a triumphant song you sing !
All the valley sings !
Nor only warblers who have wings ;
All the peach and almond blossom
Seems young carol from their bosom
In the form of flowers,
Wandering every way
On many a spray,
Rills in the blue day,
Very bird-notes in a spray,
Filling all the valley.
And I deem that, as they dally
In the summer light intense,
In the deep Italian blue,
A subtle spirit influence
May re-enchant them to a dew
Of melody pure-hearted,
Hither and thither parted,
From the bosom of the birds,
From the gaily-feathered herds,
And they would be songs again,
One rich rain !

A peach-petal flutters down,
A white moth hath softly flown,
And we hardly know sweet note
From fair vision as they float.
All the valley sings !
An angel kindles when he dips
The fig's candelabra tips
To chrysolite, while many a vine
Amorously will incline
O'er vistas of a golden trellis,
Where a cool and shadowy well is,
All overgrown with mosses wet
And maiden-hair and violet.
O'er many a shrine
Roses twine !
Light green fountains of the palm
Fall in a blue crystal calm ;
Delicate flushing lady tulips
Close their lanceolate dim dew-lips,
Their soft satiny repose
By a light hand flecked with rose ;
Golden jonquils, white narcissus,
Whisper softly, "Come, and kiss us !
Part us not from the sweet brood
Of our companions in the wood !"
Earth's fair features, every one
Instinct with spirit of the sun,
Radiate well-married hues,
Blent with air and ocean blues.
Verily I seem to stand

In a realm of fairyland,
Or I take my dazzled station
In some intense illumination
Of a missal mediæval
Yonder on the hill's upheaval,
Where we hear the convent chime,
Wrought by monk of olden time,
Whom the cloister heard intone,
And many a sun-bleached river stone,
Or the darkling cypress cone.
Cool grey clouds of olive fill
All the foldings of the hill,
While fair dawn-empetalled peaches
Gleam athwart the bloomy reaches
Of quiet harebell-mantled mountain
Gemmed with rivulet or fountain,
Shadowy evening robes, whose hem
Shines with many a water gem :
While rich oranges all golden,
In a darkling foliage holden,
Are a foil to the pale gleaming
Of oval lemon, and the beaming
Ampler cherry trees, one snow
Of blossom in the fading glow !
In pale blue evening,
Ah ! the cherry seems to sing,
With a fairy bridal dower !
Pure white chalices of flower,
Pendent in a pale blue sky,
Shadowy blossom with soft eye !

Dimlit amber mysteries
We faint surmise,
Where bees hover,
And a soft moth-lover !
Oh, I would that I might know
The secret of your bridal snow,
Soul of the pure ecstasy
Softly haunting a grey sky
With such a grace
Of spirit-lace !
For it seems a happy ghost
From the seraph host !
Never bride dissolved in love,
Never saint in realms above,
Nor lark on his own music tost,
Hath more joy than this, embossed,
Shadowy, rare,
On pale blue air ;
White cloud a-flower,
A very shower
Of still rapture unalloyed,
Too overjoyed
For sound of singing !
All the valley sings !
A clear rivulet is flinging
Warbled songs to the pure air,
Laughing, a young infant fair,
Ruffling softly, swiftly passes
Green-illumined among grasses,
Or red anemone to wander,

Where are violet, germander ;
Child pursued in play, to ramble,
After such a sweet preamble,
Among myrtle bowers and bramble.
Green-pennoned canebrakes in the river
All around grey arches quiver ;
While westering Apollo dulls
Delvèd loam, and vivid pulse,
A swart red-vestured toiler waters
From rills, who are the river's daughters.
All the valley sings !
And rings, and rings !
Ah ! Nature never would have power
To breathe such ecstasy of flower,
Vernal songs of happy birds,
The young rill's delicious words,
No iris hues might bring to birth,
No heart were hers for any mirth,
If *he* were turned to common earth !
If a child so fair, so good,
Were a waif on Lethe's flood,
If one soul-source of feeling, seeing,
Were blotted from the realms of being !
She from all delight would start,
With such a horror at her heart,
She would reel dissolved, and faint
With deep dishonour of the taint !
The very girders of her hall
Crushed, her stately floor would fall.
Ourselves are the foundation-stone ;

If thought fail, the world is gone ;
All were ruined, wanting one.
But all the valley sings !
Nature rises on immortal wings !
And soaring, lo ! she sings ! she sings !
　　There is no death !
　　She saith.
O Spring ! O Spring ! O Southern Spring !
What a triumphal song you sing !

UNDER THE STARS.

AH ! what little hearts are ours
To hold the miseries of the world!
Behind our private belts of flowers
We play, nor view to ruin hurled
Our kindred; till for us Death lowers,
And summons from the pleasant bowers.
Dare not forecast the Future—know
The doom that Fate reserves for you!
Look no World-Gorgons in the face !
Grisly madness waits that way:
Only help as help ye may!
We have to pass the loathly place
To reach yon heights of holy day,
Serenely shining far away.
So we justify the Lord,
And kiss the terrible red sword !
For throned in hidden eternal state,
Though wingless, desolate she roam,
The Soul hath chosen all her fate,
Now remembering not the Home,
Whereunto wealthier she will come.
If One who bore the wide world's pain

Heartbroken, blest and trusted God,
I may look up and smile again,
Kiss the plague-enravelled rod,
And follow where the Master trod.
Surely each is kin to all,
And man, a mirror of the whole;
Should worlds, gods, demons, aught appal
Who knows himself a conscious soul?
Give me but time, no bounds may thrall
One who hath God Himself for goal!
Ah, solitudes, immense, profound!
And lonelier solitudes within!
Ye shine, O worlds, in solemn swound;
All the discord, all the din
Of a city's moil and sin
Heard from a tower or higher ground,
Blend to one grand ocean-sound;
So from memories are lost
All we gladly would forget;
Faces white with Death's deep frost
Lose the fever and the fret;
So yonder orbs in darkness met,
Each a silver tranquil ghost,
Lose all of vext and tempest-tost;
By mortal eyes undreamed in day,
Revealed alone to darkling night,
They rest so far, so far away,
I deem their calm and gentle light
For our consoling seems to say,
"Absorbed within the Infinite,

Deforming evils fallen away,
No dishonouring care may stain,
The Ideal only rule and reign !"
Dear places, feelings, thoughts, will go,
Calm revolving worlds will fail,
But when the stars have ceased to glow,
Abideth One who ne'er may pale,
And all in Him immortal, hale,
Our life, abide; whate'er remove,
Remaineth the Eternal Love;
And surely Love will reunite
Who wander sundered here in night !
Surely Love will lead them home,
However far afield they roam !

POEMS OF THE PEOPLE.

POEMS OF THE PEOPLE.

POOR PEOPLE'S CHRISTMAS.

Hark ! the Christmas bells ring round !
Many light hearts with joy abound !
They come and go upon the wind,
"Peace and goodwill to all mankind !"

Where bleared faces of mean houses
Lean as if to touch each other,
Where idle, ugly vice carouses,
And the brown fogs choke and smother,
In a room confined, dun, damp,
Sits a woman scantly clad,
Sewing by a feeble lamp
Some lovely raiment deftly made,
Rich apparel to be worn
In splendid halls by laughing wealth,
Whose pale sister here forlorn
Leaves in it all her youth and health—

Ah ! I wonder, can it bless,
Such living lining to a dress? . . .
Take the lovely raiment off !
Hell hath given it with a scoff !
For she must toil ere daydawn dim,
Long after winter suns have set,
And even so, the Hunger grim
Slow feeds on lives she fights for yet—
Three tattered little ones who play
Faint-hearted on the mouldy floor:
She fought for other two ; but they
Have gone where want can hurt no more.

Vile fumes, with subtle poison-breath,
That fouls the throat, killed one young child :
Roofs bulge in this abode of death,
Walls totter and tumble, damp-defiled ;
While on the too scant space intrude
Rats, hustling the young human brood.
A mean bed, table, broken chair,
Furnish the degraded room ;
A print, some delf, one flower fair,
Are fain to mitigate the gloom.
Bitter winter wind shrilled through
Rotten door and window when it blew.
She, working early, working late,
Breathes no impatient word nor wail :
Her heavy task may ne'er abate,
Though eyesight fade and strength may fail.

Her husband, long through accident
Disabled, might no more endure
To watch her, burden-bowed and bent,
The wife, whom these dark dens immure,
Whom no longing love may cure,
Nor help, though she be bruised and rent.
Confused, heartbroken, he will hide
His eyes for ever under tide
Of deeply, darkly rolling Thames,
That quenches hottest human flames.

Merry Christmas bells ring round !
Many light hearts with joy abound ;
They come and go upon the wind,
" Peace and goodwill to all mankind ! "

Merry Christmas chimes rang round,
When he sought the river's bank,
Rang over him the while he drowned,
And in the depths a third time sank,
While laughing youth's swift-flying feet
To music danced in yonder street,
And in gay halls glad masquers meet.

Now the flickering lamplights float
Idly over corpse and boat ;
From tower and temple London frowns
On all this ruin of her sons ;

9

On her huge dome the cross of gold
Gleams in winter starlight cold ;
Nor storied old-world obelisk,
Nor the illumined horal disk
High orbed on stately Westminster,
Where the Parliaments confer,
Take any heed of the black spot
That doth the silver moonlight blot,
A human shape unhearing hours,
Pealed now from modern, ancient towers,
That dark on turbid water ridges
Rocks in reflected flame from bridges
Where steam-lit trains, with living freight,
Going to glad homes elate,
Near ships laden with merchandise,
Spice, or silk of gorgeous dyes,
Where men from far realms of sunrise
Wait, forgetting care and sorrow,
In hope to greet dear friends to-morrow,
While their paddle-wheel foams over
The swaying corse, a senseless rover.

He turned from life, but left some words
Dyed in the anguish of his soul ;
Deep anguish the brief page records,
Before dull waters o'er him roll.

"Upon the bed, or broken chair,
I sit and brood in my despair.

At times my brain seems all confused—
To watch my Mary's failing eyes,
And youth consumed with too much toil,
While patient at her task she dies !
I, pinioned, helpless, may not foil
Slow deaths that round my dear ones coil !
Over a new dress sits she bowed ?—
I thought it was her own white shroud ;—
Our wee Willie, like a weed,
Thrown into a nameless grave—
I am but one more mouth to feed !
They starve here, and I cannot save. . . .
I am but one more mouth to feed ! . . .
We could not even put a stone,
To show where Willie lies alone !
When I left home, my love would write
That, ere our Willie went to bed,
He, wishing father a good-night,
Kissed the written words, she said,
Ere softly slept the curly head.
Ah ! and now the boy is gone !—
We could not even put a stone !

(*Bells peal*) ". . . Well loved those chimes
  In happier times. . . .
Once more we have our cheerful home,
Around the window roses blow;
I see my Mary fair as foam,

Blithely singing, come and go,
While rosed with health the children roam. . . .
Now we are ground 'twixt two millstones—
The man that wrings the murderous rent,
Yet shelters not the naked bones
Cooped in his plague-fraught tenement,—
And vampires who suck sleek content
From human anguish, tears, and groans,
Clutch the fruit of our life's toil,
And batten upon the unholy spoil,
Throwing a wage-scrap back for fuel,
Lest man-mills stop the labour cruel,
And cease with Death unequal duel.
Shall we, chained starvelings, go, buy law,
To save us from the robber's claw?
Law is a cumbrous thing to move;
It will not come and help for love!
Buy women to starve at ' market-price,'
Gallio-Law, with looks of ice,
Smiles placid; poor man, steal a crust,
To feed them, Jefferies, judge most just,
Thee, wrath-red, into gyves will thrust.
' Church and State will guard,' saith he,
' The sacred rights of property!'
England wrestles for the slave
Enthralled beyond the alien wave;
Why doth this mother of the free
Let her strong sons with cruel glee
Crush weak sisters at her knee?
Set thine own house in order—then

Go and preach to evil men !
In feudal dungeons underground
They buried their live victims bound,
And we in our vile vaults immure
These whose crime is to be poor,
Starve babes and women innocent,
Tortured, in black prisons pent.
Feudal lords would *feed* the slave ;
But Capital from his despair
Extorts more toil than flesh can bear,
Keeps him half-living in his grave,
That serf may earn, and master have,
Till kindlier Death arrive to save.

" True men devise large schemes to heal
This gangrene of the Commonweal,
This prime injustice of the world,
That drones, who waste the wealth, may steal
From makers, to the dunghill hurled. . . .
. . . What use to watch slow murder done
On wife, and babe, and little son—
When near me glides Oblivion ? "
So, while the indifferent body rolls,
With other things that have no souls,
On the blind tide to random goals,
In lustred lordly palace hall
Radiant boys and maidens play ;
On whose cold doorstep women fall
Starved, numbed, and naked, life gone grey ;

Within, youth's agile feet to sound
Of music flying, bells ring round,
Come and go upon the wind,
" Peace and goodwill to all mankind ! "

On massy bridge, on broad-built quay,
Tumultuous tides of hurrying wealth
Sweep the marred sons of misery,
(Who thrid by sufferance, by stealth,
Their faint way; near the parapet
Cower, dull aware of fume and fret,)
Sweep them to where they may forget !
For riverward wan eyes are bowed ;
Beside whom roars the traffic loud,
And the many-nationed crowd.
See grimed and haggard him or her,
Amid the animated stir
Of throngs that leave a theatre ;
Well-dressed men cab and carriage call,
Round white shoulders fold the shawl,
Praise or blame what box or stall
Observed of acted joy or grief,
Carelessly, with comment brief—
Civic, or military pomp,
Massed colour, banner, drum and trump,
Court dames in well-appointed carriages,
Fair-favoured, fashionable marriages
Wolf-lean Hunger's eye disparages !
Wherein, as in some magic glass,

Ye may foresee your triumph pass,
Learning's vaunted vast appliances
Shattered in terrible defiances,
Flinging to the wild winds all affiances !
Do ye not hear low thunders rumble,
Ere, lightning-struck, the fabric crumble ?
Your marts are thronged, luxurious, bright,
Your magic moons confound the night,
Yet marbled warehouse, palace height,
Grey minster that hath borne the brunt
Of Time's long battle, all confront
Shame, grim Nakedness, and Want !
While close-shut doors of secret sin
Open upon hell-flames within !

Hearken ! how grand organ-strains
Shake the emblazoned window-panes,
Where priest and gorgeous ritual blesseth
Whoso prayeth, or confesseth,
In holy twilight of hushed fanes !
Yet Christmas carols from the church
Mock those dim figures by the porch,
Huddled, famished in their rags
Drink-sodden these from alehouse lurch,
And those lie numbed upon the flags,
Till, passing, a policeman drags
To ward or workhouse, "moves them on"
Somewhere, while they make low moan,
Pale spectres of dread Babylon !

But the flaunting harlot's ditty
Striketh even a deeper pity,
Cruel Want's degraded daughter,
On her way to the dark water,
Where horror-breathing, dense brown air
Grimly shrouds a dumb despair. . . .
. . . Is there a worse hell over there?

The holly and the mistletoe
Cheer our banquet, wine-cups flow,
Light laughter bubbles o'er the bowl,
And we forget no Christmas dole;
Yet our grief-burdened sisters die
Around us in slow agony,
While we are ringing in the morn
When man's Deliverer was born; . . .
. . . Ah! but our Brother too wore thorn!

Pale Mary toils; her hollow eyes
Are patient, mild, of heavenly blue;
Hourly repeats the sacrifice
That all the world to Calvary drew;
"Father, forgive their cruelties;
For they know not what they do." . . .
. . . She murmurs, "Now I feel Thee near!
My little ones I leave to Thee:
Do what thou wilt,—I trust, not fear. . . .
Thy Birthday bells ring merrily!

I am weary, and would rest,
Gentle Jesus, on Thy breast !
I shall see Willie,—yes, and Jim,
My heart's own husband ; turbid, dim,
His mind was from our suffering so ;
Therefore the Lord forgave, I know,
The unbelief that conquered him.
Ah ! but I wonder much how long
He will endure their cruel wrong ! "
    A high-born sister who had left
Her vantage-ground to help the weak,
Supplying unto these bereft
From her full store whate'er they seek,
Came that night, a nurse, to tend
The dying woman ; and she heard
Near the poor pallet, ere the end,
Low song as from some heavenly bird,
Although no human lips were stirred !
Christ came, in vision, to the dying,
Led by the hand their own lost child ;
He saith : " Love justifies relying
On him, daughter ! " and she smiled !
Near the boy a Christmas tree
Laughed with lights full merrily !
" Love justifieth your relying,
And heareth ever bitter crying
Of those whom the hard world hath spurned :
My martyrs high estate have earned."
A common workman seemed the Lord,
Standing by the poor bedside ;

Yet she knew He was the Word,
That Jesus who was crucified,
And poured contempt on human pride.

" My servants fashion even now
Justice for the commonweal ;
From toilers with the hand, the brow,
Idle men no more may steal ;
My servants seek ; I whisper how
They may find the remedy,
Save My little ones who cry:
For I am poor Myself, you know ;
The poor are Mine, and I will heal !—
Already dawns millennium ;
Soon My holy reign will come.
The man who loved you, whom you love,
Was of the faithful band I move.
Awhile I hid My face from him,
For awhile his ways were dim ;
Baser, earthlier passion jars
With spheral music of the stars ;
Yet in the end all makes, not mars !
I vindicate his human place
For every member of My race ;
Let every manhood find free scope !
Now, beasts of burden, with no hope,
Men ripen not peculiar grain,
Given to each for general gain,
The social body to sustain.

Your Churches rarely worship Me,
Who am the incarnate Charity:
They call indeed upon My name ;
But their proud Christ with crown and flame
Is another, not the same.
I made known a suffering God ;
I consecrated Pain's abode.
Yet are they refuges for faith,
Though she be faded to a wraith,
Though driven from the altar, she
Oft in the world find sanctuary.
Strong men, refrain from legal greed !
Hear the fate-smitten when they plead !—
Justice, not almsgiving, they need.
God with conscience dowered you,
With more than in mere Nature grew ;
All are brethren, all are one ;
Wound other hearts, ye wound your own !
Strong men ! poor weak worms ! when *ye* fall,
On whom, in trouble, will ye call ?
When God hath changed your countenance,
And sends you feeble, fainting, hence ? "

Then that gentle Face grew stern ;
Sun-blazing eyes confront and burn
All the Temple-shadowed lies,
The marble-tomb proprieties
Of our later Pharisees,

Pious, proud, decorous, hard ;
He blasted base content, and marred.
They shrinking wither up, nor linger—
Even as when, writing with His finger,
In the old Syrian garden, He
Shamed with a God-word quietly
Phylacteried fathers of the men,
Whose race hath the hard heart, as then.
" My birthday bells chime merrily !
Come, dear child, more close to me !
My best is evermore the prize
Of souls who nobly agonise ! "

No feeble glimmer in the room,
Heaven's own effulgence doth illume
Her spirit ; the poor sempstress died,
And Love immortal claimed a bride.

Hark ! the Christmas bells ring round !
Many light hearts with joy abound ;
They come and go upon the wind :
" Peace and goodwill to all mankind ! "

THE CHILDREN'S GRASS.

I.

WHERE the twinkling river pushes
'Thwart the dipping swan,
All his ruffling down
Very softly blown,
Lustrous blue reflects the rushes
Where the coot is gone ;
Thames, an innocent heart of childhood,
Buoying lovers from the wild wood,
Hearing boyish laughter chime
Where the flashing oars keep time,
Where they quiver
In the river :

In a sunshine sown with song
Of many a merry bird,
Three sunny children bound along,
With many a merry word.
Their eyes blue fountains of delight,
And every cheek a rose,
Their dimpled hands with grasses light
So full, they hardly close.

One fawn-like little maiden falls
Breathless upon her mother,
Telling how yonder elf who calls,
Her tiny wavering brother,
Chose to pull the tender stems
Where the dew-drop lingers,
And marvelled when the limpid gems
Fell upon his fingers.
She tells a soft-eyed rabbit brown
Near a wimpling runnel
Eyed them askance, then hurried down
Through a plantain tunnel.
In the woodland sweetly smell
Fairy grass and clover,
Sensitive in the woodland dell,
Where the bees hum over;
"O! I love the summer well;
Mother, will it soon be over?"

II.

Where the unholy river gleameth,
Deep, and cold, and dun,
Hiding secrets from the sun,
As an awful dream one dreameth,
As Oblivion:

Three little children in the reek
Of the monster town,

With a woman worn and weak,
Ere the sun goes down,
Toil by flare of ghastly light
In a dingy fume :
Two young children carry bright
Grasses in the room :
An elder sister with her mother
Decks the blades with glass,
Sprinkles one and then another,
As with dews of grass.
How the vivid verdure gleams
In the child's old face !
Starved and very pale she seems,
With a hollow place
Dark beneath her eyes, how wearied,
Lashless looking on the blearèd
Mimic grass,
Dewed with glass !
Hark ! she gives a feeble cough,
And the withered mother
Glances where some paces off
A coffin holds another
Maiden very cold and white,
Not yet hidden out of sight.
" Mother, I am very weary !"
So she moans with accents dreary :
" Mother, make my bed !"
" Child," the woman answers, " finish !
Dare not from your task diminish
Aught, for fear a watchful neighbour,

Bidding lower for the labour,
Seize our bitter bread !"
Ladies in a lustred hall
Wear them gaily for a ball
In their fair
Wavy hair.
"Mother, I can toil no longer ;
After sleep I shall be stronger !"
. . . . After sleep, the child was dead.

There the unholy river gleameth,
Deep, and cold, and dun,
Hiding secrets from the sun,
As an awful dream one dreameth,
As Oblivion :

Are not these thy children, Father ?
These—or only those ?
Are we all lost orphans rather
Of whom—none knows?

FROM "THE RED FLAG."

YOUR grand colossal edifice to-day
Rests on a yawning darkness and decay ;
Beware ! for it is ready to vanish away !
Yea, is it founded on the people's backs ?
Behold ! how as ye walk the sanguine tracks
Ye leave are slippery with human gore,
The life, the health, the souls of men your floor.
Glance not below ; yield to the organ's pealing ;
Explore the lonely grandeurs of the ceiling !
Ah ! but your tyrannous structure is atremble—
I who behold it dare no more dissemble :
God breathes upon it with the breath of doom :
Phantoms of empire summon from the tomb !
Dominant o'er us glares the cross of gold,
And haughty hierarchies manifold
Brandish the symbol for a flaming sword,
Kneel to the cross, and crucify the Lord !
Friend of the lowly, fainting on the wood,
Behold thy poor upon a golden rood !

. . . . The lonely toiler, gasping for some air,
Listens in shadowy poison of the stair,

10

Listens, a wounded beast within his lair. . . . . .
. . . . . And there is *Peace* in London !

Now trips a dame who lifts her skirt for fear
Of many a foul contamination here,
Revealing delicate ankles to the friend,
Who (to assist) his manly arm may lend.
"Think what a desperate misery may slink
In these low neighbourhoods from whence we
    shrink?"
In silver tones she whispers : "Look ! there prowl
Two terrible ragged ruffians with a scowl."
"Near our town-houses ! who could fancy it?"
Drawls out the dandy with more birth than wit.
She, with a slight, quick shiver, half a sigh :
"One's heart aches even to *dream* such poverty !"
(It jarred her nervous sensibility.)
"And yet, as Mister Glozeman said in church,
To make the vessel of the State to lurch,
To shake our ancient Order is the worst
Crime : it deserves the torture, 'tis accurst
Of God and man—he meant the Communist
Canaille in Paris."   Then the dandy hissed
With panic fury, "Shoot the draff by millions !
So may our scum here learn to make rebellions !"
To clear some stray defilement from her dress,
Bending she slightly on his arm may press ;
Then, as if breeding were a little at fault
In that last ardour of her friend's assault

Even on hereditary foes, the mob,
On swarms unclean, who sweat and starve and rob,
She waved aside the subject she had lent
Her glance in passing, drawling as she went,
" They say the poor are so improvident ! "
Half absently she spoke, to weightier themes
Turning anon—to cunning, lordly schemes
For stifling noxious popular low measures :
Then of refined aristocratic pleasures
They babbled—Hurlingham—the ducal ball—
Of a monstrous nobleman turned Radical,
Of latest fashions out, a novel tie,
Or the last sweet thing in adultery.

The lonely toiler, gasping for some air,
Listens in shadowy poison of the stair,
Listens, a hunted beast within his lair. . . . .
. . . . And there is *Peace* in London !

It happened once two gentlemen were stayed
Here, waiting some companion delayed.
Sauntering to and fro they smoking walked,
Or leant against the house-wall while they talked.
One was an oldish man ; the other, he
Spake as one claiming great authority.
His dust-hued head was growing grey in part—
From tardy fellow-feeling with his heart.
" Not to admire " the only art he knew
To keep him comfortable as he grew.

What might have moved the vulgar to distraction
Moved him to limp distaste or satisfaction.
But he had taken honours at his college,
And deemed himself a microcosm of knowledge.
A sort of sour old maid the man was born;
He could secrete but weak incontinent scorn;
Sterile to foster, organise, produce—
Aught but sophistic pleas for some abuse.
He could be lively only when he hated:
Pungent aromas all evaporated,
When he with heavy hand, with heavier face,
Apotheosised English commonplace;
A Rubens' cherub cumbersomely squat,
Labouring to upheave some royal fat
Skyward—the whole falls marvellously flat!
With ponderous platitude his smart review
Lumbers along when it proclaims the true
Plethoric gospel of the well-to-do.
Man of a *petite culture*, whose college culture
Is but a whited sepulchre sepulture
Of living manhood—his in sooth was small:
Only a castrate creature's after all.

Ah! though they give two fingers to the Saviour,
Best clothes on Sunday and demure behaviour,
Men of the world on every working day
Put the old creed with childish things away.
Measure the infinite God on pain of hell;
But do not heed Him when you buy or sell.

Call Jesus Lord decorously on Sunday,
But treat Him as a genial fool on Monday.
Lift up your pious eyes at Darwin's creed;
And try to prove him right about your breed,
Dear fellow-Christians! who live as though
Not even yet you'd struggled from below.
For beasts of prey with all their savage strife
Are still the cherished models of your life.
Ye war with all your fellows for existence,
And when you've thrown them, still with fierce
    insistence
Grind them beneath you, crush them all to death,
That you may breathe a more luxurious breath.
Hail! weaponed man of grand expanding brain,
Most formidable beast of all that stain
Our mother-earth with fratricidal blood!
Tigers but raven hungry for their food;
But thou, to fling one shining bauble more
In coffers bursting with thy gold before,
Starvest the babes and women at thy door!
Ah! what if some unshamed iconoclast,
Crumbling old fetish-raiments of the past,
Rouse from dead cerements the Christ at last?
What if men take to following where He leads,
Weary of mumbling Athanasian creeds?

How these two friends congenial conversed
Here, as the listener heard it is rehearsed,
As from his slightly varied point of view
It might have sounded to the speakers too.

" Self-interest enlightened is our rule :
Perish the pauper, and the general fool !—
Well for the luckier or shrewder man !
For he, by Heaven's especial favour, can
Lodge duller rivals in foul dens like these,
And feed them with rank garbage if he please.
Mercy is an exploded superstition ;
Men are but brutes in bloodier competition.

" The State ! what call has that to interfere ?
Are we not free-born Britons living here ?
If these like not their scrofulous dens, you know,
They're free to change their quarters ; let them go.
Why one of these may struggle uppermost !
Himself may trample on the writhing host,
They cursing him, he cursing from above—
Hatred and Hell are finer things than Love !
The State forbids that paupers should be slain
With knives and guns ; but as for stench and drain,
And putrefying styes they build so small,
'Tis suicide to breathe in them at all,
Breath turns to poison—that's another thing—
See Malthus on prolific littering !
Children are luxuries—let these dispense
With offspring—we ourselves to save expense
Lop off the babes, and the benevolence.
Mother ! with murderous unflinching eye
Gaze on your moaning babe about to die ;
Ring in the rich man's child with jubilation,
And ring the poor man's out, O happy nation !

Woman, *your* babe is 'surplus population!'
Why take such constant thought about the body?
Man shall not live by bread"—"but by his toddy,
Margeaux, and Bisque-soup rather," quoth the wag.
"Don't chaff, nor let your rapt attention flag,"
Resumed the Gigadibs, who seemed offended,
"My arguments will be the sooner ended.
What was I saying? well, these Radicals
Pamper the carnal part of pauper pals
Unduly; why not teach them to endure
With fortitude these ills they cannot cure?
Throw them a sop of wholesome moral saws—
(Ah! pestilent 'education'—*that's* the cause,
Which *makes* them carp at our existing laws)
The dogs are always yelping for a bone:
Fling them to bite a weighty moral stone!

"A man must grab whatever he can get;
We human creatures are not angels yet.
You must not stab, nor strangle, a poor neighbour;
For, if you did, why you would lose *his* labour.
No; take advantage of his cramped position
To mangle him with your cruellest condition.
Rob soul and body by superior wit
And fortune; ignorant hunger will submit.
If he should gash you, that were ugly murder:
Dribble his life-blood slowly—you're in order.
Nay, surely 'tis a very venial vice
To buy one's workman at the market price."

. . . . The lonely toiler, gasping for some air,
Listens in shadowy poison of the stair,
Listens, a wounded beast within his lair. . . . . .
. . . . And there is *Peace* in London !

A Man grew God upon the shadowy cross,
And taught the world to triumph in love's loss.
Following Him they took for great and holy,
Men helped the weak, forbore to insult the lowly;
The mighty made them ministers of woe,
Because the Lord had served us high and low:
Now Love and Chivalry lie done to death;
Stony-eyed monsters feed on human breath:
In Christ's forgotten grave we have buried weakness,
Justice, and Mercy, and Righteousness, and Meekness !

What ! shall Wealth kneel upon the fainting forms
Of millions whom scarce a raiment warms,
Draining their very heart's blood leisurely,
And shall we wonder when with frenzied cry,
Beyond endurance urged, at last they leap
To murder gorged wealth where it lies asleep?
The legal armed oppressor of his neighbour,
He who hath goaded overdriven labour,
A peaceful tyrant, the Red Flag unfurled:
He stands accurst of God, and of the world !
. . . . There is *War* in London.

POEMS OF HUMAN BEAUTY.

POEMS OF HUMAN BEAUTY.

GANYMEDE.

An azure heaven, where floats a feathery cloud,
An azure sea, far-scintillating light,
Soft, rich, like velvet, yielding to the eye;
Horizons haunted with some dreamlike sails;
A temple hypæthral open to sweet air
Nigh, on the height, columned with solid flame,
Whose flutings and acanthus-work are quick
With lithe green lizards, and whose shadows sharp
Bar slantwise inner wall and golden floor.

A locust-tree condensed the hazeless light
On glossy leaves, and let some trickle low
Among the cooler umbrage underneath;
Subdued there to a mellower quiet key,
Beholding unaware a lovely youth
Bare-limbed reclining, statue-moulded, white,
Whose dainty hand and rounded arm support
His chestnut-curled head, conscious, conquering.

Near by him, leaning on the chequered bole,
Sits his companion gazing on him fond,
A goat-herd, whose rough hand on bulky knee
Holds a rude hollow reeden pipe of Pan,
Tanned, clad with goatskin, rudely-moulded, large;
While yonder, browsing in the rosemary
And cytisus, you hear a bearded goat,
Hear a fly humming, with a droning bee
In yon wild thyme and in the myrtles low,
That breathe in every feebly-blowing air;
Whose foamy bloom fair Ganymede anon
Plucks with a royal motion and an aim
Toward his comrade's tolerant fond face.
Far off cicada shrills among the pine,
And one may hear low tinkling where a stream
Yonder in planes and willows, from the blaze
Of day coy hiding, runs with many a pool
Where the twain bathe how often in the cool!

And so they know not of the gradual cloud
That stains the zenith with a little stain,
Then grows expansive, nearing one would say
The happy earth—until at last a noise
As of a rushing wind invades the ear,
Gathering volume, and the shepherd sees,
Amazed forth-peering, dusking, closing all
Startled and tremulous rock-roses nigh,
Portentous shadow; and before he may
Rise to explore the open, like a bolt

From heaven a prodigy descends at hand,
Absorbing daylight ; some tremendous bird,
An eagle, yet in plumage as in form
And stature far transcending any bird
Imperial inhabiting lone clefts
And piny crags of this Idæan range.

But lo ! the supernatural dread thing,
Creating wind from cavernous vast vans,
Now slanting swoops toward them, hovering
Over the fair boy, smitten dumb with awe.
A moment more, and how no mortal knows,
The bird hath seized him, if it be a bird,
And he though wildered hardly seems afraid,
So lightly lovingly those eagle talons
Lock the soft yielding flesh of either flank,
His back so tender, thigh and shoulder pillowed
How warmly, whitely in the tawny down
Of that imperial eagle amorous !
Whose beakèd head with eyes of burning flame
Nestles along the tremulous sweet heave
Of his fair bosom budding with a blush,
So that one arm droops pensile all aglow
Over the neck immense, and hangs a hand
Frail like a shell, pink like an apple bloom ;
While shadowy wings expansive causing wind
Jealously hide some beauty from the sun.

Poor hind ! who fancied as the pinions clanged
In their ascent, he looking open-mouthed

Distraught yet passive, that the boy's blue eye
Sought him in soaring ! his own gaze be sure
Wearied not famished feeding upon all
The youth's dear charms for ever vanishing
From his love-longing, hungered for in heaven—
Took his last fill of delicate flushed face,
And sculptured limb, with rosy pendent foot
Slim-ankled, body dimpled, while he went.
Behold ! he fades receding evermore
From straining vision misting dim with tears,
Gleaming aloft swan-white into the blue
Relieved upon the dusky ravisher,
Deeper and deeper glutting amorous light,
That cruel swallows all for evermore.

PASSION.

O PALE my lady, where shall we ride?
Into the forest dark and wide,
Into the roaring deep sea-tide,
You and I only, side by side?

Your eyes, like stars in a well's clear gloom,
May be sinister orbs imposing doom,
Gates of life, or doors of the tomb,
Yet mellower than moonlit foam,
Your burning beauty warms the room.

Cling to me, cling to me, lady mine,
Your lips are more than the red red wine,
Your flower white glows in the rosy shine,
We quaff to-day from a draught divine,
And still I pine, I pine, I pine!

O pale my lady, and were you death,
Kissing away the soul's own breath,
I would follow, for all cold Reason saith,
Even where Ruin raveneth!

AZRAEL:

A DREAM OF PLEASURE.

" Azrael, the angel of death."

MOURN for Annabel!
The village bell is tolling, and she will
Never arise from where she lieth still,
Cold and so lovely, flowers white and red,
Old dames and tender damozels have shed
Tearful, all over her, in shadowy air
Alive with perfume curling blue and rare,
Jewels and gold and jasper glowing deep
As in a dreamland of a solemn sleep,
With solemn music plaining while the mourners
    weep.

Fair Azrael, with Annabel the child
Of Southern suns, a panther supple and wild,
Mellow and beautiful, the while one tarried
Far hence, a man she never loved but married,
Wandered in sweet communion day and night
Within her garden, shielded from the light
Of suns too violent, under pensile palm,

And aromatic, glossy-leaved calm
Orange, with lemon wedding boughs above ;
In whose green twilight bridal blooms of love
Bud, and expand their petals, till they shed
Lavish white coronals on either head,
On lustrous ebony and golden head.
They wandered where a soft Æolian sea
Fills far off with profound tranquillity
Half of the interval, which lies between
Shadowy cypresses and pines that lean
Over the sunlight ; half is filled with air
Azure as ocean ; near, a fountain fair
Singing springs ever thwart blue air and main,
A shifting snowcloud, twinkling into rain,
Drifting to fume that feeds earth's emerald :
Anon their dreamy vision is enthralled
With scintillating of a ruffled ocean
Among thin olive-foliage in motion :
Seaward from flowers around their feet a lawn
Slopes ; all the greenery's a haunt of fawn,
Or nymph marmoreal : from shade to shade
On the sea-lustre glows and glides to fade,
Swiftly and silent, many a wing-like sail
Of bark aerial ; never seems to fail
Some new surprise of freshly-flowing joy,
Wafting young lives afar from all annoy.
Eros and Psyche in white marble embrace,
Whom lustrous-leaved camellias enlace :
In light and shadow of a terebinth,
Elsewhere, upon a myrtle-inwoven plinth,

Heavenly Hebe her perennial charm
Unfolds; young Dionysos a lithe arm
Curls over love-locks, and a rounded form,
In fair profusion of lit vine-leaves warm.
When either Phidian image glows in roses
Lavish around them, or at eve reposes
Flushed with a glory, breatheth every one
Alive, a new bride of Pygmalion-
Sweet Mitylene, isle of love and song,
Two fair young lovers for an hour prolong
Reverberate modulations from the lyre,
Whose soul still haunts thee with voluptuous fire !
Sappho, Arion, and Terpander breathe
O'er hill and valley; lawny mists enwreathe
Faintly before all lovers oversea
A mountain, hued like flowers of memory;
Where Aphrodite, born of Paphian foam,
Found the fair shepherd in his piny home,
And where, on Ida, an imperial Bird
Ravished a fairer from his pipes and herd.

They read or sang sweet songs, and oft a star
Thrilled in a roseate eve to her guitar.
She wore pomegranate crimson in her hair,
Around her waist and shoulders only rare
Silk from Olympian looms, like gossamer ;
While languid pearls lay heavingly on her
Virginal bosom ; ambergris and myrrh
Enkindling breathe from ocean-blue enamel,

Whose misty fervours golden lids entrammel :
And while they taste a bright Methymnian wine,
Amber-inhaled ambrosial fumes entwine
Delicious dream around them : fingers fine
Fill often his half-laughing, amorous lips
With pleasant, garnet-hued pomegranate pips,
Or luscious, lucent dainties that her skill
Can from sweet, crimson-hearted fruits distil.
If with his wanton mouth he gently bite,
But very gently will she feign to smite.
Three interlaced half-moons of diamond
Thrill for rich ecstasy to link, with frond
Of fern-wrought rubies, on her balmy breast
Her silk translucency of filmy vest.
He wore a slumbrous oriental gold
Dusky with silk inwoven, half unrolled
From a white bosom of ideal mould.

Once when a silver-clanging chime
Told the stealthy flight of time,
They left a cedar-raftered chamber,
Where oil in opaline and amber
Gleamed, as mildest lamps are able,
Over furs of lynx and sable ;
Crimson wools, Iranian fur
Of panther, pard, or minever.
And while they went, some drowsy doves
In holm and laurel flew like loves
Over them ; the mild fire-flies
Gleamed before their happy eyes.

Fair was the night when youth and lady stept
From where their lemon-tinted villa slept,
With balustrade and roofing palely grey,
Laved of the moon, beneath a grove that lay
Under enchantment, to a hushful bower
Of bay and asphodel, with passion flower
Inwoven : it was warm and dusk therein,
And delicate foliage made a shadowy thin
Lacework suspended in aerial blue
Silvery twilight, over where they two,
Muffled in mossful secrecy, reclined
Nigh one another, Azrael behind.

"In the tree
A murmur, as of indolent shed sea
On sands at midnight ceasing slumbrously !
Through dim, uncoloured leaves
An elfin glimmer cleaves
A varying way from realms of mystery."
So sang she softly to her soft guitar,
And ceased ; and both were silent, hearing far
The bubbling fountain, and a nightingale,
That seemed to flow at intervals and fail.
Her face for him was pencilled pure and fine
Athwart the gloaming; and, "O lady mine,"
He whispered, "how adorable are you
To-night ! forgive me !" till there softly grew
A tender arm around her form, and she
Yielded and leaned on him responsively,
Until his blood ran fire when she pressed

Her dewy, ripe young lips upon his breast,
Moonwhite in moonlight; for a ray had come
To nestle in the fair, congenial home.
Then mouth burned mouth, her undulating charms
Yielding to his luxurious young arms.
Later, in sweet confusion's disarray,
Hand in hand stole they to a little bay,
Where a pale foam stole out of a grey sea,
And kissed the pale rock ever murmurously.
Cypress leaned mournful over, and a throng
Of hushful moonwhite houses lay along
Yon circling shoreside, minarets, how fair !
Arising tall and slender into air :
A chaunt was wafted from a fisher's boat,
Dozing upon the pearl with nets afloat.
Shadowy, folding mountains from the sea
Rise to enclose the bay's chalcedony :
Ida beyond, dim silvered of the moon,
Soars with her snow in some enchanted swoon :
Delicate shells with whorl, and valve, and spire
Gleam in a rhythmic phosphorescent fire.
Silently dreams near yonder myrtle brake
An egret, plumed as with a soft snowflake,
Like a pure soul by some celestial lake.
Lo ! now the lovers dainty limbs will lave
In the delicious coolness of the wave.

  " I with thee,
By fringes of the pale, enamoured sea,
On the shore's bosom dying dreamfully,

Singing in the leaves,
Love it is who weaves
Around our hearts a heavenly mystery!"
Then as they neared their villa, in a tunnel
Of oranges where purls a crystal runnel,
A rustle in the trees she thought she heard,
And deemed she saw a shadow; "'Tis a bird,"
He whispered, after pausing: "all's a dream!"
She murmured, "Ah! how heavenly a dream!"...
... Out of the shadow flashed a steely gleam:
Her own death-shriek awoke her, and she fell
At the feet of her angel Azrael.

Mourn for Annabel!
The village bell is tolling, and she will
Never arise from where she lieth still,
Cold and so lovely, flowers white and red,
Old dames and tender damozels have shed
Tearful, all over her, in shadowy air
Alive with perfume curling blue and rare,
Jewels and gold and jasper glowing deep
As in a dreamland of a solemn sleep,
With solemn music plaining while the mourners
weep.

SIREN BOWERS, AND THE TRIUMPH
OF BACCHUS.

" HERE are bowers
In halls of pleasure,
Flushed with flowers
For love or leisure ;
Breathes no pain here,
Theirs, nor yours,
All are fain here
Of honeyed hours ;
Here in pleasure
Hide we pain,
None may measure,
Nor refrain ;
Beauty blooming,
And flowing wine !
Yonder glooming,
Here Love-shine !
Breathes no pain here,
Theirs nor thine,
O remain here !
Low recline !
In Love's illuming

Woes all wane,
Of beauty blooming
All are fain !
O remain here !
Lo ! Love shining
After rain !

The air faints with aroma of sweet flowers,
Marrying many-tendrilled labyrinths
Dew-diamonded, a harmony of hues ;
And some are flushed like delicate fair flesh
Of smooth, soft texture ; delicate love-organs
Impetalled hide, depend their fairy forms ;
Ruffled corolla, pitcher, salver, cell,
Dim haunts of humming-bird, or velvet moth ;
Doves pulsate with white wings, and make soft
    sound.
Such was the floral roof ; flowers overran
In lovely riot ample, mounting pillars,
Emergent from full bowers of greenery,
Water and marble, lily, water-lily,
Columns of alabaster, and soft stone,
That hath the moon's name, alternating far,
Innumerable, feebly luminous.
A mellow chime dividing the lulled hours
Embroiders them with fairy tone fourfold ;
And we were soothed with ever-raining sound
Of fountains flying in the warm, low light
Of pendent lamp, wrought silver, gold, and gem,

Rich with adventure of immortal gods.
Fair acolyte waved censer, whence the curled
Perfume-cloud made the languid air one blue,
And linen-robèd priest on marble altar
Made offering of fruit to Queen Astarte.
　　Behind half-open broidery of bloom
The eye won often glimpse of an alcove
In floral bower, ceiled over with dim gold ;
There velvet pile lay on the floor inlaid
From looms of India, or Ispahan,
With lace from Valenciennes, with silk or satin
For coverlid ; they, with the downy pillow,
Have tint of purple plums, or apricot,
Of waning woods autumnal,
Salvia, moth-fan, plume of orient bird.
And here the storied walls luxuriant
Are mellow-limned ; for lo ! Pompeianwise,
All the young world feigned of a wanton joy,
Of Erôs, Io, Hebe, Ganymede,
And all the poets tell of Aphrodite,
Or her who lulled Ulysses in her isle,
The idle lake, the garden of Armida,
And more, what grave historian hath told
Of Rosamund, Antinous, Cleopatra.
Here forms of youthful loveliness recline,
I know not whether only tinted marble,
Or breathing amorous warm flesh and blood.
　　Now from a grove of laurel and oleander,
Plum, fragrant fig, vine, myrtle, fern, pomegranate,
Recalling Daphne, or Byblos, where the Queen

Hath cave and fane anear the falling water,
And where she wooed, won, tended her Adonis,
A masque of Beauty shone ; young Dionysus
He seemed, the leader of the company,
Who lolled in a Chryselephantine car
Upon a pillow's damson velvet pile ;
An undulating form voluptuous,
All one warm waved and breathing ivory,
Aglow with male and female lovelihood,
The yellow panther fur worn negligent
Fondling one shoulder ; stealthy-footed these
That hale the chariot, one a lithe, large tiger,
Blackbarred, and fulvous, eyed with furnace-flame,
A tawny lion one, his mane a jungle.
The face was fair and beardless like a maid's,
The soft waved hair vine-filleted ; he held
Aloft with one white arm's rare symmetry
A crystal brimmed with blood of grape that hath
Heart like a lucid carbuncle ; some fallen
Over his form envermeiled more the rose
Of ample bosom, and love-moulded flank ;
The fir-coned thyrsus lying along the shoulder,
And listless fingered by a delicate hand,
The languid eyes dim-dewy with desire.
  Some foam-fair, and some amber of deep tone
The company to rear of him, yet nigh,
Fawn-youths and maidens robed in woven wind
Of that fine alien fabric, hiding only
As lucid wave hides, or a vernal haze ;
But some were rough and red, and rudely hewn,

Goat-shagged, satyric ; all high-held the vine,
(Or quaffed it reeling), and the fir-cone rod ;
The fairer filleted with violet,
Anemone, or rose, Adonis-flower,
The rude with vine, or ivy ; syrinx, flute,
Sweetly they breathed into ; anon they pause,
Till Dionysus, from his car descending,
Tipsily leaned on one who may have been
That swart and swollen comrade, old Silenus,
Fain to enfold the yielding and flushed form,
Even as when the god wooed Ariadne ;
So one may see them on a vase, or gem.

THE TWO MAGDALENES.*

ART thou indeed repentant ? though thy look
Be concentrated on the holy book ?
Thy glowing wave of bosom makes it warm !
Thine oval face-flower leaneth on an arm
Luxuriantly moulded, negligent.
A Mediterranean-blue robe hath lent
Disclosure to the undulating form,
Reclining languid in a shadowy place
'Mid murmuring leaves, and there thy mellow grace
The Sun divines, who, passing through the grove,
Illumines throat, and bosom with still love.
Art thou indeed repentant ? all thy youth
Mantling within thee, doth the perfect mouth
Weary of kissing ?   Here 'tis cool and fresh
For musing on the frailty of the flesh,
For shadowy contemplation, and sweet sorrow !
But who may prophesy of thy to-morrow ?
The seven devils in thee, did they go ?
Or do they only sleep that they may grow ?
Smouldering slumberous in thine almond white,
They may awake with renovated might !

* The paintings by Correggio and D. G. Rossetti.

Thou, blessing the brown earth with bare light foot !
I think they only parted to recruit.
When the world leaves you, worn with use, ye turn;
Nay, rule the world-illusion while ye burn !

A later painter showed her otherwise.
Under the domination of deep eyes,
She knows no more these lovers, for the wings
Of lovelier life new-born in her; she flings
The jewels from her, for the Pearl He brings.
In presence of her Lord, no fair and sweet
She knoweth, save to lay them at His feet.
Our splendid world dies, very dull and dim;
The woman in her seeth only Him !

NARRATIVE, DRAMATIC, AND
DESCRIPTIVE.

NARRATIVE, DRAMATIC, AND DESCRIPTIVE.

THE NILE, AFRICA, AND EGYPT.[*]

Livingstone soliloquises.

THE sun is sinking over Africa;
And under shadowy native eaves reclines
A traveller upon a fur-strewn floor;
One whom no years' ignoble rust, but high
And holy toil have wasted; bearded grey,
In wayworn English garb he seems array'd;
His shoulders bow'd as from a life's long burden;
His rude wan countenance profoundly scarr'd
With noble ruin wrought by Love and Sorrow.
Reclined against the dwelling's clay-built wall,
His falcon eyes explore the moonèd East.
Athwart a wondrous land that lies before
Slow shadow steals; o'er all the fervid palms,
Broad-leaved banana, leaf-seas infinite,
Hoar unfamiliar stupendous forms
Of that primæval forest African :

---

[*] The poems from here to "The Caravan," p. 233, are from "Livingstone in Africa."

12

Slowly the shadow with declining day
Fades rainbow splendour of the forest far,
And drowns imperial purple of the hills
In one phantasmal all-confounding gloom.

Ye mountains, hiding undiscover'd worlds,
So mused in spirit the lone wanderer,
I hunger till I pass your mighty doors,
And lay my hand upon the Mystery !
African Andes, vast, inviolate,
Crown'd with the cloud, robed round with sombre
    forest,
Whose virgin snow no human feet profane
Have swept, but only the wild eagle's wing,
Of old your ghost on Rumour's shadowy breath
Wander'd abroad, O Mountains of the Moon!
And still ye are no more than a dim name:
Of old the Egyptian from your loins, that loom
Large in far realms of Rumour, drew the Nile.
Ye, couchant o'er the sultry continent,
Seem the great guardian Lion of Africa,
Who, from primæval ages all alone,
Silently stern, confronts a crimson dawn
Over fair Indian seas, with face that towers
Sunward, supreme ; feeling a warm moist breath,
Faint with perfume, turn crystals of soft snow
Among the terrors of his icy mane;
Or, where the stature of his giant frame
Declines to westward, feeling the breath change
To rain within the hollows of his heart.

All, thundering down abrupt convulsed ravines,
Scarr'd in precipitous rugged flanks of stone,
Feed wide Nyanzas; whether there be twain,
Or many waters, these engender thee,
Wonderful Nile !
           And yet I deem that I
Shall find thy parent springs remoter still.
Lualaba, with his tributary rivers,
And lilied lakes his loving bounty fills !
Yea, some have told me, and I well believe,
There are four fountains clear and deep as day,
Welling unfathomable, perennial
Among low hills as yet unseen, the last
Subsiding roll, it may be, of one range
Named of old Rumour, Mountains of the Moon.
Behold the shrine of living waters !   Here
From one immense rock-temple stream the Souls
Of many lands and nations, whispering
In dim enchanted caverns; East and North,
And West emerging, sunny wings unfold :
Shouting they plunge in joyous waterfalls,
To roll a priceless silver all abroad,
Each to his Ocean, whose illustrious names
Are Congo, Nile, and long Leeambayee !
Whom Mother Ocean, in her awful arms
Absorbing, ever engendereth anew,
Gendering a holy Cycle evermore.

  When royal Sun his Oriental bride,
India's Ocean, fiercely fervent woos,

While She dissolves in his delightful love,
What time He fronts earth's equatorial zone
On his way North to Cancer, then the waters
Rise in a tide of life upon the lands,
Lying athirst and barren in his blaze.

. . . . My soul, unbow'd in face of failing years,
Though Hope may falter from unwearying
Hindrance of blind baseborn vicissitude,
Swears to resolve the alluring Mystery,
At whose cold feet our mightiest have fallen,
Yearning to find the sacred Source, and die;
Nor have prevail'd; but if the Lord allow,
I and my fellow-labourers will prevail!

I seek the birth of that immortal River,
Who bears great Egypt in her watery womb,
Who nursed the world's prime empire on her bosom;
And Moses, more illustrious than all
Pharaohs, her earth-enthralling conquerors,
Throned in their golden hundred-gated Thebes,
Tomb'd in hoar wonder of the pyramids.
At thy most holy source, primæval Nile!
The Greek drank wisdom; yea, in solemn halls
Of Memphis, in columnar stone forests
Of mighty Karnac, rich with hieroglyph,
And pictured symbol and weird shapes of Gods.
Only the solar beam, the Obelisk,

Now from green palms and verdure and pure rills,
As then from sacred fountains of the Sun,
In olden time, in Heliopolis,
Still points with mystic granite flame to Heaven!
This mighty gnomon of a sun-dial
Moved then a shadow, lengthening among signs
Upon a porphyry or a brazen floor,
Among blithe forms of Pharaonic time;
Now o'er young corn and red anemone!
There came Pythagoras to learn the lore
Of stars, and suns, and gods, and human souls;
There Moses mused, well nourish'd on rich stores
Of priests and sages; communing with truth,
And in his spirit sifting dust from gold.
Only this one most ancient monument
Stands of thy glory, Heliopolis!
Earliest seat of learning, where the seer,
Illustrious Plato, came from Academe,
And sweet Ilissus; fairest star of all
The fair young band who follow'd one wise master.
Here a stone astrolabe explored the night,
Measuring solemn wanderings of stars;
Laboratory fires were glowing here;
While some astrologer with mystic rites
Drew horoscopes, or cast nativities:
But then our Earth, who in her equable
And proud obeisant motion round the sun
Hath in twice ten millennial periods
Her inclined axle measurably perturb'd,
Lean'd otherwise her pole among the skies;

Another Polestar ruled the mariner;
Another Ocean shrined thy radiance,
O Christian constellation of the Cross !
While otherwhere in every tranquil night,
Among cool calm abysses of pure space,
Shone Sirius, Arcturus, and Orion.

Here too the holiest Child of mortal race
Rested in humble guise with a pure Mother.

At thy most holy source, primæval Nile !
The Greek drank wisdom; learn'd a Dædal art,
That in his pure white light of genius,
In that pellucid æther of his clime,
Among pure breezes of Castalian hills,
And delicate unrobed consummate forms
Of radiant heroes, bloom'd in glorious
Marble immortal gods for all the world.

Here he beheld the blazon'd Zodiac
On loftiest firmaments of broad hewn stone
Within dim fanes, or solemn tombs of kings;
Stupendous vaulted chambers in the heart
Of flame-hued mountain, silently aware
With populous imagery of men and gods,
Hawk or ram-headed; on wide wall and ceiling
Beheld a constellate celestial river
Meandering around a crystal sphere,
And navigated in twelve lives of Moons

By that resplendent Father of the Kings;
Kings lying here in glory, all embalm'd,
And jewell'd o'er with slumbering talisman,
Asleep in their immense sarcophagi.

Yonder, on burning sands of Libya,
Unmoved the tranquil-featured Sphinx beheld
Abraham, Homer, Solon, all the wise
Of every clime, who came, and saw, and wonder'd;
Who pass'd, leaving a heritage to man;
Beheld dissolving dynasties of Kings,
And all their people, pageant-like unroll'd
Before His face; they, with o'erwhelming pillars
Of desert sand before the whirlwind's breath,
Pass'd in loud pomp, and were not any more;
The silent Sphinx regarding, as to-day,
Beyond them all, serene Eternity!

There that colossal Memnon, while the Nile
Pour'd like another morning all around
Sweet life-engendering waters musical,
Murmur'd melodious salutation,
When first Aurora, his celestial mother,
Smiled blandly on him from the Orient.

Fresh from fierce thunder of the cataracts,
Tortured among dark demon-blocks of stone
Fireborn, divine Nile smoothes his ruffled flow;
Lingers a tranquil, a celestial lake

To embrace fair Philæ, Philæ, fairest isle
Of all earth's islands! fringed with mirror'd palm,
And lotos blossom on the crystalline
Laving her bosom; she hath lotos blossom
For capitals of her hypæthral fane,
Quiet in heaven, tremulous in the river:
Where, sundering flowing phantoms of the stars,
Boats glide by night, aslant on broider'd sail,
Freighted with youth, and love and loveliness:
Balmy night breezes, all alive with song,
Laughter, and rhythmic plashing of light oars,
(While coloured lamp-lights lambent on the ripple
Stream from fair vessel, or embower'd shore);
Wave slender-fountain'd palms among the stars;
As strange slim forms of a most ancient age
Land on pale quays of that so stately temple,
Sonorous with a gorgeous ritual.—
Now on a roofless column builds the stork!
Here, they believe, slumbers a mighty god,
Osiris, Love incarnate, and the Judge;
Also the Solar orb, and sacred Nile;
Who, with moon'd Isis and her little child,
Shadoweth forth a triune Deity.
His awful name none dare to breathe aloud:
An oath avails to bind for evermore
One who hath sworn "by Him that sleeps in Philæ."

Most ancient realm of all this ancient earth,
Thought faints to sound thy hoar antiquity!
Europe and Asia were not when thy form

Brooded in solemn grandeur, as to-day,
Over dark ocean ! when Dicynodon,
Ancestor of thy huge Leviathan,
Ruled over mightier seas and estuaries;
When melancholy vapours veil'd strange stars,
Ere man's wan yearning unavailing eyes
Awoke to wonder ! ere the cataclysm
Rent all thy rocks, and summon'd forth the rivers . . .
. . . When came the Negro?—and the dwindling
    Dwarf?
I have found bones of immemorial age :
Their living families surround me now !

Wilds more unknown than yonder ghostly Moon,
Beyond the bounds of Earth ! whose ruin huge
Of awful mountain, Albategnius,
Or Döerfel, whose abysses of dead gloom
Herschel in his enchanter's glass reveal'd !

Africa ! vast immeasurable Void,
Where no imperial march of History
Solemn resounds from echoing age to age !
Haunt of light-headed fable and dim dream !
To whose fierce strand the Heaven-shadowing bird,
Enormous Roc, long deemed a wild romance,
Was wont to fly of old from Madagascar !—
In whose blue wave floats fragrant ambergris ;
Whose shores are blushing corallines most rare,

Where ocean-fairies wander mailed in gems,
Silently gliding through the branching bowers,
While far inland strange palaces are piled
Profusely with pure ivory and gold—
No lynx-eyed peril-affronting pioneer,
Since the beginning, until yesterday,
Dared violate thy sultry somnolence,
Couch'd, a grim lion in thine ancient lair ;
Sullenly self-involved, impenetrable !
Or if one ever bearded and aroused,
Thy winds have spurn'd his unrevealing dust !
Yea, in thy fiery deserts, in the pomp
Of lurid evenings, crimson, warm, like blood,
Thou dost devour thine own dark children, crouch'd
About thy cruel knees, dark Africa !

THE EXPLORER IN AFRICA.

YET mine are higher, holier purposes ;
For I will cleave this darkling continent,
As with a sword of intellectual light ;
Lead these lost children to a living Father,
And tell them of a Brother who has died.
Yea, if my nature's weakness have rebell'd
Against what seems the world's indifference ;
Men treading their unarduous wonted round
Of common care, oblivious of mine,
Who battle alone, afar from all ; who waste,
Ignobly sinking here in sight of goal,
For bitter need of help I hoped from men,
At leisure in their calm abounding homes ;
Bales for exchange or tribute ; healing herbs ;
Wherewith to calm this fire within my veins,
And tame the ravening, hungry heathendom—
Thou knowest, O Lord, my prime solicitude
Was for the work thou hast to me unworthy
Confided in Thy Providence unachieved,—
And yet I know the Holiest never fails
For lack of service ; but allows to each
The measure He in wisdom hath ordain'd.

For all the land is foul with monstrous wrong,
And desolation of the sons of Hell.
Surely the long, long wail of human woe
Ever ascends from all our earth to heaven !
But here the mist of blind unending tears
Hangs undissolving, and abolishes
Yon very Life-Light from His shining halls,
And hides the Father from His orphan'd sons.
Hell is let loose ; and jubilant cruelty
Tortures a feeble, lowly-witted race,
Poor fallen outcast of humanity ;
Inflames the lurking, savage brute that haunts
A wilding blood to fratricidal war,
To thrall its very kindred, for the sport
Of paler, large-brain'd fiends, the common foe,
And glut their markets with the flesh of men.
Shoot them and drown them ! from convulsive arms
Tear small sweet clinging babes, and fainting brides
From lovers, who with unavailing life
Stain them in falling, or themselves enslaved,
Yoked, goaded, pinioned, tramp the burning wilds,
To bleach with beast-gnawn bones the wilderness ;
Or huddled in a slaver's pestilent hold,
Writhing and raving, rotting while alive,
Are flung to gorge sleek monsters of the sea !
Lo ! in dusk offings of ensanguined seas,
At sunset doth the torpid slaver droop
Her guilty sail ; while evil strangers brand
Dark women on a golden strand with fire ;
Who are mute with endless woes unutterable !

Nay ! the long wail of wounded innocence
Hath ne'er been squander'd on a voiceless Void !
But every tear of every helpless child
Sinks in a warm, unfathomable Love :
And armèd Righteousness awaits her hour,
Albeit Her lightning slumber in the cloud.
These human shambles shall be purged from blood :
This charnel of the world shall reek no more,
Plague-spot of all the starry universe !
For I will flash the light of Europe's eyes
Full on the tyrant, till he quail and cower,
And vanish, a mere snowflake in the sun.
England, inviolate Ark of Freedom, launch
Thy thunder as of old ; and hurl them low !
Fulfil thy mission ! fallen heroes want
Yonder in heaven their crown of blessedness,
Till the last bondsman clasp unfetter'd hands
O'er the last slaver, whelm'd beneath the wave !

But I abide until my task be done.
And if they slay their mortal enemy,
It is the Lord who calls, and it is well—
When they had thought to murder ; reft from me
All I most cherish'd on a former day ;
Killing my converts, even the little ones,
Or sweeping them into captivity ;
I said, " I am not less resolved than they :
They do but save me wills and codicils !"
I turn my face indeed, as they intend,

From this my labour of long years o'erthrown;
And yet not homeward, baffled as they deem—
For lo! my face is toward the world unknown,
That seem'd almost the very world in sooth,
" From whose dark bourne no traveller returns."
I take the plunge, and I am lost in night!
Lost to the life and tumult of mankind:
No voice may reach me from the homes of men;
No voice of mine may penetrate to them.
Five times twelve moons have filled their horns and
 waned;
My memory is failing from the world;
Only a ghostly rumour murmurs low
How one has seen a strange white wanderer,
Somewhere inland; none certainly knows where;
And once more rumour whispers, he is dead.
Empires may rise and fall; great wars may thunder;
And peace may follow war; and I not know,
More than the drown'd who slumber in the sea—
Yea, have they ruin'd me at Kolobeng?
Behold I wrest from them all Africa!

For I will never cease from journeying,
Until the length and breadth of all the land
Shine forth illuminate from shore to shore!
My life is one long journey; and I love
Peril, and toil, and strange vicissitude;
Exploring all the wonder of the world
On sea and land; wonder for evermore;
And all the marvellous miracle of man.

I am urged ever by a restless ghost,
And may not fold my hands in tranquil sleep.
Yet when we have grown old, we want the glow
Of our own generous children in their prime,
Warming our twilight ; they love thought for us,
As we of old for them ; their little ones
Play, like a dear last dawn, around our age ;
And I too long to be at home again
By the sweet firelight of my northern land !
At Christmas-time, the room is bright with green,
And far bells faintly peal athwart the snow :
Then quiet firelight, wavering with soft sound,
Pleasantly ruddies gold and silver hair :
But in the summer, little children sing
Anear a shimmer of slim aspen leaves,
Fluttering with sound of summer rain.
Ah ! shall I never cease from journeying?
Urged ever onward by a restless ghost,
I may not fold my hands in pleasant sleep !

When I surmount some unfamiliar height,
Behold ! an alien realm mysterious
Unroll'd in twilight ! ghostly, drear, and wan ;
Stain'd with what seem huge bombs of shatter'd iron,
Hurl'd from a weird infernal enginery.
And then I muse what eerie living things
Dwell far beyond among the mists of night—
Whether the wanderer may wander on
For ever in the waste, hearing no sound,
Save of his own footfall ; or yonder dwell

Dark unimaginable human lives ;
Wearing what uncouth forms, allied to some
Misshapen horrors of the forest wild—
Weird startling mockery of immortal man ;
Shocking the soul with chill mistrustful fear,
And doubt of her pre-eminent destiny—
Brute-brow'd, brute-maw'd, huge hirsute prodigies,
Challenging with a vast appalling roar
Whoso disturbs their monstrous monarchy !
Dark unimaginable human lives,
Ever alone in this most ancient realm,
Immured in a stupendous sepulchre,
Afar from man's tumultuous chariot-race
Of sounding splendour ; somnolent aware
How the dull tide of dim inglorious years
Moves ever foul and lurid with the scurf
Of ruin'd blood, and gold, and scalding tears !

Some veer small restless, rambling, apelike eyes ;
Their clicking gibber mimics flittermice ;
A skeleton people plucking roots and berries
For starved subsistence, grubbing shallow holes,
Or sheltering in borrow'd dens disused. . . .
What people lies before me ? some affirm
That there be men sepulchred verily
In subterranean chambers like the dead ;
Burrowing human moles, fleeing from light,
By their free choice, and immemorial
Usage ; though Rumour murmurs her wild tale
Ever with a light head confusedly.

Shall I behold some dark terrific cave,
Reeking with bats, and owls, and doleful things,
High among crags of a precipitous mountain,
Strewn with fresh bones of men, that hideous ghouls
In human form, foul anthropophagi,
Have gnawn for food ; a loathsome den defiled
With dripping human members, torn for meat ?
A desolate wind howls ever dolefully
Around the dismal open mouth of hell,
Howls like a murdered man's avenging soul !
While among boulder-ruins of the mountain
Climb beasts obscene, scenting a horrid feast !
At night a thunder of great lions rolls,
Rebellowing from basalt precipices :
At night a fervour of infernal flame,
With cruel yells of hellish revelry,
Affronts pale stars ; what time the unearthly fiends
Grimy, and gash'd with knives, and foul with earth,
Squat mumbling bodies of lost travellers,
Whom they decoying fell'd with monstrous clubs.
But underneath the floor of their black vault
Deepens a hollow murmur, far withdrawn
Within the haunted heart of the dread mountain.
It may be mutter'd wrath of slumbering fires ;
It may be secret waters wandering ;
But they believe it of another world ;
And shuddering pour libation to the god.

Sometimes by night a mightier thunder even
Than thunder of roaring lions, like an ocean,

Bursts all the boundaries of ruinous heaven
In one wild flood of universal flame,
With sound as of upheaval of adamant ;
Towering wrath of Powers immeasurable,
And roll'd war-chariots of tremendous cloud :
Sound the great mountains in their chasms and
    craters,
Bastions, and inviolable towers,
Rebellow ; hurl abroad ; mutter in gloom ;
Brood over in their dim and sullen souls.
Perpetual seas of broad purpureal flame,
With intervals of momentary night,
Dark as the darkness of a man born blind,
Possess the sky's unfathomable concave ;
Wherein appalling growths of more intense
Fire with seven branches, like gigantic trees,
Spring up and vanish ! . . .
Behold yon perpendicular crags, like flame,
Whose melaphyre and porphyry condor crests
Threaten the valleys ! their profound ravines
Of deadly twilight ne'er a sun may see,
Unsoften'd of a tiniest herb or flower !
Now furious torrents toss white manes of foam
Down their long solitudes ; the firmament
Sunders, and pours dense watery deluges,
Illuminate with deluges of light ;
Howls the tornado ; 'tis the reign of chaos !
Great lions lashing tails in grim despair,
Mingling their roar with elemental thunder,
Climb from the floods, or struggling drown therein !

Ah ! would the blinding falchion of swift lightning,
That crimson wounds the mountain flank, but hurl
One of those loosen'd bounding blocks of rock,
So as to stop for ever the black mouth
Of that infernal cavern of the fiends,
Where still a madden'd laughter peals among
Commotions of Divine wrath flying abroad,
Reiterate from all their haunted halls !
Lo ! the tornado, and the levinbolt
Have fallen upon yon tree's enormous bulk,
Hard by the cave ; blasting, and wrenching it
Loose from a cleft it grappled for centuries
With serpentine huge roots ! it creaks and crashes !
Headlong it topples to the gulf that boils !

Some even tell a marvellous dim tale
Of a tribe buried somewhere in the wild ;
A satyr-race of clovenfooted men,
Hairy and tail'd, with cloven feet like swine !
Where are the Pigmies ?   Homer sang of old
Their yearly war with southward-flying cranes !
They wear enormous heads upon their shoulders ;
They build their pigmy booths in dim recesses
Of some impenetrable forest world !
Two travellers lately came upon their traces.

MISSIONARY AND SAVAGE.

My long life moves before me like a dream.
Behold ! our mission-house at Kolobeng :
These labour-roughen'd hands have builded it.
Nor for myself alone, but for the dark
Children of whom I am the father here,
I labour with strong hand, and heart, and soul.
I smelt rude ores ; and, fervid as large eyes
Of wrathful tigers, ringing iron yields
Upon mine anvil, hammer'd heartily;
While a bow'd native plies the goatskin bellows.
Lusty and hale, in manhood's vigorous prime,
I startle the lone woods with stalwart blows ;
While cream-white splinters fly from stubborn trunks,
Whose leafy pride falls headlong shattering ;
My wife with finger nimble, dexterous,
Moulding the while a hundred things at home.

There is a power enthralling human souls
In equal dealings, in a lofty life,
And lowly Love's unwearying ministry.
One who inherits wisdom's treasure-house,
And lives endow'd with more than wonted grace

Of human faculty, may forge the gold
Thereof to ignominious chains for men ;
Or twine the spiritual wealth, for their
Deliverance, to cords of fair persuasion,
Wooing their own endeavours after God.
I wielding for the common use, not mine,
A wider knowledge and a riper skill,
Bestow'd free counsel or sincere reproof ;
Tended my children when their bodies ail'd ;
Lent a large heart to small perplexities,
And simple tales of hourly human woe. . . .

Sun of the living ! Hesper of the gloom !
Surely Thy dusky children call for Thee,
Unknowing whom they call—the wail resounds
Yet in mine ears of some funereal dirge
For one beloved and vanish'd ; when the moon
Wavers, as if in water, among leaves
Of air-moved umbrage ; and a bark-built village
Lies in pale elf-light, with embowering palm
And silvern plantain ; lonely forest shades
Of over-frowning mountain-presences
With stealthily mysterious forms aware.
A bitter, long, monotonous human wail !
More poignant than the cries of animal lives
In unreverberate torture ; 'tis a wail
Of one that's cloven to the depths of being,
Maim'd in the vitals of an immortal soul.
To me it seems alive with the wild prayer,

This poor blind people hath so oft preferr'd,
Crying with dumb yet infinite eloquence,
"O wise white man ! we pray thee give us sleep ! "
So moans a hollow voice reverberate
In long-drawn aisles of some sepulchral vault ;
So moans the mystic growth Mandragora,
Feeding on human ravage in a ruin
Under a gibbet, when one pulls the root.
How long have these then cower'd here in night,
Mouthpieces of creation's misery,
Wailing the world's wail in closed ears of God ?
Whom now lament they ? some beloved friend,
Chief, mother, bride, or child, who turn'd so cold
And strange and silent ; who may not abide
Any more here in sweet sunlight with them,
Or pleasant interchange of word and smile ;
Gone forth for ever from them to the chill
And cheerless realm of dreams impalpable.
Nevermore ! wails the burden of the strain,
Burdening, as it seems, the very sleep
Of a serene, fair incense-breathing earth !
Ever it wails, low, dreary, and desolate,
Oppress'd and muffled in a solemn sorrow ;
A dirge world-weary, an old-world requiem,
Trailing a slow wan length along the dust,
Faint from the fount of immemorial tears ;
A shadow, whose maim'd wings are plumed with
     awe ;
Sunken so deep from ghostly woes and fears,
And broken hearts of all ancestral lives ;

Phantoms aroused by a fresh living pain
To haunt the labyrinths of a living soul,
And all the dark slow movement of the dirge !

One cabin stands a little way apart
From all the rest upon a higher ground.
Hence flows the wail ! A man laments his son.
It is an aged warrior of the tribe,
Who cowers, and sways himself upon the floor,
Before an ember glow, that he beholds
Only in dreaming; while a warm, red gleam
Falls on the brown of rude encircling wall,
Leaving a smoke-beclouded roof in gloom ;
Falls on barb'd javelins, and bows and arrows,
And many hunting spoils of him who lies
Near to his father, silent, stark, and cold ;
Ruddies the dark bare limbs of life and death.
Rich furs are under and over the young form ;
Furs golden, furs of lynx, and ocelot :
A small uncomely dog, with pointed ears,
Presses his faithful body to the corpse.
He was a comely boy, a mighty hunter,
A bold young warrior, hope of all the tribe,
And his infirm old father's only stay.
When humid morning, chill, and pale, and wan,
Stares at those intervals between the boughs
Of wattled wall, yon ashes will be grey,
And still the old man be cowering by the dead !
Then the fond faltering sire must wander forth

Alone; away from this unpitying herd
Of yet unwounded men into the wild;
There to fade slowly; with a feeble hand
Plucking the berries, pulling up the roots;
A living skeleton, grim woe and want
In dim, scared eyes; until the wolf and raven
Find him low laid, their unresisting prey!

The father's wail, like mournful waves unseen,
Dies on the ear, and moans alternately;
But later, figures gather in the open,
Lamenting by a fire new-made the dead. . . .
What wizard, with his incantation curst,
Blasted the living; changing to a foe,
And chilling fear, what was so amiable?
Over the shoulder timorously glance
They, at the very rustling of a leaf,
To where the dead lie yonder in the forest,
Strewn with some humble offerings they need:
Food, bowls, or ivory, arms, and hunting gear.
Now beat loud tamtams; rattle hollow drums!
So scare away the dim unhomely ghost
With yells, and shouts, and drunken revelry. . . .
"Ah! shadow-muffled panther, with fierce eyes,
Prowling and mumbling yonder, art thou he?
Ah! whispering leaves of darkling forest trees!
Ye are ill whispers of infernal fiends!
But we will drown the bitterness of woe,
Frowning, foreboding, and bewildering fear!"

THE NEGRO.

I CANNOT loathe nor scorn the colour'd man;
Nor deem him far below my Master's love.
I know about the sutures of his skull;
But I have proved him verily my brother.
And I have heard of Toussaint L'Ouverture!
(Perchance I am not so fastidious
As those who have great genius for words;
Yet we dumb doers crave some standing room,
O ye, so deft and dazzling with the tongue!)

   Well I remember, after all my toil,
When within grasp of a momentous prize,
Earth seem'd to glide from under; all was failing,
Even as now! my very faithful friends—
Who had plunged in drowning floods to rescue me;
Who had interposed their bodies to avert
The deadly javelin aim'd against my life;
Who, pressing princely favours on my need,
With more than counsel, with material aid,
Further'd my humanising pilgrimage;
When Christian Levites would have pass'd me by,
Jingled their gold, and sneer'd " Utopia!"—

My well-tried Makololo, *they* desert me!
Shrinking at last from more long sacrifice,
Bitter and boundless, it may be unavailing—
I shall not reach those Lusian settlements
Upon the long'd-for coast! all urge return.
．　．　．　．　Return I will not!
" Return *ye* then, my people!　I will go
Alone, if so indeed it needs must be!"
With heavy tread, with heavier heart, I enter,
Weary and fever-stricken, my small tent
Under a tamarind; and I lean my head
Upon my hand to offer up a prayer.
Silence is all around me in the noon—
Yet only for a little—then I hear
Footsteps approaching; timidly one peers,
And sees me by the tent-pole; first the one,
Then more, have push'd the canvas fold aside;
Falling upon me like repentant children,
Sobbing, with tears they pray to be forgiven:
" We never meant it!　We will never leave thee!
Our own kind Father! be of better cheer!
Where'er thou leadest, we will follow thee!"

And that poor African, who when I sail'd
For England supplicated to be taken!
It was with bleeding heart I said him nay.
I told him he would perish of the cold
In my bleak country, but he sobb'd with tears:
" O let me come, and perish at your feet!"

Sebweku had a stronger claim than he.
Alas ! Sebweku !
The sea was rolling mountains high, when all
Embark'd at Kilimane in a boat.
Ascending gliding turbid mountain-slopes,
Their toppling hissing foamy summits broke
Drenching upon us, and submerged our bark :
Giddily slid we deep into the trough,
Whose seething waterwalls hid all the masts
Of that great vessel which awaited us :
We struck the massy bottom with a shock,
That made our stout planks quiver ; slanting up
Another beetling journeying watercliff,
Second of three great billows lightning-crown'd.
Poor Sebweku, so valiant on land,
So wise and skill'd in dealing with the many
Tribes of his continent, strove strenuously
To be as brave in my fierce water world,
Ghostly, unknown, terrific unto him :
Yet as that awful play of leaping foam
Struck us, and nearly swept us all from life,
He clutch'd my knees, crying with face of fear,
Faintly illumined by a poor phantom smile,
Like a wet timid gleam among wan clouds,
"Is this the way you go? is this the way?"
But when we had made a perilous ascent
Into the British war-brig anchor'd near,
His fresh fantastic marvelling child-soul,
So little tutor'd, ponder'd evermore
On all he saw within the war vessel ;

Cannon, great coils of cable, ponderous chain,
Hammocks, and kitchen of the floating town,
Her sailors, and well-order'd soldiery;
On the interminable water world,
Strewn with dark swimming snakes, and plants;
    where roll
Dolphins and whales; where azure fishes fly,
And birds gleam in a momentary ray
Out of dull storm that raves among the shrouds.
Reeling to starboard and to larboard, he,
By swaying lamplight, in the midnight hour,
Lies wakeful, hearing labouring timbers groan,
Or shouted orders, piercing all the roar;
And clear struck bells, dividing hour from hour.
He, creeping up lone glimmering hatchway stairs,
Beholds a gleam from that mysterious shrine
Where, under lighted crystal, a slim needle
Trembles for ever toward the hidden pole;
Notes a bronzed mariner's strong vigilance
Revolving with both arms the straining wheel,
Beyond wet decks, wash'd over by fierce seas;
Beholds tall masts, more tall than forest kings,
Robed in broad shadowy windy sails and booms,
Circling among wan stars in rifts of cloud.

All made him welcome, and they liked him well;
But the new wonder-world inflamed his brain;
Kept his mind whirling ever night and day;
Until, when we approach'd Mauritius,

A steamer steam'd from forth the harbour mouth—
Wonder of wonders to poor Sebweku !
Fiery smoke outbursting from her funnel,
She churns the water with a rushing wheel ;
Slanting and swiftly swims upon the wave :
He cries : " It is some fiend of the wild sea ! "
Alas ! my friend. . . .
. . . . When we are calmly moor'd,
In a mad frenzy plunges—and is drown'd !

SAVAGE LIFE.

METHINKS I hear some solemn state palaver,
Held in the grand unwall'd assembling-place,
Thatch'd with bamboos and branches, when blue
 morn
Glows golden, while cool shadows at the doors
Of a leaf-bower'd village minish fast.
Morn lies a lake of light amid the bloom
And billowy wealth of forest foliage;
Young Sun, ascending, shines on thatch like snow,
Revealing veins of herbs, and draining them;
Glancing among high senatorial boughs
Of feathery tamarind, or mahogany;
While dews of slumber rustle, rainbow rain
In sylvan, solitary silences
Of Nature's own cathedral sanctuary.
A spear is in the dusky orator's hand,
And spears are planted black athwart the day;
Dark bearded elders hearken solemnly,
Resting on logs, all polish'd from long use.
Perennial founts of eloquent, warm words
Are these untutor'd children of the sun!

Now reigns the blazing furnace of full noon:
And save for little rills that want no sleep,

Silence, before the intolerable glory,
Falls on a cowering world of beast and man.
Bird-song has waned, and even the stridulent
Cicala sleeps ; a rare bee drowsily
Explores a twilit labyrinth of flowers ;
Delicate blossoms dallying in warm airs,
Bowing and yielding to the velvet lover ;
While heaven-blue elves with pulsing fans alight
Over a ruin of red leaves, or sail
From light to shadow, like a jubilant
Song, failing in a tenderer low minor.
Gorgeous insects of metallic gleam,
Waver, and glance, and glimmer on the fronds.
Low, murmurous sound pervades all emerald isles,
As though the floral earth and leaves were breathing,
Life teems ! a myriad hidden mandibles,
Amid lush herbage, under moss and loam,
Clear away life superfluous, and death.
Gorgeous fungi here and there reveal,
Where sun can pierce, traversing shadows thrown
Athwart them from some silken spider's line,
To and fro glancing when a zephyr breathes ;
Bending long grasses wheresoe'er it hangs.
And hark ! the honey-bird invites to steal
Delicious honey-combs from hollow boles.

　　Hearken again !
A sound, how plaintive and melodious,
Swells in the green gloom ! it is like one note
From a sweet vibrant lyre—a hidden bird !

Women have gone, with infants slung behind
   them,
Toward a spring, light pitchers gracefully
Poised on their heads by steadying of dark arms
Curl'd over; or they bruise with iron hoes
The hopeful soil; plant yams and manioc;
Pound in wood mortars these, or maize and millet;
Hem with some thorn, or fish-bone for a needle,
And fibres of a leaf; weave grassy cloths
In looms, or spin with immemorial spindle.
Some men have gone with quiver, targe, and spear,
To hunt the beast for food; some loll at ease,
Like their own gourds, luxuriously idle;
Listless and vacant dumb black animals,
Who spurn the accursèd yoke of thought and toil—
They never roll the stone of Sisyphus!
No fool's ambition ever goads their lives
To rouse a restless rumour, while they roll
Into fate's mortal darkness, and to leave
A hollow murmur for a little time
In some poor space of insignificant earth!

Now Sun steals westward; and his fading light
Glows golden, while cool shadows at the doors
Of leaf-embower'd villages are long.
Burning he falls into the forest sea,
Inflames leaf-billows with purpureal fire;
Drawing down souls to caves of the under-world;
Whence in twelve hours he royal will arise

From holy nenuphars upon the river !
Fragrance and song, released from royalty
Of his fierce presence, timid lift their heads ;
Grey parrots crying flutter home to roost.
Hunters return, with many a gay halloo,
And whoop light-hearted, bearing various game,
About whose way hilarious women throng,
Calling them by pet names, and fondling them,
Prattling, intent to hear of all the sport.
Boys in gourd bowls bring frothy plantain wine
From cool leaf-cellars in low boughs of trees,
Presenting it with clapping of their hands :
Anon there smokes a savoury repast,
Viands of venison, nuts, and season'd yams.

THE DANCE.

DANCING and singing under tender stars,
In serene purple air ! a rising moon
Charming all harshness from the fuming flame
Of resinous torch, and lowlier village fires,
Mild as evanishing fireflies in the shade !
A night of love for lovely youths and girls,
Of revelry, and wine and flute playing,
Psaltery, reed, marimba, or cithern ;
Rude sires of more harmonious instruments,
String'd with a root, a snake-skin strain'd athwart—
One sang me a small song about the dance.

The dance ! the dance !
Maidens advance
Your undulating charm !
A line deploys
Of gentle boys,
Waving the light arm,
Bronze alive and warm ;
Reedflute and drum
Sound as they come,
Under your eyelight warm !

Many a boy,
A dancing joy,
Many a mellow maid,
With fireflies in the shade,
Mingle and glide,
Appear and hide,
Here in a fairy glade:
Ebb and flow
To a music low,
Viol, and flute and lyre,
As melody mounts higher:
With a merry will,
They touch and thrill,
Beautiful limbs of fire!

Red berries, shells,
Over bosom-dells,
And girdles of light grass,
May never hide
The youthful pride
Of beauty, ere it pass:
Yet, ah! sweet boy and lass,
Refrain, retire!
Love is a fire!
Night will pass!

THE RIVERS.

I TRAVELL'D over many lakes and rivers,
In floating trees men hollow'd with an adze
For a canoe, my rowers with wild song
Paddling or poling, in accordant time
Of oar and voice, chanting some ancient stave
Of river-song in tones Gregorian,
Solemn and strange, ancient as Pharaoh !

How wonderful it was to float along the river !
Dreamily hearing water plash and gurgle
From my canoe's advancing sides and oars,
Washing among green rushes of the shore !

Onward we glide, and twine meandering
On a moss-colour'd water, till the gale
Relieves my merry rowers ; we expand
A little sail, filling with soft sweet air,
Like some soft bird's white bosom heaved with
    song,
White as a foam of waterfalls ; we glide
Merrily among wave-enchanted flowers,
Glossily heaving while we gently pass ;

Or splendid twinkling trees, immersed in light,
From shadowy bosoms offering fruits of Eden ;
Breathing a perfume as of Paradise
From their soft islands ; islands of the blest,
Bower'd to the marge, re-echo'd in the water ;
With many a fleecy cloudlet sailing slow.
Small richly armour'd quaint iguanas bask
On every sunniest bough ; while startled eyes
Of glorious lithe beasts flash for a moment
Out of the solemn, sylvan opaline
Of hoary forest boles, and swiftly vanish :
Little agamas nod their orange heads ;
A lovely praying mantis, green as leaves,
Rests on green leaves ; and green cameleons.

ASPIRATIONS.

AND I would have wise lovers of mankind,
Dwelling through all the land in colonies;
Gendering new necessities of life,
Desires entwined with all the nobler growth
Of reason, mutual reverence, and love;
Arousing men with sturdier enterprise
To stir the virtues of a virgin soil;
Fostering civil arts of mutual peace,
That ask for interchange of services.
So shall they cherish honourable trade
In all the wealth of Ethiopia;
Ebony, amber, gold, and ivory;
A care to barter these for what is wrought
By fiery familiars of the brain
Yonder in Europe, in our world sublime
Of godlike labour, triumph, and despair;
In realms more wonderful than Africa!
For in our Europe and America,
Sun, ocean, earth, are vassals unto man;
For whom he moulds huge organs all inform'd
With a blind emanation from the soul—
Wheel within wheel of giant enginery,

Thunderously storming, wailing, murmuring,
Cow'd slaves of his creative human will;
Eager to mangle the slight taskmaster,
If God plunge him among their whirling limbs. . . .

But with a gauntlet of stern iron crush out,
England! the foul snake coil'd voluminous
About this desolate land, feeding on blood!
Forbid, stamp out, the accursed trade in men:
Nor dare neglect the mission of the strong,
To bind the oppressor, and to help the poor!

Then shall these glorious immemorial rivers,
And inland seas, mine eyes have first beholden,
The Lord's highways of holiness and peace,
Alive with white-wing'd ministers of heaven,
Waft sunnier glory to the jubilant shores
Of Ethiopia, and the Maurian's land
Lift up her dark deliver'd hands to God!
I may not see it! Like Israel's leader, I
Am but a pioneer to bring the people
Out of their bondage: as on Pisgah's height,
May but behold the promised land from far. . . .
I have flung wide the portals of the night:
Children of hope and morning, enter ye!

THE LION.

A LION once, a mightiest male lion,
Whom my good rifle's bullet had but maim'd,
Sprang in his wrath; one huge and ponderous paw,
Striking my shoulder, hurl'd me under him.
Over me stood the vast dilated beast
Growling; his paw weigh'd on my shatter'd shoulder;
His great eyes glower'd; his fangs gleam'd terrible;
Like a simoom, his breathing scorch'd my face;
With tawny wilderness of mane aroused,
Frowning, aloft he swung his tufted tail.
But God removed all terrors and all pain:
When the brute shook me, numb indifference
Stole over all my being, while I watch'd;
Yea, look'd into the formidable eyes!
(So Love tempers inevitable blows
Of Fate for all the sons of suffering:)
A comrade fires; the lion springs on him;
Then fainting staggers,—ponderous falls—and dies.

THE SLAVE-TRADE.

I HAVE come to pleasant places on my way:
Angels beholding might be lured from heaven !
And in the course of my long wandering
I have return'd once more to visit them.
Alas ! how changed !
. . . Bowery villages roll volumed clouds
Of fiery smoke, staining the limpid light ;
Rich harvests, charr'd, or trampled, or ungarner'd
Idly luxuriant, meet the mournful eye.
While, even beside a golden, rich array
Of bounteous corn, a few starved boys and women,
Gaunt as yon skeletons around them strewn,
Crawl ; listless, hopeless famine in their eyes ;
All that were dear, slain, tortured, or expell'd
By arm'd assaults of the fierce slave-driver.
And ah ! these skeletons ! the tales they tell !
Beside fair river-banks, beside wreck'd huts,
Under green trees, under red rocks, in caves,
Ghastly anatomies, in attitudes
Of mortal anguish, writhed, and curl'd, and twisted,
Mutually clasp'd in transports of despair !

In one closed cabin, when mine eyes conform
To its faint twilight, on a rude raised bed
Appear two skeletons in mouldering weeds;
The head of one fallen from its wooden pillow;
And piteous between them a small form
Of a starved child, nestled by sire and mother.
The dead, and living wounded, and the babes,
Are flung by those contemptuous conquerors
To feed loathsome hyenas, that assemble
Through lurid smoke of sunset, gaunt and grey;
With obscene screaming vultures, heavily
Wheeling, or swooping; rending the live prey.
One infant darling, weeping, wilder'd, still
Solicits the cold breast of a dead mother!

I have seen Lualaba's mighty rolling water
Red with the blood of a blithe innocent people,
Who, unforeboding slant-eyed treachery,
Chaffer'd, and bought and sold, as was their wont,
In a populous fair by the worn river-marge.
And there was melody of mandolin,
And dulcet flute; with dancing, and warm love
Of gay young lovers, under broad brown eaves,
Sheltering from a hot ascending day;
Where clear young laughter blent deliciously
With falling notes of bowery turtle-doves,
Mantled in hues of tender summer cloud.
Hearken!—a rush! a trample of arm'd men!

A sudden deafening crash of musketry!
Hundreds of blithe love-dreaming youths and
    maidens,
Bathed in their own life-blood, and one another's,
Fall with one last death-quivering embrace:
While women in rude violating arms
Of strangers struggle; and the flower of men
Strain their necks impotent in yokes of iron,
Grappled around them by their insolent foes.
Hundreds in panic blind—man, woman, child—
Plunge among waters of deep Lualaba;
Whose drowning bodies the swift current hurries;
These, maim'd swollen corpses, drifting far away,
Hideously-croaking famish'd alligators
Fight for possession; lashing furious trains,
Pulling asunder human trunks and limbs!

But follow ye the stolen journeying slave!
Behold her toiling shackled, starved, and goaded
Upon her weary way through wild and wood,
Under the sunblaze; till her bleeding feet
Refuse their office; till she faints and falls!
Whom the tormentors, with a curse and jeer,
Torture to sense of cruel life once more:
Two burdens doth she carry; one, her babe:
She cannot bear them both; they snatch the babe
From her, for all the wailing and wrung hands;
Tossing it crush'd upon a mossy stone.

They goad her on; full blinding tears have darken'd
All the parch'd earth; she cannot stumble far—
Now shouts arise to kill her—it is done!
Christ saith to Satan: " Hold! the child shall sleep!"

MOSI-OA-TUNYA.*

SMOOTH river water holdeth softly furl'd
Thee, hoarded wonder of the wondrous world !
Ere thy tempestuous cataracts are hurl'd,
  Mosi-oa-tunya !

Twenty miles away thy sound
Travels from the gulf profound
Of thine earth-convulsing bound,
  Mosi-oa-tunya !

Five great cloudy columns rise,
To uphold the rolling skies :
Morning clothes with rainbow dyes
  Mosi-oa-tunya !

Awful phantoms in the moon
Rise to thy tremendous tune :
When the fiery evening falls,
Hell sulphureous appals,
While thy blazing thunder calls,
  Mosi-oa-tunya !

  * Cataract on the Zambesi.

The huge Mowana, and the Mohonono,
Like silvery cedar-trees on Lebanon,
Wave, with light palms, upon the pleasant isles
And shores, ere Leeambayee vanishes,
As though annihilate in his proud career :
Motsouri-cypress, yielding scarlet fruit ;
All noblest equatorial trees adorn
His mile-wide water, clear as a clear day,
Gliding like lightning into the abyss.

Clear a moment, ere thou blanch
Into a mile-wide avalanche,
Snowfall lapsing twice the height
Of Niagâra in his might !
Born of thy resounding day,
Myriad meteors o'er thee play :
There is an evergreen dark grove,
Guarded by thine own awful love :
Her inner melancholy no sun may move,
Mosi-oa-tunya !

Tall ghostly forms of sounding cloud
Clothe her in a rainbow shroud ;
No bird of hers carols aloud,
Mosi-oa-tunya !

Down the rock's tremendous face,
Foam-rills, tremulous like lace,
Flow from roots that grasp the place,

To where thy vaporous cauldrons hiss ;
But ere they may attain to this,
Smoke roaring, whirl'd from the abyss,
Licks them off precipitous stone,
High into a cloudy zone,
          Mosi-oa-tunya !

Water and wind jamm'd in a chasm profound,
Tortured, pent-up, and madden'd, with strong
    sound
War in world-ruining chaos, fierce rebounding ;
A wild tumultuous rumour, earth and heaven con-
    founding.

After, the river rushes, a long green
Serpent, convolved about dark promontories
Of sternest basalt, in the unfathomable
Chasm to and fro, a swift fork'd lightning-flash ;
But all the promontories are crown'd with trees,
Gorgeous blooming herbage and tall flowers.

On a green island, hanging o'er the flood,
Even where it falleth, lovely flowers are wooed,
And with eternal youth imbued,
By a lapse of gentle rain
From the cataract's hurricane :
Love celestial in showers
Falls from devastating powers !

Under the foam-bow and the cloud,
Here where thunders peal aloud,
Human souls with trembling bow'd,
    Mosi-oa-tunya !

  Cruel lords of all the isles,
Though a heavenly rainbow smiles,
Only feel bewildering annihilating terror ;
Offer human lives to thee in blind, bewilder'd
    error.
Love abideth still, sublime
O'er the roar and whirl of Time,
Foam-bow of a sunnier clime,
    Mosi-oa-tunya !

THE JOURNEY; AND WIFE'S DEATH.

My long life moves before me like a dream !

The cheerful bustle of the morning march !
Shouts of the driver ; scuffling of loud beasts !
Delicious swims and baths in some lone pool,
With chestnut-colour'd leaves in the blue glass,
And gorgeous birds reflected as they fly !

Appears the dear wild nightly bivouac
In some dim forest,—I upon a couch
Of woven rushes, under a furr'd hide,
Shelter'd, it may be, by a roof of boughs.
A grimy cauldron slung athwart the blaze
Held our repast of savoury buffalo-meat :
(Ere sunset had my rifle slain the beast)
But now my dusky troop surround the fire,
That ruddies their swart forms and visages,
Leaping to flame, with crackling faggot piled ;
Subsiding soon to embers deeply glowing.
Illumined smoke drifts fragrant, wavering
Amid the maze of long involved llanos,
That seem in the red, hesitating light,

To move alive, like pythons watching prey.
There breathes a strange, delicious woodland smell ;
Resinous amber glimmers to the stars ;
Richly-dim blossoms, many-hued, immense,
Droop fragrant heaven, a milky way of flowers,
Wherein by day the nimble monkey hurries,
And gorgeous parrot screams—now all is hush'd.

My trusty followers, my Makololo,
Astound the rest, relating how they toil'd
Athwart the continent ; arriving last
On a subsiding ridge of table-land ;
Whence without warning burst upon their view,
Ocean !
        Vision never dreamed before—
On Him in His sublime infinitude,
Soliloquising awful in the gloom ;
With one intolerable rift of light
Vibrating in the immeasurable waste
Of massy, torn, wan water that ascends,
To meet confusion of the hurrying cloud,
Releasing misty momentary rays ;
While in this shifting gulf of utter light,
A snowy sail shows black as ebony.

"Spell-bound we pause : we had follow'd this
        our Father,
Him of the honest heart, our wise white friend,
Through weal and woe, a weary, weary way,

From our own homes; in face of all the people
Spake, while we journey'd through their several
    lands,
That never white man brought an African
Here to the coast, save only to enslave;
But we would trust our father; we had proved
Him well, and he had promised; yea, we know
The English have good hearts for Africa!
And yet we pause at the sublime surprise.
For we had faith in what our Ancients told,
That the great World continueth evermore;
And now the World Himself saith unto us,
'Lo! I am ended! there is no more of me!'"

   Well I remember, O my splendid Sea,
How thy salt breath blew o'er me, as alive!
After interminable deserts drear,
And dank hot jungles of the savage race,
To come upon thee, Ocean, unaware,
Dear native element of all the free!
With British tars, and British hearts of oak,
And the old fiery flag upon the wind!
Tears blind my vision—yonder England lies!
A grey gull, in his strong deliberate flight
Hover'd and slanted, dipp'd his breast in brine,
Exulting in the wind and turbulent foam;
While half the mortal languor left my limbs,
And I rejoiced with him. From sea to sea!
I traversed all the dark, blank continent;

And proved it not, as timid idle dream
Surmised, an evil waste unprofitable,
Huge blot on God's most bountiful, fair world ;
Rather a promised land of living waters !
Like that king's daughter in the fairy tale,
Asleep, awaiting her Deliverer.

How clearly do mine inner eyes behold
The dear, wild nightly bivouac of yore,
When I was in my manhood's vigorous prime !
If it were in the prairie, or the desert,
Sinbad, my riding ox, with other oxen,
Would lie beside the looming bullock-wain,
Audibly ruminating, couch'd at ease
Upon his shadow, in a luminous moon.
If it were in a forest, such as last
Appear'd before my musing memory,
When I have heard awhile my followers' tales,
I weary close mine ears in first faint sleep,
Half hearing only broken words, and names
Of tribes or places, weird, and all germane
To the mysterious realm of forest wild.
But later silence all inviolate reigns ;
Save for a low communing of weird wind
Among high crowns of leafy ebonies,
Moving and murmuring, while star-worlds pass
    over.
When I awake, dark forms are lying round :
Firelight warms faintly mighty sylvan pillars,

Rising from gloom to gloom : they seem to my
Drowsed senses ancient phantoms of the night.
Thousands of years, some say, the huge Mowana
Flourishing lives, while mortal men around
Fall with his leaves, and wither at his feet.

And since she died,* rapture of my young years,
Love, and abiding pole-star of my life !
A marble cross, that gleams amid the gloom
Shines ever in dim vistas of my soul ;
And I desire to lay my toil-worn limbs
Under still leaves of some primæval grove,
As she, my well-beloved, resteth hers.

* His wife.

THE STARS.

SOLEMNLY purple night reigns over me,
With all the solemn glory of her stars.
Sublime star-worlds, who never have disdain'd
To be my friends, consolers, counsellors,
Guiding faint footfalls of a mortal man !
How often, when the moon among your lights
Glided, with her wan face beholding day ;
A slim canoe, carven from tender pearl,
Confused to many crescents as I gaze ;
Noting the very punctual moment, I
Besought my faithful sextant to reveal
What interval of cavernous clear gloom
Lay now between her orb and one of you !
I found how high above your brilliant
Image in my small pool of mercury
Ye rose in heaven on my meridian.
So, in the least conjectured realm of all
These pilgrim feet have found, my whereabout
On this our Earth discovering I record.
But the barbarians, when they saw me place
And note the readings of mine instrument,
Deemed me magician ; some beneath their breath,
Viewing my quadrant's ivory curvature,

Whisper'd : " The Son of God hath come to us ;
And lo ! the moon was underneath his arm !
He holdeth strange communion with stars."

Yours are fair faces of familiar friends
To the lone traveller in a lonely land,
Ye constellations, slowly journeying west !
And some of you, my best beloved at home
May not behold ; but some of you, with me,
Their eyes and mine may gaze upon together.
Glorious worlds, unknown to mortal men,
My spirit yearns to you from hollow orbs !
Soon shall I slake my longing all divine
Even in you, with higher powers than these
Of this poor worn-out body !
                                        Now my soul
Seeks those immortals, who have passed away
From earth to yonder infinite star-worlds :
World within world, sun, planet, comet, moon,
All in their order and their own degree,
One crimson, and one golden, and one green,
Harmonious hearing a low voice of Love !
Star of the Nile ! resplendent Sirius !
Whom here men name " Drawer of all the Night ! "
Planet of Love ! Ntanda,* fair firstborn
Of evening, tremulous dew in a sweet rose !
(She is so large, and clear, she sheds a shadow :)
Aldebaran, Orion, Fomalhaut,
Altair, Canopus, and the Southern Cross !

* Native name for planet Venus, meaning "firstborn."

Now fades yon pyramid of nebulous light
Zodiacal, that, paling as it soars,
Tinges mild splendour of the Milky Way
A delicate orange; but Magellan's clouds
Revolve around our starless Southern Pole.
And all is silence—only a night air
Rustles a palm, dreaming among the stars,
From whose dim languorous long fronds they rise,
Slow disentangling their celestial gleam.
No human sound disturbs the solitude,
Only a cry of some far florican,
A chirping cricket in the herb afar,
Or doleful forest-muffled living thing.
Also I hear a distant ghostly voice
Of plangent surf, alternately resounding
And ceasing, on wild Tanganika's shore.
But a low thunder booms at intervals.
Some say it is a surge, wandering in caves
Unfathomable of a mighty mountain range,
For off to westward, nearer Liembâ.
And some affirm a river under earth
Rushes in yonder mountains of Kabongo,
Breathing a strange low thunder on the wind . . .
England! my children! shall I see you once
Again before I perish?—nay the end
Is very near: here I shall die alone:
I am weary, worn, deserted, destitute!

THE CARAVAN.

LAST in rude bark of a great tree they bear him
Toward the isle of clove and cinnamon,*
Bulbul and orange, and pomegranate flower ;
Carrying their dead Leader to the sea,
Who in glad triumph should have brought them
    there !
A solemn, strange, a holy Caravan !
When was the like thereof beheld by man ?
Slow journeying from unconjectured lands,
Behold ! they bear him in their gentle hands ;
His dark youths bear him in the rude grey bark,
As though their burden were a holiest ark.
Embalm'd they bear him from the lands of Nile,
As men bore Israel, Abraham, erewhile.
Weary and weak, and faint and fallen ill,
Through desert, jungle, forest wild and still,
By lake, and dismal swamp, and rolling river,
Slowly their dark procession winds forever.
How would the Chief exult at every sight !
Alas ! those eagle eyes are seal'd in night.

* Zanzibar.

Behold them winding over hill and plain,
In storm, in sunshine, calm and hurricane !
And if they may not hide what thing they bear,
Men banish them with horror and wild fear,
Far from all human dwelling ; nor will feed ;
Nor furnish aught to fill their bitter need ;
Assailing them with hindering word and deed.
But though their burden may not wake to cheer,
The Hero-Spirit hovers very near :
Upon them rests the holy Master's power :
His soul before them moves, a mighty tower !
They, and the body, rest beneath the stars,
Or moonèd ghostly-rainbow'd cloudy bars ;
Until at length they hear the sounding sea,
In all the grandeur of Eternity !
A solemn, strange, a holy Caravan !
When was the like thereof beheld by man ?

THE DEATH OF LIVINGSTONE.

I.

" No mortal power shall turn me : I arise,
And will go forward, with my face for ever
Toward those fountains of the sacred river,
River still guarding from all mortal eyes
The hoary mystery of mysteries."
So vowed the pilgrim, chief of a strong band,
Who toil to wrest from Death the twilight land.
A deep resolve, more grand than midnight skies,
Glowed in his countenance ; but face and form
Were marred and writhen with the lifelong storm.
While life's dark winter snowed upon his heart,
All wrathful elements howled forth, Depart !
Heaven with remorseless frown above him bowed ;
Earth rose in whelming floods to help the cloud.

II.

Whelmed in the wild and terrible morass,
He wades, he swims, he flounders ; he is borne
Upon the shoulders of dark men forlorn,
To whom the grandeurs of his spirit pass
By glorious contagion ; a foul mass

Of foes malignant o'er the man outworn
Clamour; disease his vitals doth harass,
Draining the life-blood; mortal pain hath torn:
Until his faithfuls weave him a soft bed
Of boughs, and bear him among flowering reeds
And lotus-paven waters: overhead,
Languid from anguish, he in dreaming heeds
An eagle at dawn, whose ghostly voice is hurled,
As though he called one from another world.

III.

A world of waters—sounds of solemn sea,
As wind soughs wandering in rushes now:
But they have built with grass and limber bough
A hut for him who fainteth mortally.
"Lord, let not Hell prevail! be with me Thou!
May I sustain the load allotted me;
And ere in England falls the winter snow,
May I be there, at home, with Victory! . . .
. . . Deep is the desolation of my soul:
It may be I am failing ere my task
Full-ended: in my wake no champion
Of light is following; where waters roll
On fair Nyassa, Death's dark navies bask!
Mary lies in her forest grave alone!

IV.

"Alone her face, and one more, dear as hers,
Avail red haunting horrors to dispel.

O my dark race, plunged in the abyss of Hell !
Sweet babes and women, beneath slow murderers !
Tortured I start from slumber—weeping blurs
Mine eyes for memories no words may tell.
. . . Ere the young linnet in a soft nest stirs,
I would be home, my work accomplished well ! "
. . . Drearily day faints, moaning into night ;
The dark men sadly lose their fading sight,
Cowering silent by the watchfire light.
Beasts growl in jungles of Ilala land ;
Far nightbirds wail on Lulimala strand ;
Trees fire-illumined murmur, a tall band.

V.

" Is it our people who are shouting so ? "
The dark and tender follower replies,
" A buffalo from far corn-fields with cries
Men scare." . . . The spirit wanders to and fro,
Like some dim waters' aimless ebb and flow ;
" Is this the Luapula ? " . . . whose surmise
Gently the man dissolves : then in a low
Alien tongue, and with faint, filming eyes,
The weary wanderer wistfully inquires,
" How far is Luapula ? " falling soon
To slumber. . . . Later, after night's chill noon,
His boy-attendant, running toward the fires
Out of the hut, where both were sleeping, said,
" Come to the Master ! for I am afraid."

VI.

They, rising, hasten to the cabin door;
Where, by a feeble taper, which adheres
To a worn wooden travelling-case, appears
The form of one who kneels upon the floor,
The head bowed in the hands enclasped before
The body.   Reverent they pause: none hears
A sound of breathing; louder than of yore
The low watch-pulse affronts foreboding ears.
At length one, timid, touches the grey head.
Stone-cold, and silent!   Livingstone is dead!
Lifting his arms to God above the crowd
Of trampling furies, broken, but not bowed,
His mighty soul went out: the slave in chains
Moans: the ghost-eagle calls: Hell laughs: Night
     reigns!

VII.

The cold hands call upon abysmal Gloom:
Strange frondage murmurs in a darkling morn:
Orphaned men cower round the fires forlorn:
Nile shrouds his fountains: the dim living tomb
Of Africa still closed, Death's blank-eyed doom,—
No face beloved, no land where he was born,—
Guerdons the warrior!   No prayed-for bloom
Of home-love crowns him ere the year outworn;
But while faint eyes look far away with trust,
Death spurns the soul's quenched altar in the dust!

. . . Is all, then, failure? Lives no Father there?
Do living hearts but supplicate dead air?
Is this the end of the Promethean
Indomitable, all-enduring Man?

VIII.

Who calls it failure?
     God fulfils the prayer :
He is at home ; he rests ; the work is done.
He hath not failed, who fails like Livingstone !
Radiant diadems all conquerors wear
Pale before his magnificent despair ;
And whatsoever kingdoms men have won,
He triumphs dead, defeated, and alone,
Who learned sublimely to endure and dare !
For holy labour is the very end,
Duty man's crown, and his eternal friend ;
Reason from Chaos wards the world's grand whole ;
All Nature hath Love's martyrdom for goal.
Who nobly toils, though none be nigh to see,
He only lives,—he lives eternally.

IX.

Night melts in glory ; royal-robèd Sun
Glowingly deepens, like a martial blare,
Awakening mountain, lake, and forest fair ;
Assumes all Africa for royal throne.
Slaves, to the height of their great master grown,

With souls unfettered, and free limbs, prepare
The wondrous march, whose Europe-shaming care
Made all his faithful fortitude our own,
Enshrined for men the man magnanimous,
A beacon for all races and for us !
Yet if no rumour had survived the grave,
If all were whelmed in dark Ilala-wave,
Yon very woods and waters in their dim
Hearts would have lost no memory of him !
They, in their mystic message to all time,
And all the worlds, have thrilled with the sublime
Story of man ; God reassumes the life ;
He crowns unseen the labour and the strife.
Labour is full fruition in the bud,
And faith, possession dimly understood.

Mortal defeat blows oft the clarion
Of resurrection o'er an indolent world
Death-dreaming, louder than hath e'er been blown
From visible triumph ; the freed soul unfurled
A conquering flame, arousing the dull plain
Of common souls to kindle in his train,
Heroic-moulded, woke the silent dust
To songful flowers of helpful love and trust ;
Inspired the world's dead heart to throb victoriously ;
So they awake to life, who warring desperate die !
Yea, in the smile of some Divine deep Peace,
Our faithful find from storms of earth release.

LONDON.

ANOTHER sound,
Akin to the sea-sound, was in mine ears,
Resembling some huge roar of a far furnace,
Whose sullen flare through wallowing mists impure
Burned like the fire-flush from those realms of Dis
In that deep-mouthed verse of the Mantuan.
Huge murmur from the throat of Babylon !
Illimitable leagues of piles confused,
Dome, tower, and steeple, stately palaces,
Islanded in a welter of dim street ;
Mean habitations, warrens of dun life,
Tortuous, swarming ; sullied, pale, cramped life,
With, in the midst, a large imperial River,
Turbid and troubled, the town's artery,
Spanned by tumultuous bridges ; o'er them clang
Steam-dragon, chariot, horse, and laden wain,
With hurrying people of the human hive ;
Whose shores are thronged with warehouse, opulent
    wharf,
Whose turbulent tide upbuoyeth bark and barge,
Throbbing, foam-trailing steamer, russet sail,
And stately ships from far sea-sundered lands.

16

But over all a brown Plutonian gloom
Of murk air dismal and defiled, the breath
Of our so monstrous town—her visible sin,
And weight of wan woe, blotting out sweet heaven !
Behold the River ! a guilt-laden ghost,
How he hurries all unlingering below,
Away, away, through horror of deep night,
Pale with the guilty secret of the city !
Like that sin-burdened victim, driven forth
In Israel to the wilds, ashamèd Thames
Rolls headlong, tarries nor to look, nor listen,
Hastens to hide himself in the great Deep,
There to confide, unbosom, bury there,
The tomb, the womb, the unfathomed other-world,
Absolving and absorbing Mother Ocean,
The ineffable oppression at his heart,
The horror of unutterable wrong !
How changed, O Thames ! from in thine earlier
    hour
Of child-like dallying among reeds and lilies,
White swans, and flowers, and boats of lingering
    lovers,
By Marlow, Maidenhead, or Cliveden Grove !
   O whirling wheels ! O throngs of murmuring
    men !
Where is the goal of infinite endeavour ?
And where your haven, O ye fleeting faces ?
High Westminster, like some tall ghostly father
Of olden time, stands wildered, while for crowds
Of modern men, swift eddying at his feet,

His reverend grandeur void of consolation
Broods ; for no warriors, consecrated kings,
Kings who were crowned here through the cen-
    turies,
Nor bard, nor saint, emblazoned on the pane,
Canopied under marble in the aisle,
Whose shadowy memories haunt his heart, may
    help.
These are unsceptred ; time trends otherwhere ;
Their slumber is by channels long deserted !
His hoary towers, with melancholy eyes,
Dream in their own world, impotent for ours ;
Or if he speak, who may interpret now ?
He wakes in vain, who slept for centuries,
For he awakens in some alien world.
    Doth Hope inhabit, then, the sister-pile,
Whose stately height hath grown to overshadow
That hoary minster ?   This in sooth avails.
And yet methinks more health is in the old,
Renewing youth from fountains of the new,
Than in rash overthrow of all men built,
With salt of insolence sown in holy places.
    Therefore, O secular, and sacred towers,
Confound your glories by the river-shore,
And marry mighty tones in ordering time !
Cathedral organ, roll insurgent sound,
As though the archangel would arouse the dead !
Our firm foundations on the invisible,
Build we the ever ampler, loftier state,
Till unaware we walk the City of God !

Yea, for I deem the fathers we revere,
Shrined in cathedral glooms, embolden us
With eyes of silent counsel, and dumb power,
Approving backs turned on their empty tomb.
But who may slay the irrevocable Past?
The Past, our venerable Sire, who girds
Bright armour round us, like some grand old knight,
With benediction sending forth fair youth
To battle, crowning what himself began!
　　When England bathes in shadow, the tall tower
Of that great palace of the people shines,
Shines to the midnight like a midnight sun.
While crowned, inherited incompetence,
And while law-making men laborious
Through long night-watches, in their golden chamber,
Wage wordy wars of faction, help the State,
The dreadful river rolls in darkness under,
Whirling our human lights to wild witch-gleam!
See yellow lamps in formidable gloom
Of both the shores, night-hearted haunts of men;
Terrible water heaped about great piers
Of arches, gliding, gurgling, ominous!
But on the vasty parapet above
Those Titan tunnels, ghastlier for the glare
Of our electric mockery of moons,
Appears a moment a fate-haunted face—
Wan Desolation, plunging to the Void.
Then swirls a form dishonoured among gleams,
Which eddy as light-headed; what was man,
With other offal flotsam, flounders, rolls.

But now for one who mused upon the bridge,
Of pier and arch tremendous, the huge reek,
And sin-breathed exhalations of the city,
Transfigured by an alchemy of power,
Burned with all colour ; the broad river rose
Aslant horizonward, and heavenward,
One calm aerial glory of still dream ;
Thronged habitations on the shadowy shore
Blend solemn, disembodied to a bloom
Ethereal, bathed in evening ; fair, enchased,
Or diapered upon the delicate air,
Hull, mast, sail, tiny bark, or barge, or steamer,
Poised darkly in mid primrose of the tide,
Like carven fretwork on a golden shrine.
All monstrous hostels, with interminable
Glazed bulks that over-roof the clanging train,
And all our builded chaos doth repent,
Converting into beauty ; while I muse,
The mild and modulated cadences
Of lemon fruit, shy violet, dove-down,
Deepen to very pomp and festival
Of dyes magnificent ; one diapason
Of hues resplendent, crimson, gold, and green,
And purple gorgeous, like robes of kings,
Or caves of sun-illumined sea-treasure,
Or glories blazoned in cathedral aisle,
Heart of white lily, fruit of passion-flower,
Or fervid eagle-eyes ; a parable,
One nuptial-feast of marrying glow and gloom,
A wondrous parable of life through death !

While yonder haughty heights of Westminster,
Where once fierce feuds of our illustrious dead
Sleep reconciled in monumental calm,
Mary reposing by Elizabeth,
And where with throes of living, loud debate
Are brought to birth the still behests of Heaven ;
With ancient consecrated privilege
Of lordly Lambeth on his stately sward ;
These, and the grand dome, and the four grim towers,
Haunted by phantoms of long-wandering crime,
And harbours thronged with navies of the world,
Glow fair a moment with supernal fire.

THE COAST OF CORNWALL.

FOR me, true son of Erin, thou art rife,
Grand coast of Cornwall, cliff, and cave, and surge,
With glamour of the Kelt.   Strong sons at strife
With wind and wave if healthier influence purge
Not wholly yet from wrecker's blood, nor merge
All in mild manners, yet there do not fail
Ancestral hero hearts and lives to urge
Their native virtue, that will never pale
In any strait, nor cringe, nor need to wear a veil.

Tired hearts' refreshment, friend, glad life was mine
Hearing rich music in Lamorna's bower ;
And where thy whelming, tawny dunes incline
Saint Piran ! waveward, many a siren hour
Me and my village friend through shine and shower
Crowned, pacing level sands by foamy flood ;
Tintagel, thy dark legendary tower
Dreams o'er the seas of Tristram and Isoud ;
By cliff and cavern gleam Romance's aery brood !

Toward thee, wild Treryn Dinas, oft I steer,
From whose weird form wake melancholy wings

Of cloudy memories divinely dear ;
Thou lookest all unutterable things,
Haunt of some mystic atmosphere that clings
From faintly-imagined, vanished Druid time,
While a low wind, like one demented, sings,
Or murmurs a lorn, incoherent rhyme
Of mariners wrecked here since Earth was in her
    prime.

I love Bedruthan's frowning, storm-swept steep,
Saint Columb's minster-caverned purple gloom,
Where bosoms of the babe-waves heave in sleep :
Around Tol-Pedn's sombre height they boom ;
Through tall fantastic arches glancing foam ;
By grey Saint Levan, surge-ringed Rundlestone,
Whose bell wave-tolled hath learned sad sounds
    from Doom,
How often do I wander all alone,
With quest bewildered hearing the sea's monotone !

BALLAD OF THE DEAD MONK; OR,
BROTHER BENEDICT.

I.

THE monk upon the bier lies dead ;
  Seven tapers burn by him ;
Robed brethren at the feet, the head,
  Chaunt a low requiem.

II.

Deep gloom involves the vaulted church,
  Save where the moon's pale face
Shows through unbarred doors of the porch
  A misty mountain grace.

III.

He came, a knight of high degree,
  His former life untold ;
The noble proud served lowlily,
  With thoughts that self-enfold.

IV.

Self-scourged in stony cells he prayed ;
  Himself did sore afflict :
Thorned sarks on delicate flesh he laid ;
  Men called him Benedict.

V.

Or he would roam the lonely hills,
  Where faintly floats the chime,
An eyrie the far cloister dwells
  Upon the crag sublime.

VI.

The brother came in bygone years,
  A wild-eyed penitent ;
Now famed for vigil, fasting, tears,
  The brethren o'er him bent.

VII.

They kissed the hands, they kissed the feet ;
  God dowers with gifts of healing
A saint so pure, for Earth unmeet,
  Ripe for Heaven's revealing. . . .

VIII.

. . . Yet under the monk's shadowy cowl,
　On that carven countenance,
Do writhen anguish, and a scowl
　Mate with heavenly trance ?

IX.

In pace requiescat ! roll
　O solemn, dirgeful sound !
Fill pause in prayer for human soul,
　Vast torrent-boom profound ! . . .

X.

. . . What ails the body on the bier ?
　What trouble shakes the dead ?
All shrink aloof, heart-chilled with fear !
　The corpse, eyes open, said :

XI.

" By the just judgment of the Lord,
　I am damned ! my spirit
For evil life now reaps reward,
　Hell-fire my sins inherit.

XII.

" Mine own ill-deeds environ me,
   Build dungeons of deep sorrow,
The live pit-walls laugh loud their glee,
   Yesterday, now, to-morrow !

XIII.

" Ye lambs my selfish pleasure stained,
   Who once were virgin snow !
O burden not to be sustained !
   Pity !   I suffer so !

XIV.

" Nay, look not with your dovelike eyes
   On me, your murderer !
The death-shroud o'er my spirit lies,
   Your blood streams over her.

XV.

" O'er lonely realms I wander far,
   Following a marish-gleam ;
Me ever the false elfin star
   Eludes ; I do but dream.

XVI.

" O dreadful luring breasts and arms !
    Witch banquets with no name !
Bondslave am I to baleful charms,
    That feed on me like flame.

XVII.

" By ruined shores I rove alone,
    Dull rain, storm-beaten brine !
By cliff and cave heart-broken moan,
    Low light on the sea-line,
    Dim, desolate, like mine !

XVIII.

" Mine own unquenchable desire,
    Ambition, lust, consumes,
Clothes me with a shirt of fire ;
    I mourn among the tombs."

XIX.

. . . The phantom words were like a wail
    Of low wind in the vault ;
Resuming, " May your prayer prevail
    To loose me from my fault ! "

XX.

They prayed; less poignant grew the tone. . .
  . . . He seemeth to converse
With one invisible, unknown,
  Who lighteneth the curse.

XXI.

A monk affirmed he saw and heard
  A semblance in the air,
As of a child, pale, tattered, marred,
  Of aspect little fair.

XXII.

" Who art thou, dear ? " saith the dead brother,
  With accent marvelling ;
" Not know me ? left by mine own mother,
  You found me wandering.

XXIII.

" In that black bitter night of snow ;
  So faint I scarce may move ;
Food, shelter, clothes, were mine with you ;
  And more you gave me—love.

XXIV.

" You took me home, and by your side
  Set in my rags and dirt,
You found me friends ; I early died ;
  My father none shall hurt.

XXV.

" Thou father of my heart, so dear !
  I am but a poor child ;
Yet I may use the Name they fear,
  These, lurid, and defiled.

XXVI.

" Avaunt, foul torturers, in the Name
  Of Him who died on cross !
Now will I lead thee from thy shame,
  Although thou suffer loss.

XXVII.

" Fly with me where the healing streams
  From bloomy hills descend ;
Where leafy groves with birds and beams
  Melodiously blend."

XXVIII.

The vision-gifted monk beheld
  What men by him discerned not,
Whose eyes wide-wondering were held,
  A rigid form that turned not.

XXIX.

Transfigured was the common boy,
  The form grew radiant ;
The face, a sunrise of deep joy,
  Like Christ, the child of want.

XXX.

Now one whom he hath injured most
  Brings pardon of her love ;
The weak twain were a mighty host,
  And through great armies clove ;
  His own will heartened strove.

XXXI.

She came, the woman he did wound,
  Lay weeping on his breast ;
She loosed him, in the grave-clothes bound,
  And lulled despair to rest.

XXXII.

Intent the straining senses drank
  Looks, words, of soft repose,
And then poor eyelids gently sank,
  As when Love's fingers close.

XXXIII.

Each awed to his own cell hath gone ;
  Night folds the world in gloom ;
The dead are sleeping still as stone ;
  So ends a tale of doom.

THE GEMONIAN STAIRS.

ONLY a slave in Rome of old,
   A slave for whom none cares!
Slaughtered in dungeon-deeps, and rolled
   Down the Gemonian stairs;
Insulted, marred, exposed to view,
   With other human lumber,
There in the Forum, where the Roman concourse
     grew
   Around his mortal slumber.
There in the Forum, by the mighty walls,
   And columns hero-crowned,
Whose mourning voice upon the slumberer calls?
   The whine of a poor hound!
He will not leave the swarthy clay,
   He licks the rigid face;
Harsh-laughing, stern men in long-robed array
   Gather about the place:
One pitying hath offered bread;
   The dog but lays it down
Before the dumb mouth of the master dead;
   Whose body later thrown

In turbid Tiber's flood he follows,
   Borne headlong by the river,
To lift it from the strong, loud gulf that swallows,
   Struggling, till both have sunk for ever.

A gleam is for a moment cast
   Over oblivion:
The dead slave, whose dog holds him fast,
   Drifts, passes,—all are gone. . . .

THE POLISH MOTHER.

A DRAMATIC MONOLOGUE. *

SHE looked a matron from the ancient world
Of Roman grandeur, tall, pale, proud, black-robed.
Strong passion chained, with poignant suffering,
Held down by stern hand, crouched, yet writhed alive
    alive
In her fine countenance; whose graven lines,
White hair, death-pallor, and deep caverned eyes,
That lustrous burned with fierce intensity,
All prophesied the death-doom imminent.
She was a Pole of ancient lineage,
Whose son, Count Român, made a prisoner
In those great hopeless battles, which the race
Fought, for the right to be, with the strong Tzar,
Had been condemned to labour in the mines
Of far Siberia perpetually.
    Now she conferred with one, whom suffocation
Of all free thought and speech in Russia made

---

* Founded on a real incident, mentioned by Liszt in his *Life
of Chopin.*

Wild to wrest freedom by main force, a lady,
Young, fair, fanatical; to whom she told
The story of the wrongs, that wrung consent from
    her
To violent counsels of conspiracy.
    "I could not kneel; my knees were turned to
      marble;
I could not save my son, my only child!
And yet you know well how I loved him! how
I had waited for him, tended from the birth,
Fed from my own life's fountain; when he ailed,
Bent over, watching wakeful by the bed,
Hearing him breathe, and soothed when he awoke.
Myself I ministered to want and whim;
My being hung on his; my thoughts returned
Thither, however far afield they flew,
Hovered around him, birds about the nest.
Ah! boy beloved, my heart's home was in thee!
    Hours of our early love, the balmy moons
By drowsy, lisping seas in the warm south,
Were they more dear than later summer evenings,
When, after favourite tale, accompanied
By rippling laughter from my baby boy,
Mother undressed him (nurse had holiday,
Sweet birds were warbling, the young rose was blown)?
We sang our simple songs, dear, you and I,
Until you only crooned them, half in dream,
Then softly glided into slumberland,
Away from mother; but her heart still held you!
    Where is he now? In some profounder sleep.

Where is he now? . . . they say I might have saved
   him.
I was too proud.   My God! I might have knelt!
There was one moment only—I could not!
  My son, the Count, fought like a patriot Pole
Against our old hereditary foe.
Made captive, Nicholas himself had added,
When signing the imperial decree
Of lifelong death in far Siberian mine,
Whence none emergeth more to social day,
'Thither shall he go manacled, on foot.'
Ha! do you know what that means? 'chained, on
  foot'?
It means to tramp long winter through to summer,
Athwart interminable steppes, and snow,
To that bleak outcast region beyond hope,
With one coarse convict yoked a bondfellow,
Defiled in body, and defiled in mind,
With him to tramp, to feed, to lie by night,
Subject to every brutal outrage from
Soldiers who love to wreak indignity
Upon one outlawed, of high grade, refined :
And if his strength (but he was weak, and ailing)
Sustained through that dread journey to the goal,
Live burial in the nether deeps of earth,
Toil so repulsive, so interminable,
That men have killed their guard, to win the grace
Of being knouted to a speedier death—
Or else malignant years, that beat men down,
Each with his own peculiar stroke, combine

Here their slow malice into one supreme
Assault, and turn the young man deaf, blind, grey,
Quench in a year the fading faculties,
Render imbecile ere the very end.
Or men escape in winter weather; then
They may lie down, and faint out in the snow. . . .
And this was he who lay upon my breast,
And drew warm life I stored up there for him—
For whom I would have parted with all mine. . . .
Why, then, did I not save him? why? God knows!
If God there be—but when the tyrant came,
An evil sneer upon his curving lips,
My knees were turned to stone; I could not move—
Kneel to the insolent murderer of my people,
Who now would torture my poor child, in wrath,
Because he paid his country what he owed her—
You know not the conditions the man made,
Indignities designed to break my pride—
To break the pride of Poland—of one born
Illustrious as any emperor.
On such conditions, if I craved for pardon,
(Pardon forsooth! and mercy! and from him!)
He would toss me the freedom of my child,
Contemptuously as you toss bone to dog—
Exemption from his own injustice, his
Inhuman sentence—nay, there is a God!
This man must needs be punished for his life!
These degradations I refused; for honour
Is more than life; more even than one's child.
At last, the Empress, pitying me, arranged

That I should ask an audience of her;
Then he the autocrat would cross the room,
And I upon my knees might crave for grace. . . .
He entered, while we talked; I never moved.
So she, supposing that I knew him not,
Rose, and I rose too; but he slowly passed,
Staring, incarnate Insult, in mine eyes,
The stare of arrogant autocracy,
With sneer that relished our humiliation.
He slowly passed, looked, lingered, and went out.
The Empress seized my two hands, and she cried:
' You have lost your only opportunity ! '
    Face to face with the murderer of my country,
I was the daughter of Poland, and no mother !
In that brief moment I beheld *my* Mother,
Poland, my Mother,
Dishonoured, and dismembered; felt them part
Her frame, yet warm, assigned among three
    tyrants. . . .
What did I see?   I saw in vivid vision
Our green fields bloodied, corpses in the woods
Of fair, brave brothers—felt them beaten to death
By Tartar soldiers, maddening in dungeons
Deprived of day, dank, loathsome, for the love
They bore our common Mother; saw corn, food
Trampled by hooves barbarian, crushed down
Under the mangled bodies of her sons;
The flaming smoke rolled up from ruined homes,
And women sobbing on the unroofed, wrecked
    hearths—

And not one heart, but multitudes of hearts,
True hearts—lay broken in the mines of hell ! . . .
What did I hear ? I heard the syllables
We loved to lisp in childhood on loved knees,
Silenced for ever among living men,
Forbidden to be spoken by the children. . . .
Ah ! ah ! the children ! wailing they were dragged,
Dragged from mad mothers' arms, and heaped in
 waggons,
Jolted along the frozen snows, for nurse
The brutal Cossack, cursing when they cried,
Their mothers following the dwindling carts,
And floundering into snowdrifts ; happy they,
If to remain there ! while the children's cry
Dwindled to silence; all became so still ! . . .
Supreme stroke this of cynic cruelty—
Infants torn from their native land, to learn
Upon an alien soil from mortal foe
Forgetfulness of our parental love,
Indifference to their people's agony,
That so young Polish hearts might ossify
To Russian ! trained to arms for their oppressor,
Young Poles made Russian soldiers, and degraded,
Cajoled by demons to abjure themselves. . . .
Seeing and hearing which, how could I kneel
To him, in whom our injury was summed,
And centred ; radiated, from a deadly sun ?
I could not kneel, not even to save my child. . .
But I am going to Român ; all is well;
If not to meet him, then to rest in sleep.

He sleeps, he rests now.   Very soon I with him.
Ah ! so is best ! much better than if Time
Slackened the close clasp of Love's fingers, ere,
Wearying of His mumbling fools, He broke them   . . .
And vengeance only slumbers: work your will
Upon the tyrant ! I will help ; take gold:
Earth will be cleaner for one stain wiped out."

JUBILEE, AND THE GOOD EMPEROR.

BEHOLD an empress-queen, who nobly reigns,
And an ideal womanhood sustains
Upon a throne, who wisely rules by laws,
From long deliberation, clause by clause,
Grown fair, and growing, fed with patriot blood
Of Tyndale, Hampden, Sidney, and the good
Martyred, unnamed illustrious multitude.
Her fifty years of dedicated toil
To all self-pleasing tyrants are a foil,
Who only nurse their poor prerogative,
Whether the starving people die, or live.
Her large, full heart goes forth to all that mourn,
Itself, alas ! wrung, lacerate, and torn.
Our monarch hath a grander coronet
Than any mighty predecessor yet,
With many a subject people's jewel set.
First, orient India, fount of morning's beam,
Realm of Avâtar, and the wondrous dream !
Australia, young with earth's glad primal power,
Who weaves weird visions in her lonely bower,
Arms for defence her well-knit, stalwart sons,
And launches navies, iron-mouthed with guns,

To assure the Mother-mistress of the seas
Dominion more unchallenged over these !
In you, blithe land of long lake, frost, and fur,
Vast volumed waters of St. Lawrence pour
Their foaming thunders with an ocean roar !
All ye sent children armed for many a mile,
To help us nobly by Egyptian Nile.
Court gentle Peace ! and yet be well prepared !
Without our England, ill the world had fared !
Arm ships and soldiers ! ill may they be spared !
Distrust world-citizens, who fain would loose
Thine argent armour, deemed of no more use !

And thou, dark Afric's tempest-beaten Cape,
Around whom Gama dared his course to shape,
Sublime sea-comrade of Columbus bold,
By perilous water-ways unknown of old,
Thou, in the crown a diamond-beaming star,
Art sending sons to jubilee from far !

The pageant of her triumph proudly shone
With warriors, led erst by Wellington,
And that Black-armoured Prince ; red, sable, grey ;
Plumed horsemen, helmed, with steel and colour
    gay,
Swart Indian jewelled, in dim gold array ;
Elect Colonials, powerful of frame,
With nation-founding faces, known to fame ;
From every quarter of the world her guard !
Whose people throng the chariot way ; they ward
Her throne from danger ; love is great reward.
Bending with royal grace and beaming eye,

Moves the good queen, whose name is Victory.
The stately triumph of her glory moves
With loud acclaim, upborne by all the loves
Of all the people; kings and princes ride,
Her escort, with no ill-beseeming pride;
Her chariot rolls, surrounded by her sons,
Of whom the nobler, grander port he owns,
Who wedded England's daughter; who will be
Magnanimous Emperor in Germany;
He, though great empire his mild rule embrace,
Hath character more lofty than his place.
    Here towering with eagle-crested casque,
Face, form, proclaim one born for his high task.
He, a more gentle, just, God-fearing Saul,
Hath waged grim conquering battle with the Gaul;
Will wage a deadlier with the dire Disease
That lays him low; yet, scorning his own ease,
Conquereth here too; patient, cheerful, brave,
While borne in strong midmanhood to the grave,
Bends calm, composed eyes on the public good,
Who in his long death helps the multitude,
Country, and well-beloved; who will not swerve;
For if Death numbs the right hand, left will serve;
But when one symptom "*apathy*" they named,
Then all divined that Death at length hath claimed,
If to the lover his dear world grew dim!
A Light and Hope of Europe quenched in him!
Alas! for her, to whom he gave white heather,
In Caledonia, in blue lover's weather!
 He lies in state, he lies in his long rest;

And she hath laid the sere wreath on his breast,
Laurel, wherewith she crowned her Paladin,
In war proved, as in peace, a king of men.
   Our queen moves royally to Westminster.
Fortune hath dealt in gracious mood with her.
Yet one irreparable bereavement laid
A scathing hand upon her heart ! Snows weighed
Heavily, fallen from care-laden years !
Changed, since that early hour of April tears,
When young-winged Morning in the minster shone,
Illumed with Heaven, her, wearing earthly crown;
Changed, since her marrying the wise prince she
     lost,
Before chill autumn, and the winter frost ! . . .
   But the broad highway laughs with various hue,
That seems to pour from forth aerial blue :
Roof, balcony, door, window, all the street
Teem with a happy people, fain to greet
Her, whom the loyal, glad, tumultuous sound
Doth welcome, Love's loud answering rebound
From her Love-loyal reign, re-echoing round ! . . .
Yet if this monarch were not good and just,
To Heaven the pageantry were only dust.

GORDON.

GORDON, England's Red-cross Knight,
With many a dragon born to fight !
Great Gordon, waving a mere wand,
Rouses warriors who despond !*
With genial beam of his grey eye
Summons men to victory ;
Creates an army out of nought,
Unconquerables from hearts distraught :
His character, and equal laws
Enthrone secure the better cause.
And now alone o'er desert sands
He rides to Ethiopian lands,
Where his mere presence is a spell
For yon dark race that loves him well,
Where righteous, simple, true, and brave,
Long he toiled to free the slave,
Tender as a woman, strong
As a man to punish wrong ;
Human lover, trampling self,
Scorning fame, and power, and pelf.
Who, bursting on the boy of blood,†

* In China.
† Suleiman, son of Zebehr. See Gordon's "Journals" in
the Soudan.

Walled in with his man-murdering brood,
A dark armed threatening multitude,
Slight, travel-marred, almost alone,
But leaning on the mighty One,
Dominated the fell clan
With a power Promethean,
Power of greatest over least,
Of human tamer over beast.

Arrived, he welds to one strong blade,
Men disunited and dismayed;
Burns the rods of tyranny,
Breaks fetters from captivity;
At his well-loved name they gather,
Hail him Lord, and Saviour, Father,
Proclaiming equal law for all,
He bends to lift the weak who fall;
That large heart holds the dark young slave,
And our white waifs beyond the wave,*
Whom he, delivering, with love
Follows wheresoe'er they rove.

At sunrise how alert and eager,
Where the dusky swarms beleaguer,
Behold him from the palace roof—
Morn-flushed wave, and waste aloof—
Serene, yet anxious, watching Nile,
Where he winds for many a mile,
Surveying grim besieging host,
His rabble armed, and guarded post,
Waiting till the redcoats come,

* His Greenwich boys.

To save his people in Khartoum !
Confronting cataracts, sands, rocks,
Thronged foes' indomitable shocks,
How they stem the adverse tide,
All British discipline, pluck, pride,
Panting to be at his side !
While England longs to rend the curtain,
That shrouds her hero's fate uncertain.
Too late ! the man deserted, fell,
Whom only treachery might quell !
Gordon, England's Red-cross Knight,
With many a dragon born to fight !

THE LIFEBOAT.

THE manhood of our rugged coast,
Nelson's indomitable host,
Our manhood braves the raging seas,
Deaf to prayers of siren Ease,
Or warm Affection's humid eye,
To rescue shipwrecked souls who cry. . . .
Hoar ocean's wrathful night-usurping noise
Warns, like a dread god's doom-denouncing voice ;
They lean athwart the solid wall of blast,
Blinded with flying froth from forth the vast,
That spits contumely from moving mountains
Of toppling water torn to foam-white fountains ;
The maniac surge leaps furious while they launch ;
Falls a dead-weight upon the bark so staunch ;
But may not shake the mighty hearts that use
All strength of stalwart limbs and iron thews
To strain their oars athwart the swirling brine :
Big-booted, and large-chested, they incline
Broad backs together ! grim face and set eyes
Of coxwain fail not, nor strong hand that plies
Swift function of the tiller : how they bound
Up, down, abysmal cliffs of night profound,

That flash fierce scorn of them, engulfed beneath,
Hiss up to Heaven, and threaten with white teeth !
Hark ! through the storm-embroilment a faint sound
Of guns appealing ; piteous rend the sky
Red signals from the wreck's extremity !
   Their lifeboat battles with the wave ;
Grace Darling's countrymen will save,
Or perish ! . . . perish ! on the shore
They are thrown lifeless 'mid the roar !
Now mothers, wives, and children weep. . . .
All mothers, wives, and children weep :
All England bends above their solemn sleep :
Hear her intone their requiem full, and grand, and deep !

SEA KINGS. *

Who are these three, that in a little boat
Have dared upon the Antarctic surge to float,
Journey from Durban round the Cape of Storm,
Which hero hearts again to-day transform
Into a promontory of Good Hope,
As when grand Gama, and Diaz did grope
Their all unknown dim waterway of old ?
These Scandinavian mariners, more bold,
In a frail bark they hollowed far inshore,
Built from pitch-pine, and to the ocean bore,
In a frail open bark ten months will beard
Atlantic dark and formidable, steered
By their own sea-gnarled hands with dauntless
　　　strength,
Till they attain to our green land at length.
From where grim bastioned Table Mountain frowns,
And with the cloud his brooding forehead crowns,
To the caged eagle-emperor's arid isle ;
By flowery Azores they rest awhile ;
By Mauros, Corobeda, tempest-driven,

---

* See log of the *Homeward Bound*, exhibited at the Crystal
Palace on her arrival.

They arrive in England's welcoming white haven ;
The wonderful heroic voyage passed,
Through all vicissitudes come home at last.
Ah ! courage-consecrated little bark,
Men come to view thee, as wert thou sacred ark,
Or very Argo of the Argonaut !
With tokens of Sea's rough embraces fraught,
Rent canvas, cordage, bruised wood, plainly tell
Of rude storm-buffets ; tangled weed, and shell
On keel and plank now long contented dwell !
By half-amused, half-indolent contempt,
Or admiration for the bold attempt,
Was Ocean held from drowning the three men ?
Rather the God they worshipped in His ken
Kept, gave swift vision, accomplished craft, with
    power
To stem, surmount, and baffle danger's hour.
  O'er beetling cliffs of water, lo ! they bound ;
Engulfed now in a reeling chasm profound,
Obscure, foamed, swirling ; storm-breath on their side
Lays them, and plays with them ; and yet they ride,
Storm-seasoned hearts of oak, on the wild tide !
Endurance, vigilance, strength, iron nerve,
Tense, ne'er relaxed, allowing none to swerve
One hair's-breadth from his function, even for stress
Of wet, cold, hunger, thirst, or weariness,
Strain unrelieved on every faculty !
If caught off guard one moment, they shall die !
  In peril from the monsters of the deep,
In peril from wild, ruptured surge's leap ;

Fierce blast drags down, ere they may reef the sail,
Wave's weight half fills the hollow pine, bids bale
For very life, yet never great hearts fail.
 It blew great guns; stars blinked, and were blown
  out,
Or re-illumed; they saw the raging rout
Of billow smoking skyward; squall-slung spray
Smote, stung like hail; then louder than the roar
Of breaker thundering on a rock-bound shore,
A sound more terrible than aught before
Appalled their ear; some supernatural scream
Advanced toward them through the drifting steam:
And they beheld prodigious ocean herds,
Whales spouting geysers, porpoise, dolphin, birds
Rushing in headlong wild pursuit of shoals,
Menacing wreck, so hurling to their goals!
Buffeted bows drove piles in the hard sea;
Storm, waving vast vans, howled tumultuously.
 Dies from the cloud-range conflagration red,
And from long roller, taking hues of lead,
Sombre, oil-lustrous, fading dun and dead.
Cloud-mountains massed on pale horizons lower;
Grim monsters follow, hungry to devour.
One all unknown, and horrible remains
Beside them, while blood-chilling twilight wanes,
Huge, livid-backed, dim welters, and to mock
Their own mast, two long spectral rods that rock
Protrude in polished outgrowth from the spine:
Sinister, *that* lurks near them on the brine!
While on their masthead sits a weird, wild glare,

Like Death's pale lanthorn : ha ! what doth it there?
And what is that, which writhes upon the bare
Pole, like what writhed upon the lance's head
Of Dürer's knight, on his faint war-horse led
Into the forest gloom by Hell and Death?
What means the Portent? doth it breathe life's breath?
Immured in deep night the world seems to be,
Save when flashed flame lets out the boiling sea. . . .
But in long languor of clear ocean calm,
When the loose tiller held in listless palm
Made easeful noises with the lapping wave,
Dear home-thought stole upon the heart so brave ;
While loved familiar constellations rise,
When they draw nearer native Northern skies ;
High planets hold communion with them,
Pure worlds arising from heaved Ocean's rim ;
Luminous lives, how still and soft they move
In the grey wave, akin to stars above !
While elfin phosphorescence from the prow
Slopes in two murmuring, widened folds below.
Or in blue day the momentary gem,
Lovelier than a fairy diadem,
Twinkles innumerable on the rolling
Blue billow ; yellow birds for their consoling,
Pale yellow, flying o'er the lisping foam,
Alight upon the ocean-cradled boom ;
The gentle giant Olsen fondly feeds ;
Till they, relying on his kindly deeds,
Perch on his shoulder, lilting blithe and gay,
Who sorrows when he finds them flown away.

Often before a merry breeze they flew,
A wake of simmering silver in the blue ;
Many a nautilus with filmy sail,
And fishes panoplied in rainbow mail,
And flying fish with blithe young hearts they hail.
Or ample-pinioned, gleaming albatross,
That swooped and circled, dipped in soft sea-moss,
Then sunward soared, on calm, unwearied wing,
With plaintive white mew, air-meandering.
Alone upon the inward-murmuring sea,
Alone with God in the Immensity !
With worship, pious, temperate men, they call
Weekly together on the God of all.
Kingcraft and overlordship of the seas
From Olsen, Nilsen, Bernhard, such as these,
And their Norse kindred, Nelson, Franklin, Drake,
For men of other blood 'tis hard to take.
They prove the race of heroes not extinct,
By whom our common-seeming years are linked
To those that loom more fair in the dim past,
When Gama loosed his canvas to the blast,
And Raleigh in strange waters anchor cast.
Not ease, but hardship, suffering, privation
Root, toughen, hearts of oak, and mould a nation,
Bear witness Holland, Athens, Albion !
Columbia, Teuton, Italy, made one !
By toil, and strife, and agony 'twas done.

A SWAN.

Now in the lower reflected gulf of blue
A swan sails tranquil with a stately neck
Arched long, with orange beak, and lifted wing
Sail-like on either side, how soft and pure !
Have they not fallen these wings from yonder blue,
Out of the soft white cloud there, so akin
They seem to it ?   And O the tenderness
Of the blue shadow, scarcely shadow or blue,
Haunting yon dells of down behind the wing !
Surely the white cloud when it fell from heaven
Fell with the heavenly motion lingering in it,
For do but note how tranquil and how still
The cloud sails yonder and the swan sails here !
Yet lo ! a sudden impulse of the bosom
Thrills all the placid water feeling it
To dimpling smiles that waft luxurious light
Into the pendulous faces of sweet flowers,
Lush grasses, harebell, eyebright, sorrel leaves
That fringe the flood whose heart enshrines them all.
While his dim double the swan floats upon
Flickers beneath him with the twin-born ripple
From his breast sloping either side away,

Melts like snow dropped in water, yet remains.
He ruffles yielding wavering images
Of church and tree, and of the sky above,
But all the fragments gather as he goes.
Thus if a dream, a passing fancy, glide
And mar thine image for a moment, Love,
Within my heart, it glides and passes by ;
But thou art, Love, mine own abiding sky,
More undisturbed nor faithfuller than I.

REFLECTIVE, PHILOSOPHICAL, AND ALLEGORY.

REFLECTIVE, PHILOSOPHICAL, AND ALLEGORY.

DE PROFUNDIS.

I.--NAY.

How may we trust Thee, Majesty Supreme !
We whose dim life fleets by, an idle dream,
Amid the ruining welter, and the wash
Of shattered Faiths, and holiest Hopes that flash
To annihilation in a moment, or slow wane,
Till what lay desert desert lies again,
Fooled for an hour with visions of ripe grain,
Withered ere harvest ! Oh, the weary round
Of life and death halting within a bound
Of adamant, and fluctuating, ever
Goaded to dissonant, impotent endeavour !
Warring, we swarm to scale a phantom height,
We whose feet fail in some drear infinite !
Piteous human bones upon the waste
Jeer, as we wander, our infatuate haste.

Where now the goal and beacon of strong youth?
Where those far havens of Eternal Truth?
Fabled Atlantis islands of the blest,
In shadowy sunset kingdoms of the West,
If we may reach you, we may find you naught,
Mere human visions, hollow and glamour-fraught!
Where now the morning-land of Love we saw?
Vanished, a pure white snow-wreath in a thaw!
Where youth's high hope to order the wild world?
A once-bright banner, mouldering and furled!
The stern resolve to mould a world within?
Dead in deep jungles of inveterate sin!

Or may the race prove conqueror, tho' we fall?
Through long-vexed infancy the tribes grow tall,
Then slow declining, falter to the grave;
Nor wiser, happier, they who bloom and wave
In their rank ruin: whatsoe'er the gain,
Some earlier glory of the flower will wane!
No sweet sound food, the fruit of wrong and pain.
Ah! dear young children, cankered in the bud,
Surely the harvest battening on your blood
Must be transcendent, ere we may embrace
Meekly the holocaust of all your grace!
Nay! for no triumph splendid as the sun
Were an atonement for the loss of one.
Poor hearts expiring rend with wail sublime
God's vast world-palace, founded upon crime,

Whose ponderous, hell-poised blocks for their cement
Have meek red blood of all the innocent !
Nay, some faint protest of a humblest heart
Should shame and shatter such infernal art !
If He be lord who builds it, we will not
Worship, in how fierce fires soe'er our lot
He appoint for our rebellion ! but I deem
'Tis only fever that so makes it seem !

    Interminable armies ever wend
O'er maimed and martyred comrades to their end
Of blind, unused extinction, tho' the hope
Of infinite Love and Justice while they grope
Be kindled in their bosoms for a lure,
Fooling their hearts the torture to endure
Of false life longer, ere immersed in night
They feed some monstrous Blossom on the height
Of this infernal column of a world :
For it their souls one refuse-heap were hurled,
Bleeding and writhing, to annihilation,
For some sleek mortal god to inhale oblation
Of waste breaths, wrung from sentient agony,
A vampire draining life of these who die !
So that fierce carnage, cast in foemen's bronze,*
Mounts serpentine to swell Napoleon's
Inhuman triumph, whose proud solitude
Stands pillared, purpled with the people's blood !

    * The Vendome column in Paris.

The hecatomb of myriad-fold dumb lives
Invokes a clinging curse on Him who thrives
From their long torture; inarticulate calls
Man's beast progenitor ! lo ! from hopeless falls
Under the precipice of grand endeavour,
Beautiful youths and maidens, mute for ever,
Piteously silent, utter loud reproof
On Him who holds Himself unseen, aloof,
And makes Him sport, engendering their vain
Faith, effort, prayer, the longer to sustain
This miserable mockery of life
Wherewith He endows them, grim and cold, and
    rife
With cruel humour, with insane, fierce relish
For wine of anguish wrung from tortures hellish
Of souls and bodies ! lo ! we all pass by,
Saluting Cæsar, men who are to die!
    Or is it but inevitable, blind
Dull monster Force, that doth terrific grind
Forth idle aspiration, and fond fears,
Illusive bliss, and terror, and wild tears
From one dim, boundless chaos of a womb,
Till, white with horror of the waking doom,
All cower for refuge in their natal tomb?

Hath God, like mortals, a divided will,
Drunkenly reeling from weak good to ill?
Yea, there be throned gods, fallen dignities !

But high beyond we lift our longing eyes !
Ye may not fold your thoughts at such a goal,
Impelled to seek the spiritual Pole,
Ideal lodestar of the pilgrim soul !

What meaneth, then, this horrible array?
Abortions seizing hard breath for a day
When they have mangled, mad with famine-rages,
Foul mates through dark interminable ages,
Loathsome with low lust, anguish, desolation !
Until awakes Man's mournful generation
From the colossal ruin of lost life ;
And lo ! his infinite, opening eyes are rife
With hunger for eternal days, and good,
Piteously craved as necessary food !
Reveal from whence the holy hunger comes !
For all the mute onlookers turn their thumbs
Doomward around the immense arena spaces,
As Man, the victim, peers in their dread faces,
Implacable, though all the beauty-flower
Of the young gladiator plead with power !
Say, whence this thirst for truth and righteousness,
If there be no eternal Spring to bless,
No Arm to quell the tyrant, or redress
Mad earth's injustice?   Myriad-fold we grovel,
A human swine on palace floor, and hovel,
Bound by a Circe, albeit half aware
We are fallen gods in some sublime despair !

19

O monstrous Nature ! human-headed Beast,
Thou cannibal at some unnatural feast
On thine own offspring ! who hast whelped the fiend,
And man, whose offal-feeding frenzy gleaned
The hell-field of foul horrors, left unreaped
By devils ; his black coward heart full-steeped
In outrage, lies, and murderous lust for pain,
Whom all the unbounded tortures bigots feign
May purge not from the abominable stain !

O monstrous world, where innocent children jostle
Fiends from the pit ! where snakes constrict the
    throstle,
Singing of Paradise ! infuse the fire,
And gloat upon her pangs till she expire,
Her music foundering in confusion dire !

Surely there be twin fountains of the world,
And Love brought forth what Hate to ruin hurled !
Love looses lucid waters, and they sing ;
But ever one squats to pollute the spring !
Ah, Lord ! who willest well ! Thy lame hands falter,
While Death and Sin defile Thy Bride before the
    altar !
Poor Love ! and couldst not Thou preserve Thy
    daughter
From infamy and ravishment and slaughter ?
I know not ! only know that we are blind. . . .
Thou wilt divide this kingdom of the mind,

Thou threatenest if I dare behold Thy face,
Nor cower obsequious in my native place?
I see Thy doom-engraving fiery finger!
I hear Thy loud anathema—and linger!
Tho' jealous, Thou arraignest for high treason
Our Babylonian banquets of the reason.

We, scowling outcasts, branded sons of Cain,
Hear with a vast, ineffable disdain
Sleek minions of prosperity prate peace!
While wrung upon the rack we claim release,
Or with gnawn entrails clench firm teeth, nor cry;
Let one call to us from the abyss of agony!
Speak Jesus!—lo! we listen ere we die.

II.—YEA.

And what if all the death, and all the dolor
Do but imbue with life of lustrous colour
Alien natures? if the blood we bled
Grow substance of another heart full-fed?
Thrice aureoled the sacrificial Lamb,
Rolled in a fair victorious oriflamme
Of His own slaughter! fiery pangs of glory,
Wherein a life dissolves to blend one story
With God's world-triumph, so alone fulfilling
True personal being, through the ordeal killing

Mere individual semblance of an hour;
While in the end all martyrs find a power
To joy in each redeeming martyrdom,
When Love's own royal reign hath wholly come.

Thrice happy he who keeps the mournful tryst
By some wan wave of weeping with the Christ,
Wearing all sombre emblems of the Passion,
In deep dim valleys of humiliation,
Whose weeds glow with Divine Humanity,
Discovering what we are, were, and shall be!
For he is driven from all earthly shows
To find the Spirit's own divine repose;
The Spirit, whom no æons brought to birth,
Nor ever-rolling ages doom to dearth!
He lightly fondles every lovely thing,
As well aware he may not closely cling,
For joy alit here hath a wandering wing,
Fair evanescent gleaming of the true,
Abiding ever tranquil out of view.
Yea, these shall feel Love's own rare vintage prest
From sin, and sorrow, and the world's unrest;
Calvary's midnight, with the cross of shame,
The very heart of Love's immortal flame!
While agony weighs common mortals down,
Our heroes lift, and wear it for a crown:
A bow that none save hallowed hearts may bend,
A sword that will the weakling wielder rend,

Spell for a mighty Mage to conjure with,
Confounding fools who are not of their kith !
But woe for him who is contented here !
Tho' lordly gold adorn his lonely bier,
Dead, self-involved, and stark, a thing of fear !

One justifies the sweet nest-building birds,
And blind prevision of the honied herds :
Shall Nature only disappoint, and flout
Her fairest Son, who floundering in doubt,
Yet lifts child-eyes in dim pathetic trust,
With, " Mother, wilt thou leave me in the dust ? "
Ye, scarred with moral ulcers from the womb,
Who can but fester for a moral tomb,
Whom penal strokes, and groping cures immerse
More deeply in the virus of your curse !
Mine own dear children, of hope unfulfilled !
Ye myriad maimed souls, who seem but spilled
Vainly in void abysses ! you, ye germs,
Who perish in dark cherishing earth ! poor worms
A careless delver wounds ; all lowly creatures
Or man or nature rends ! your very features
We may discern not : only through a veil
We feel some form : and our wan cheeks are pale,
Deeming the selves inviolable may fail,
With their own shows of being ! On a moment
Of your eternal lives we pass vain comment,
Judging by sense, in place of Love's deep reason

Whence our wild insult and reproach ; high treason
Against that Mother-heart of all the world,
Who hath all souls beneath her warm wings curled
Invulnerable ! however they may tremble,
And though her love one bitter hour dissemble
For their maturing ; with a pitying smile
She views our wilful wandering awhile.
All are in all they were, and yet shall be,
Dawning to conscious self-identity.
For all is spirit, and the world is wrought
In one live loom of myriad-minded thought.
But what if all sink in the abyss of wrong,
And so by dark experience grow strong ?
Embryo souls, who tortuously mount,
Like fallen water, to their natal fount !
Fair glories of a future flower feed
On degradation of her buried seed.
Tho' spheral music in dull hearts may sleep,
Sound but their own note, they will laugh and leap,
Even as dumb chords, or flames quiver and sing,
If their peculiar tone be vibrating.
The sun-god lies not dead within the shroud,
Tho' shorn of beams he dwindle in a cloud.

Yea, all the vaster souls in whom we fell
By right divine will rouse them from their hell,
To claim the royal heritage of sons.
And whatsoever beast, or elfin runs

Through alien regions of the realms of being,
Where every pilgrim haply halts in fleeing
From God to God, accomplishing the round
Allotted, when he hath won the vantage-ground
And heights of destiny, unrolled sublime
Beneath he will behold the vales of time,
And every station where he made sad pause,
'Mid ranks unseen, breathing unheard applause,
Who helped, with touch impalpable of soul
On soul, the spirit journeying to her goal :
Nor in sad sooth unhindered by the host
Of royal rebels, whom we count for lost,
Yet who, like men, are only gold and clay ;
Nor by some loathly haunters of the grey
Breath from low-lying pestilential mud,
Earth's hideous lusts leave in their filthy flood.

But some are so enamoured of dark Death,
They only long to be relieved of breath.
Yet, saving folk whom the fell Fury's goad,
Or stern Despair drives from our hard abode,
Who but a coward self-involved may crave
Unending sluggard sleep in the dull grave?
His own poor comfort so repleteth him,
One drop of earth's pale vintage can so brim
A human want we counted infinite,
Or one defeat so daunt the whim to fight,
That how God's armies fare concerns him not,
If he may lie at ease, and idly rot !

Shall one, whose mind co-operates to found
The vision of a world with ne'er a bound,
Merge into some mere image, or a feeling
From forth an alien spirit swiftly stealing?
Material appearance can be naught,
Save in a human, or a foreign thought.
All this imperial fabric of the sense
Is but our own dull rendering of intense
Supernal realms of righteousness and love,
Fair shadow of a fairer realm above.

The spirit grows the form for self-expression,
And for a hall where she may hold high session
With sister souls, who, allied with her, create
Her fair companion, her espousèd mate.
Ever the hidden Person will remould
For all our lives fresh organs manifold,
Gross for the earthly, for the heavenly fine,
Ethereal woof, wherein their graces shine.
And there be secret avenues, with doors
Yielding access to inmost chamber floors
Of the soul's privacy; all varying frames,
Responsive to the several spirit-flames.
The vital form our lost now animate
Is one with what in their low mortal state
They made their own; the corse mere ashes, waste,
For all grand uses of the world replaced.
A larva needs no more the unliving husk,
When soaring winged he rends the dwelling dusk.

A rabble rout of Sense light-headed pours
Into the holy Spirit-temple doors,
Where many a grave and stately minister
His place and function doth on each confer.
These Forms inhabiting the sacred gloom,
Whose name is legion, Present, Past, To Come,
One, Many, Same, or Different, evolve
Sweet concord from confusion ; they resolve
The Babel dissonance to a choral song,
Till in divine societies a throng
Sets with one will toward the inmost shrine,
To feed there upon mystic Bread and Wine.
The Bacchanals are sobered, and grow grave,
In solemn silence treading the dim nave :
On their light hearts bloom-pinioned angels lay
Calm, hushful hands of married night and day.

It is a changing scene within the pile :
New shows arrive, and tarry for a while :
But if one living Spirit-fane could fall,
His ruin were the knell of doom for all.
Their being blended each with every one,
If any failed, the universe were gone.
These conscious forms inhabit every mind ;
All selves in one organic self they bind ;
The bloomy beams, and all the shadowy blooms
Are pure white Light eternal that illumes
A universal conscious Spirit-whole,
Fair modulated in each several soul

To many-functioned organs of one Will,
Whose sovran Being who prevails to kill?
We may expand our being to embrace,
And mirror all therein of every race;
Each is himself by universal grace.
Dying is self-fulfilment; and we cherish
His life, who, wanting ours, would wholly perish.
The Father may not be without the Son;
No love, will, knowledge, were for Him alone.
And change is naught
Save at the bar of a sole personal thought,
Enthroned for judgment, summoning past time
With present, hearing now concordant rhyme,
Now variance among voices vanishing,
That so win semblance of substantial thing.
But how conceive that there may ever be
Change in the nerve of change, our known identity?

If we, poor worms, involved in our own cloud,
Deem the wide world lies darkling in a shroud,
Raving the earth holds no felicity,
One child's clear laughter may rebuke the lie,
A lark's light rapture soaring in the blue,
Or rainbow radiant from a drop of dew!

Nor let a low-born Sense usurp the rule,
Who is but handmaid in a loftier school,
Where Love and Conscience a lore not of earth

Impart to Wisdom, child of heavenly birth.
O Thou unknown, inscrutable Divine !
I deem that I am Thine, and Thou art mine !
And though I may not gaze into Thy face,
I feel that all are clasped in Thine embrace.
The Christ is with us, and IIe points to Thee :
When we have grown into Him we shall see ;
Behold the Father in the perfect Son,
And feel, with Him, Thy holy will be done !

Love may not compass her full harmony,
Wanting the deep dread note of those who die.
And as with master-hand IIe sweeps the grand
    awakening chords,
Our wailing sighs leap winged, live talismanic words,
Dull woes and errors tempered to seraphic swords;
Love's colour-chorus flames with glorious morning-
    red,
IIis alchemy transmuting the poured heart's blood of
    our dead,
And lurid bale from murderous eyes of souls who inly
    bled !

Whose mortal mind may sail around the ocean of
    Thy might,
Billowing away in awful gloom to issues infinite ?
Bind Thee with his poor girdle ?   Surveying all thy
    shore !

His daring sinks confounded, foundering evermore,
In his dazed ear reverberating a tempestuous roar !
. . . Who sounds the abyss of Thine immense design?
 We rest,
Aware that Thou art better than our best.

"THE SEA SHALL GIVE UP HER DEAD."

TIME spake to me : " Behold !
I slay your dearest one !
And with him, dead beneath the churchyard mould,
Your living heart I bury from the sun !"
More scornfully he said :
" When you have anguished long,
I will erase remembrance of your dead :
You shall arise, singing an idle song,
As were you glad again ;
For you were glad of yore !
New circumstance, new care, shall cause to wane
His very image, till your eyes no more
Behold him in the deep
Dark mere of memory ;
Although you peer therein, and wail and weep,
You shall but find a vacant, smiling sky;
Till with faint listless wonder you espy
Wan, withered Love, who falters there to die !
Even from your heart's shrine
Your idol shall be torn ;
As erst your joys, so now your sorrows fine
I scatter with cold scorn !
All ye shall jeer at your own oath

Of infinite fidelity;
Ye shall forswear yourselves, and be to both
Heaven and earth, and your own selves a mockery !
Poor fool ! I will extinguish every ember,
Love, hope, grief, all remaining of you yet !
Yea, though thou vow to God thou wilt remember,
Thou shalt forget !"

   And I replied to Time :
"Thou shalt abolish me,
Ere thou dissolve all sanctities sublime
Of mine own being ; when I perish utterly,
I moan no more in pain, nor lie foredone,
Self-scorned, a hissing to white orbs that roll,
Flawless, annealed, obedient to their sun.
If thou hast plunged in night his precious soul,
How wilt thou hinder me
From taking sanctuary
In that eternal gloom from woe and shame ?
A holiest Altar, if the child who was all free from
   blame
Be lying mute before
The dim grey stone of Silence, cold for evermore !
Ah ! there I shall be free
From pain, from sin, from folly, and from thee !
There he and I shall rest in peace,
Nor know what may be born, nor what may cease,
Nor any God may torture us with false hopes of
   release !"

I spake again to Time:
" Thou liest in thy throat !
All may change, or fall, or climb,
Yet all lives self-retained in change, tho' never so remote,
Yea, the old form I knew
Abideth out of view,
Now first fulfilled in other,
For each is by a brother ;
In some alien guise
The dead are risen ; lo ! to longing eyes,
When Occasion calls aloud
To the Past within the shroud,
When Destiny, the omnipotent, shall wave
Her hand, the Past shall start from his deep grave
And Memory restore
What seemed in wan Oblivion buried evermore,
Sea that moans for human ravage, ever hungering
    for more !
All abideth in a sphere
Aloof from mortal eye and ear ;
Faith discerns in flowing time
Fair reflex of a holier clime,
In ruffled mirrors of dark memory
The still face of Eternity.
Yea, and every tiny sprout
Of bloom or leaf is yonder still,
Though many a wind may waft us doubt,
And they play hide and seek at will
In the spirit's fairy fountain,
From holy halls of night divine so musically mounting !

" Doth not the aged man recover
What seemed long perished of his primal youth ?
Once more he is the child, the blithe boy-lover,
Who lay concealed below life's lavish later growth.
And though the soul bewildered err from life to life,
She shall possess them all in God, afar from mortal
    strife !

" Oft on me in dream
My blessed one will gleam,
All palpable as when at first
He quenched my spirit's longing thirst ;
I fold him close, I feel him kiss,
I feel his hands, his hair ; the bliss
No fuller was of yore,
And asking for no more,
I thank the Lord for this.
Howbeit I clasp him closer than of old,
As if I knew I only may enfold
For a brief moment, dim divining why,
Foreboding him compelled anon to fly.
Troubled I own that somewhat seems amiss,
And nor asleep nor waking may I unravel this !
Often I am aware that he hath died,
And yet I hold him living by my side.
Enough ! he gleams upon my lonely tomb,
Among stern crags, from wan night-clouds, he gloweth
    in my gloom ! "

Nature reveals high lineaments of souls,
Confused from sad suffusion of our eyes,
Veiled with our tears ; in these poor earthly shoals
Of low-lapsed life, she may not wear the guise
She wore when we were innocent and wise.
And while I muse, the cold tremendous Shade,
Who spake the cruel words, appears to fade.
I know Time for a shadow of man's mind
Thrown on the wide world ; human souls are blind ;
And lo ! the Lord is shining from behind !
Ah ! strengthen, purge our eyes ! we would behold
    Thy day !
Then error, wrong, and sorrow shall vanish all away !

BEETHOVEN.*

THE mage of music, deaf to outward sound,
Rehearsing mighty harmonies within,
Waved his light wand; the full aerial tides
Ebbed billowing to rear of him, o'erwhelmed
All listening auditors, engulfed, and swept
Upon the indomitable, imperial surge
To alien realms, and halls of ancient awe,
Which are the presence-chambers of dim Death:
The grand departed haunt this mountain-sound!
Cliffs, and ravines, and torrent-shadowing pines,
A pomp of winds, and waters, and wild cloud
The enchanter raises: then the solemn scene
Evanishing, lo! delicate soft calm
Of vernal airs, young leaflets, and blithe birds,
The cuckoo and the nightingale, with bloom
Of myriad flowers, and rills, and water-falls,
Or sunlit rains that twinkle through the leaves,
And odorous ruffled whirlpools of the rose.
Anon, some wondrous petal of a flower,
An ample velvet petal, slides along

---

* Beethoven grew deaf, and conducting could only *see*, not *hear*, the acclamations of the assembly.

A luminous air of summer, visibly
Mantling a vermeil glory in the blue;
And now thin ice films clearest water; now
Our youngest angel whispers out of heaven,
And all the choir of his companions
Let loose their rapture on swift sudden wings,
Sunshine released unhoped-for from a cloud!
Slant rays of opal through the clerestory;
Dawn over solemn heights of lonely snow,
Aerial dawn, that deepens unto day;
A congregating of white seraph throngs,
Who hold the realms of ether with white plume,
And with a sweet compulsion lift to heaven!
Ye, Harmonies, expand immeasurably
The temple of our soul, and yet are more
Than earth can bear; within the courts above
Ye may expatiate majestical,
Native, at home! poor mortals hide their tears,
With caught breath, nor may follow: mountain stairs,
Platform on platform, ye aspire to God!
His infinite Soul who bore you is immortal,
And ours, in whom reverberates your appeal!
O music-marvel! how your royal river
Mirrors our life; there breathes exhaled from it
Sorrow and joy, and triumph and despair;
Your eagle flight is through the infinite,
No barriers to prison from the immense.
Yours the large language of the heights of Heaven!
Now lonely prows, exploring realms unknown,
Unpiloted, beneath wan alien stars,

Your strain recalleth, keels of lonely thought,
Wandering in some sublime bewilderment,
To pioneer where all the world will go,
Now merry buoyancy, as of a boat,
That dips in billowy foam at morning tide.
Ye are alive with yearnings of young love,
Or sombre with immeasurable woe,
Sombre with all the terror of the world,
Wild with the awe and horror of the world,
Begloomed like seas empurpled under cloud,
Reeling and dark with horror of the wind,
Or pale, long heaving under a veiled moon.

Then, with the fading symphony, the master
Drooped, earthward fallen through mortal weariness,
From heights empyreal; he faced the slaves
Now silent, with stilled instruments, who wrought
A fabric for his high imagination,
A chambered palace-pile of echoing sound,
A shadowy fane within the realms of sense.
Drear Silence seems to him to reign; when lo!
A touch, at which he turns! the audience,
Vast, thronged, innumerous have risen before him!
Unhearing the loud storm of their applause,
He sees the tumult of their ocean joy
Thunderously jubilant, in eloquent eyes,
And flashing gems, waved kerchiefs, and moved feet!
So then the solitary master feels
The heart-clasp of our infinite human world,
And bows rejoicing not to be alone.

Ah! brothers, let us work our work, for love
Of what the God in us prevails to do!
And if, when all is done, the unanswering void
And silence weigh upon our souls, remember
The music of a lonely heart may help
How many lonely hearts unknown to him!
The seeming void and silence are aware
With audience august, invisible,
Who yield thank-offering, encouragement,
And strong co-operation; the dim deep
Is awful with the God in whom we move,
Who moulds to consummation where we fail,
And saith, " Well done !" to every faithful deed,
Who in Himself will full accomplish all.

BYRON'S GRAVE.*

NAY! Byron, nay! not under where we tread,
Dumb weight of stone, lies thine imperial head!
Into no vault lethargic, dark and dank,
The splendid strength of thy swift spirit sank:
No narrow church in precincts cold and grey
Confines the plume, that loved to breast the day:
Thy self-consuming, scathing heart of flame
Was quenched to feed no silent coffin's shame!
A fierce, glad fire in buoyant hearts art thou,
A radiance in auroral spirits now;
A stormy wind, an ever-sounding ocean,
A life, a power, a never-wearying motion!
Or deadly gloom, or terrible despair,
An earthquake mockery of strong Creeds that were
Assured possessions of calm earth and sky,
Where doom-distraught pale souls took sanctuary,
As in strong temples.   The same blocks shall build,
Iconoclast! the edifice you spilled,
More durable, more fair: O scourge of God,
It was Himself who urged thee on thy road;

---

* At Hucknall the sexton said to me, "You are standing just over where the head lies."

And thou, Don Juan, Harold, Manfred, Cain,
Song-crowned within the world's young heart shalt
    reign!
Whene'er we hear embroiled lashed ocean roar,
Or thunder echoing among heights all hoar,
Brother! thy mighty measure heightens theirs,
While Freedom on her rent red banner bears
The deathless names of many a victory won,
Inspired by thy death-shattering clarion!
In Love's immortal firmament are set
Twin stars of Romeo and Juliet,
And their companions young eyes discover
In Cycladean Haidee with her lover.

May all the devastating force be spent?
Or all thy godlike energies lie shent?
Nay! thou art founded in the strength Divine:
The Soul's immense eternity is thine!
Profound Beneficence absorbs thy power,
While Ages tend the long-maturing flower:
Our Sun himself, one tempest of wild flame,
For source of joy, and very life men claim
In mellowing corn, in bird, and bloom of spring,
In leaping lambs, and lovers dallying.
Byron! the whirlwinds rended not in vain;
Aloof behold they nourish and sustain!
In the far end we shall account them gain.

A VISION OF THE DESERT.

METHOUGHT I saw the morning bloom
A solemn wilderness illume,
Desert sand and empty air :
Yet in a moment I was aware
Of One who grew from forth the East,
Mounted upon a vasty Beast.
It swung with silent, equal stride,
With a mighty shadow by the side :
The tawny, tufted hair was frayed ;
The long, protruding snout was laid
Level before it ; looking calm away
From that imperial rising of the Day.
Methought a very awful One
Towered speechless thereupon :
All the figure like a cloud
An ample mantle did enshroud,
Folding heavily dark and white,
Concealing all the face from sight,
Save where through stormlike rifts there came
A terrible gleam of eyes like flame.

Then I beheld how on his arm
A child was lying without alarm.
With innocent rest it lay asleep ;

Awakening soon to laugh and leap;
Yet well I knew, whatever passed,
The arm that held would hold it fast.
Nor ever then it sought to know
Whose tender strength encircled so,
Living incuriously wise
Under the terrible flame of eyes.
In those sweet early morning hours
It played with dewy, wreathing flowers,
Drinking oft from a little flask
Under the mantle: I heard it ask:
Yea, and at other times the cooling cup
Gentle and merciful He tilted up.

But when the sun began to burn,
I saw the child more restless turn,
Seeking to view the silent One:
Then, growing graver thereupon,
It whispered, "Father!" but I never heard
If any lips in answer stirred.
Yet if no answer reached the child,
I know not why he lay and smiled,
Raising his little arms on high
In a solemn rapture quietly!

The shadow moved, and growing less,
A blue blaze ruled the wilderness.
The child, alert with life and fire,
Gazed all around with infinite desire.

Erect he sat, contented now no more
To nestle, and feed upon the homely store :
He searched the lessening distance whence they came;
He peered into the clear cærulean flame ;
His hand would mingle with the shaggy hair
Of that enormous Living Thing which bare,
Whose feet were planted in the powdery ground
With ne'er a pause, with ne'er a sound.
Yon fascinating, wondrous Infinite
His clear young eyes explored with keen delight :
He gazed into the muffled Countenance,
Undazzled with the rifted radiance :
Then, giving names to all that he espied,
He murmured with a bright triumphant pride,
" I hold their secret ; lo ! I am satisfied."
Oh ! it was rare to see the lovely child,
As with a gaze ecstatical he smiled,
Following with eager, splendour-beaming eyes
A bird magnificent, who sailed the skies
On vast expanded plumes of sanguine white,
Enamoured of transcendent azure light,
Higher and higher soaring to the sun ;
Claiming a share in his dominion ;
Elate with ardour, like unwearying youth,
Imperially at home in awful realms of Truth !

But ah ! the sun beat fierce and merciless
Upon the boundless, barren wilderness.
Then soon, responsive to a slakeless thirst,
Behold upon his ravished sight there burst

A vision of a far-off lake most fair,
Where many a palm was dallying with air,
And soft mimosa : how alluringly
Smiled the sweet water in a blinding sky !
Can he not hear a gentle turtle coo
Among light leaves, yea, very wavelets blue
Lapping among green reeds upon the shore,
Calling him to abide for evermore ?
Ah ! how doth he impetuous entreat,
And chide the silent, never-lingering feet !
Yet was it strange—for as the feet advanced,
The lake receded, and the waters danced
An eerie dance with all the belts of trees,
And mingled with them, till the sand with these
On the horizon made a marge that wavered,
And all blew sidelong, thin white flame that
    quavered—
Then one low whispered, "'Tis the Devil's water !"
While in his ear there pealed cruel, unearthly laughter.
On this the child fell ill with fever,
Made many a vain yet wild endeavour
To fling himself from forth the grasp
That held with ne'er-relaxing clasp,
Murmuring, "None holds me fast ;
I am a plaything of the blast."
But the Rider from the girdled store
Ministered to him as before.

    And while the shadow veered by stealth,
A measure of his primal health

The boy resumed : an air that fanned
Blew veritably o'er the sand ;
And little birds before them flew,
Vested in a sober hue,
A paly brown, to suit the home
Where 'tis their destiny to roam.
Yet I am sure that ne'er a bird
Fluting more soft and sweet was heard
Among the lawns of Paradise,
Than these in such a humble guise,
Who, without any rest or haste,
Travel warbling o'er the waste.
Moreover in the sterile soil
Some spots of verdure, while the travellers toil,
Arise ; yea, even the sweet oases,
That vanished with the feigning, undulating graces,
Were fair and real delight, however fleeing,
With law distinct of transitory being ;
Only illusion for deluding eyes,
That yearn for what nor waste nor world supplies,
Some dim ideal of the soul,
That ever loves, and grows toward the illimitable
    whole.

But ever, as they two solitary range,
And as the immeasurable horizons change,
Upon the child more burdensome doth lie
Sense of impenetrable mystery.
First he imagined that he chose to go ;
But now he feels, whether he will **or no**

One carries him : he joyed to be in life
For possibilities of boundless strife,
Wresting resplendent secrets bold from all :
Now the unmasked immensities appal,
Weighing incumbent on the sense and thought,
As on a dwindling grain of dust, as on a thing of
    nought !
A moment looking toward the shrouded Face,
Now is he fain his timid eyes to abase :
" Father, unveil !" he tremulously cries,
Fearing he asks impossibilities.

    Yet hearken ! voices musical
Like dew upon the desert fall,
Rising and falling,
Calling, calling !
Very plaintive, sweet, and low,
As the lonely pilgrims go :
Are they spirits of the wild,
Calling, answering low and mild ?
Is it a voice of one departed,
Plaining gentle, unquiet-hearted,
Vainly hungering to enfold
His beloved as of old ?
Severed from our living kind,
In a feeble, wandering wind
Wandering ever ? none can tell
Whence the mystic murmurs well :
But oft an Arab, roaming far
Over sands of Saharâ,

Hears the sweet mysterious measure
With a solemn-hearted pleasure,
Saying, " No wind among the stones
Breathes the rare unearthly tones ! "
And howsoe'er it be, they tell
The soul of things ineffable,
Of a life beyond our death or birth,
Of a universe beyond the earth !

Monotonously weary seemed the way,
While light declining faded slowly away.
Some haze obscured a gradual westering sun,
And all the oppressive firmament was wan.
In it voluminous appears to form
From the horizon a continent of storm,
A ponderous bulk of gathering indigo,
Tinged in its formidable overflow
With hues of livid purple poison-flowers.
In ghastlier whiteness for the night that lowers,
Strewing forlorn the desolate desert pale,
Some grinning skeletons of men assail
My vision ; while a monstrous bird of prey
From a putrescent corpse rends fierce away
The clinging flesh with horrid sound of tearing,
Its beak abruptly plunging, pulling, baring;
Bald-headed, hideous neck low crouched betwixt
The pressure of strong talons curved, infixed:
Now the proud brain, like fearful Madness, mangling,
Like Sin now with the recking bosom wrangling;

Like ignorance, disease, war, tyranny, starvation,
Eating the vitals of a noble fallen nation!
This creature, as they pass, a moment glaring
Voracious-eyed, with vasty vans that cover—
A little further on obscene doth hover
A grey hyena, and he laughs a peal
Of beastly laughter, scraping up a meal
Loathsome from forth the sand: there is a howl
Dolefully borne from where the lean wolves prowl!
Then silence falls upon the deepening gloom,
And sultry air forebodes the smothering Simoom.
Looking toward the child with deep dismay,
I noted his fair ringlets grown to grey,
And sparse like withered bents upon his head:
His pale, worn countenance was drawn with dread:
Yet in his eyes there burned a grand resolve,
No sights of terror lightly might dissolve.
And now I heard him murmur, " Mighty Father!
I trust thee: yea, to thee I cling the rather,
Albeit I may not see thine awful face!"
Then I was sure he felt the strong embrace
Tighten around him, though a Skeleton
Came stalking from the night to lead them on:
A far-off murmur swelled into a wildering roar;
A hurricane of flame and sand whirled like a con-
    queror!
And when the o'erwhelming terrible death-tempest on
    them broke,
The shrinking child crept nestling close under the
    Father's cloak.

Then darkness swallowed the portentous plain.
When faint it dawned upon mine eyes again,
Lo! there was moonlight in a sky serene:
All lay at peace beneath the melancholy sheen.
No voice was heard, no living thing was seen.
Yet ere I was aware, that awful Apparition
Once more emerged upon my mortal vision—
The shrouded, dim, unutterable Form,
With eyes that flame as through the rifts of storm,
Mounted on that colossal Living Thing,
Bearing the child now, softly slumbering—
While all confused immeasurable shadow fling.
Peacefully lay the boy's pale, silent head:
And, looking long, I knew that he was dead.
Then all my wildered anguish forced a way
Through my wild lips: " Reveal, O Lord, I pray,
Whither thou carriest him!" I cried aloud:
No sound responded from the shadowy shroud;
Only methought that something like a hand
Was raised to point athwart the shadowy land;
And while afar the dwindling twain were borne,
I, gazing all around with eyes forlorn,
Divined the bloom of some unearthly morn!

Where was he carried? to an isle of calm,
Lulled with sweet water and the pensile palm?
Vanishing havens on the pilgrimage
Surely some more abiding home presage!
Or must the Sire attain always alone

The happy land, with never a living son?
O! awful, silent, everlasting One!
If thou must roam those islands of the west,
Ever with some dead child upon thy breast,
Who would have hailed the glory, being blest,
Eternity were one long moan for rest!
For do we not behold thee morn by morn,
Issuing from the East with one newborn,
Carrying him silently, none knoweth whither,
Knowing only all we travel swiftly thither?

THE TEMPLE OF SORROW.*

THE Minster glory lies engulfed in gloom,
With mournful music throbbing deep and low,
And all the jewelled joy within Her eyes
Slumbers suffused ; the saint, the warrior,
On tomb recumbent, kneeling panoplied,
Blend far-away mysterious presences
With a wide-seething multitude, alive
Through all the pillared grandeur of the nave,
A human sea ; the gorgeous full pomp
Of civil, militant, imperial pride,
And sacerdotal splendour, cloth of gold,
Chalice bejewelled, silks imbued with morn,
Flows in blue twilight of a perfumed air,
Flows, flashing into momentary gleam
By altar and shrine, for lustre of the lamps,
Silver and gold suspended, or mild shine
Of tall white wax around a central Night
In the mid-transept ; there the Catafalque,
The Shadow dominates, reigns paramount
O'er all the temple ; 'tis the hollow heart,

* Suggested by the fire in the Ring Theatre at Vienna, after
which to the poor as chief mourners was allotted the post of
honour in St. Stephen.

Dispensing Darkness through the frame supine
Of that colossal Cross, which is the Fane.
The huge vault under yawneth, a deep wound,
Filled full with Horror ; Death abideth there :
Ay, with our lost Ideals, our lost Loves,
Baffled Aim, palsied Faith, Hope atrophied !
All the circumfluent glory-glow of Life
Mere tributary to the awful throne
Of this dread Power; all cast their crowns before It.
Yea, as blithe waters from the abysmal womb
Of caverned Earth dance buoyant into Day,
So here from fountains of primeval Night
In very deed Life seemeth effluent.

And some there be most honoured in the crowd,
From whom illustrious prince, with emperor
And noble stand obeisantly aside.
Who are they ? for they wear no bravery,
Nor badge of high estate within the realm,
Whose garb uncourtly sombre shows and mean.
No confident bearing, claiming deference,
As of right full-conceded, suns itself
Proudly on these ; we judge them of the herd
Of rugged toilers, whom the stroke of Fate
Despoils of floral honours and green leaves,
Fells for rough use, not leaves for leisured grace,
Or putting forth the loveliest that is theirs.
Lowly their port, whose dull and earthward eyes,
Heavy with weeping, droop beneath rude brows,

Whose light is with their heart, quenched in the abyss
That holds their best beloved, torn from them
In fierce embraces of devouring fire ;
Whose souls were so inextricably involved
With these that perished, in the ghastly fall
They too were wrenched low from the living light
Of placid, self-possessed familiar day
Down to a desolate disconsolate wild,
Haunt of grim Madness, hollow Doubt, Despair :
Only the dead, more happy, seem to glide
Lower to nether caverns of cool sleep.
  Grief is their patent of nobility;
Sorrow the charter of their right to honour.
Smitten to earth, behold them cowering,
Mocked, buffeted, spurned, spat upon, effaced
Under the blood-red executioner,
Whom some name Nature, and some God, the Lord.
These do but threaten feebly with a mouth
Or hand, more feeble than a delicate beast,
Lashed for hell-torment by a learned man,
Lashed for hell-torment in the torture-trough ;
The unregarded Sudras of the world,
Bleeding to slow death from an inward wound,
Deep and immedicable evermore.

  To these the proud and prosperous of earth
Pay reverent homage ! it is marvellous !
And yet no marvel ! such fate-stricken men
Are armed, and robed imperially with awe !

Who flame sublime to momentary wrath,
Peal with mad mirth, then grovel impotent;
Who affirm not their own selves, who falter lost,
Like foam blown inland on the whirlwind's wing
From ocean, there dissolving tremulous
Where kindred foam evanished only now,
So they in the lapsed being of their dead.
They are one with these they cherished and adored,
Not separate, individual any more:
Lieges are they of Sorrow, pale crowned Queen
Over man's miserable mad universe.

What might have been fair Body grows to Soul;
From false-appearing palace halls of sense
They are delivered, into mournful worlds
Of Peradventures all unfathomable,
Forebodings infinite, wild hope, surmise,
Faith, love, sweet longing; yea, they are disturbed
From dull content with earth's inanities
By revelation of what hollow hearts,
And loathly shapes they hide; afire with thirst,
Now will they sound the eternal deeps within
For living water, clouded and disused,
Cumbered with ruin; their dull eyes are roused
From low rank plains to interrogate the height
Of perilous attainment or endeavour,
Where snows hold high communion with stars,
Where from aerial eyrie sails the eagle,

Calm in clear air, familiar with Heaven.
They are made free of God's eternal spirit,
Ever abounding, inexhaustible;
Consumed, that they themselves may truly be.

Behold! the Minster cruciform and grand,
Grows human, more than human, as I muse,
The Holy House of Life, the Crucified!
What seems the World, the Body of the Lord!
Expanded arms, and frame pulsate with blood,
Close-thronging individual lives; His Heart,
Death, haloed with pale anguish and desire.
Even so the Sun eclipsed, a sable sphere,
Is ringed around with his corona flame,
Wherein appear weird members of red fire.
But as the Sun behind this ominous orb,
That is the spectral shadow of our moon,
Smiles evermore beneficent, so Love
Veils Him in gloom sepulchral for awhile,
That we who sound the abysses of Despair
May weave pure pearls, Her awful bosom hides,
Into a coronal for our pale brows,
And He Himself, descending to the deep,
Bearing our burden, may win lovelier grace
Of Love's own tears, which are the gems of God.

Ever the plangent ocean of low sound
Fills all with midnight, overwhelms my heart.
Lit tapers faint around the Catafalque,

And fair-wrought lamp in sanctuary and shrine.
The wan expanse seems labouring confused
With what feels like some glutinous chill mist,
Close cobweb-woof; the great Cathedral quakes,
As from sick earthquake throes; the pillars tall
Heave, like huge forest-peers, that agonise
In tides of roaring tempest: will the pile
Vanish anon to assume an alien form?
For all the pillars hurtle aloft to flame
Flamboyant, cloven, pallid, while the roof
Reels riven; yet there is not any sound.
Lo! every Christ on every crucifix
Glares with the swordblade glare of Antichrist!
While on the immense-hewn flanking masonry,
Scrawled, as by finger supernatural,
As in Belshazzar's banquet-hall of old,
Behold the " *Mene! mene!* " but the realm
Divided is the royal realm, the soul!
The guilty soul, ingorged by the dim fiend
Of loathsome, limbless bulk, Insanity!
In dusk recesses how the shadows wax
Palpable, till they palpitate obscene,
Clinging, half-severed; our sick souls are ware
Of some live Leprosy, that heaves and breathes
Audibly in the impenetrable gloom.

Hear ye the moans of muffled agony
By yonder altars of the infernal aisle?
Marmoreal pavements slippery with blood!
While all the ghastly-lit ensanguined space

Quickening teems with foul abnormal births;
Corpse faces scowling, wound about with shrouds,
Sniffing thick orgy fumes of cruelty,
Steal out, or slink behind in the shamed air.
Vast arteries of the dilating pile
Pulsate with ever denser atom-lives
Unhappy; do mine eyes indeed behold
Those holy innocents, whom she of yore,
The Voice in Ramah, wept so bitterly,
Rachel, sweet spirit-mother of their race ?
They are holy innocents of many a clime,
And many a time, some murdered yesterday,
And some still languishing in present pain :
Dumb women, with marred faces eloquent,
Hold their wan hands ; while all around, behold
Among their feet, what seems a harried crowd
Of gentle beings, who are man's meek friends !
They in the reeking shadow yonder fawn
Upon dyed knees of things in human shape,
All hell's heat smouldering in lurid eyes,
And Cain's ensanguined brand upon their brow,
Who on those altars, prostitute to sin,
Offer the innocents to fiends whose names,
Obsequious to the inconstant moods of man,
Vary elusive, and deluding ; now
They are called Moloch, Baal, Ashtaroth,
Hatred, Revenge, War, Lust, Greed, Might-is-Right,
Now Church, the Truth, the Virgin, or the Christ,
But in a later time Expediency,
Weal of Man, Nature, Lust of Curious Lore.

The accurst oblation of fair alien lives,
None of their own, they pour to satiate
The hydra-headed, demon brood obscene.
These are devoured with ever subtler pangs
Cunningly heightened, fuelled, nursed, prolonged
By cold, harsh hearts, one adamant to woe,
Or cruel, infamous appetite for pain.
Ay, and of horrors loathlier than these
The verse dares name not, thrust on beautiful
Maidens and babes defenceless, of such feasts
The God-deserted souls are gluttonous.

White victims, immolated for the world !
Ye tyrants, ye alone are miserable !
For whom Hate hath left loving, though a beast,
Is nearer God than you, removed from Him
By all the hierarchies of all worlds !
But these have fallen to abysms of pain,
And you to sloughs of inmost infamy,
That all the spheres may learn for evermore
The treachery of sweet ways that are not Love.
Yet if some God be lingering in you,
Your own eternal selves consenting not,
(Which are by lapse, and by recovery)
Touching the lowest deep ye shall recoil !
When in the furnace heated sevenfold
More than the wont, fierce furnace of God's wrath,
Blasted, ye shrivel, your inhuman pride
Stern, stubborn metal swooning to weak air
In the white heat of Love's intolerable,

Ah ! then will not the innocence ye wronged,
Leaving her own bliss for you, fly from heaven
To heal you by forgiveness ?　May it be !

Yea, there are fleeting gleams from the All-fair,
Playing of children, larks, and lovers gay,
Beautiful image, grand heroic deed,
Cheery content ; but ah ! the grim World-woe
Absorbs all vision, overwhelms the heart !
A few, with seraph pity in clear eyes,
And flashing swords retributive unsheathed,
Sore-pressed and wounded, wrestle with the foe,
Defeated, slain, delivering ; while aloft
We seize anon some glimpses of august,
Benignant countenances, with white wings,
As of Heaven's host invisible drawn up
For battle ; but I know not who prevail.
A few pale stars in chasms of wild storm !
Aliens, alas ! no potentates of ours.
We are in the power of Darkness and Dismay,
Anguishing God-forsaken on the cross !
Yea, sons of Belial with jaunty jeer
Ask where thou hidest, Lord ! the Avenger ! God !
Devils a priestly scare to them, who know not
Devils allure them blind into the pit.
Could they but hear low ghastly mirth convulse
Shadowy flanks of these live Plagues in air !
Mine eyeballs seared with horror, and my heart
One writhing flame, I prayed that I might die,

And lay me down to sleep with *him* for ever !
A sevenfold darkness weighs upon my soul :
I hear no groans, no music ; all is still,
Even as the grave : one whispers of the Dawn :
Once I surmised the morning grey, not now :
Nor in the chancel, whose wide wakeful orb,
Solemnly waiting, ever fronts the East,
Nor in the cold clerestories of the nave.
One whispers of the lark ; I hear no bird.
And yet I know the seraph eyes of Dawn
Find in her last, lone hollow the veiled Night.

Hearken ! a long, low toll appals the gloom !
Like a slow welling blood from a death-wound
In the world's heart, that never will be stanched,
Crimsoning the void with waste expense of pain !
Another, and another, vibrating !
A phantom bell tolls in the abysmal dark
The funeral of all living things that be.
I, turning toward the Catafalque, desire,
Plunging within the gulf, to be no more. . . .

When, lo ! some touch as of a healing hand.
For while I knew the mourners only saw
Flowers on fair corses and closed coffin-lid,
I grew aware of souls regenerate
Afar, sweet spirits raimented in white,
Who leaned above the Terror with calm eyes ;

And for a moment their purged vision cleared
Earth-humours from mine own, till I beheld
No deadly Dark—a lake of living Light,
A mystic sphere, the Apocalyptic main !
Heaving with happiness that breathes, a home
For all dear spirits of the faded flowers
Outrageous men have pulled and thrown away ;
Clouds in blue air reflected in a mere,
Or roseflush in rose-opal, a shy dawn
In lakes at morning, so the souls appeared.

My little children, do I find you here?
All here !   Among you smiles our very own.
Each little one hath, nestled in his bosom,
A delicate bird, or elfin animal.
White-clustered lilies, beautiful as morn,
In wayward luxury of love's own light
Eddying, abandoned to love-liberty !
Joy-pulses of young hearts unsulliable
Weave warbling music, a low lullaby.
I fancy they have syllabled a song :

We are fain, are fain
Of mortal pain,
We are fain of heavenly sorrow;
As a gentle rain
She will sustain,
Wait only till to-morrow !

Among death-pearls
Of dewy curls,
O little ones in anguish !
The Lord hath kissed,
I would you wist
For all the world ye languish !

The loveless world
Lies love-impearled
From innocency weeping ;
Wan wings be furled,
And you lie curled
In Love's warm haven sleeping.

For when ye know
What glories flow
For all from childly sorrow,
A flower will blow
From your wan woe
Within the wounded furrow.

We are fain, are fain
Of mortal pain,
We are fain of heavenly sorrow ;
As a gentle rain
She will sustain,
Wait only till to-morrow !

So pure, pellucid fays enjoy the calm
Of summer seas, and woven waterlights
In faëry cavern, where the emerald heart
Lies heaving, or blue sheen on a warm wave.
And ye are fair-surrounded with lost Love,
Celestial Vision, vanished Hope, Desire,
Lovelier recovered, gloriously fulfilled
With a Divine fulfilment, more than ours.

There, in the midst, the likeness of a Lamb,
That had been slain, whose passion heals our hurt,
Wearing a thorn crown, breathing into bloom !
Lo ! if ye listen intently by the light,
Ye hear a winnowing of angel wings,
Nearing, or waning : while from far away,
I'the Heart of all, what revelation falls ? . . .
A sound, oh marvel ! like a sound of tears !

Pain ever deepens with the deepening life,
Though fair Love modulate the whole to joy.
A myriad darkling points of dolorous gloom
Startle to live light ; subtle infinite veins
Of world-wide Anguish glow, a noonlit leaf.

All vanish : there is dawn within the fane ;
Born slowly from the wan reluctant gloom
Conquering emerges a grand Cross of Gold,
And all the nations range around serene.

ELEGIAC.

ELEGIAC.

LAMENT.

I AM lying in the tomb, love,
Lying in the tomb,
Tho' I move within the gloom, love,
Breathe within the gloom!
Men deem life not fled, dear,
Deem my life not fled,
Tho' I with thee am dead, dear,
I with thee am dead,
O my little child!

What is the grey world, darling,
What is the grey world,
Where the worm lies curled, darling,
The deathworm lies curled?
They tell me of the spring, dear!
Do I want the spring?

22

Will she waft upon her wing, dear,
The joy-pulse of her wing,
Thy songs, thy blossoming,
O my little child!

For the hallowing of thy smile, love,
The rainbow of thy smile,
Gleaming for a while, love,
Gleaming to beguile,
Replunged me in the cold, dear,
Leaves me in the cold,
And I feel so very old, dear,
Very, very old!

Would they put me out of pain, dear,
Out of all my pain,
Since I may not live again, dear,
Never live again!

I am lying in the grave, love,
In thy little grave,
Yet I hear the wind rave, love,
And the wild wave!
I would lie asleep, darling,
With thee lie asleep,
Unhearing the world weep, darling,
Little children weep!
O my little child!

DARK SPRING.

Now the mavis and the merle
Lavish their full hearts in song;
Peach and almond boughs unfurl
White and purple bloom along
A blue burning air,
All is very fair :
But ah! the silence and the sorrow !
I may not borrow
Any anodyne for grief
From the joy of flower or leaf,
No healing to allay my pain
From the cool of air or rain;
Every sweet sound grew still,
Every fair colour pale,
When his life began to wane!
They may never live again !
A child's voice and visage will
Evermore about me fail ;
And my weary feet will go
Labouring as in deep snow:
Though the year with glowing wine
Fill the living veins of vine,

While a faint moon hangs between
Broidery of a leafy screen;
Though the glossy fig may swell,
And Night hear her Philomel,
While sweet lemon blossom breathes,
And fair Sun his falchion wreathes
With rich depending golden fruit,
Or crimson roses at his foot,
All is desolate and mute!
Dark to-day, and dark to-morrow!
Ah! the silence and the sorrow!

DEAD.

I.

WHERE the child's joy-carol
Rang sweeter than the spheres,
There, centre of deep silence,
Darkness, and tears,
On his bed
The child lay dead.

II.

There a man sat stolid,
Stupefied and cold,
Save when the lamp's flicker
To poor love told
Some mocking lie
Of quivering eye,
Or lip that said,
" *He is not dead.*"

III.

Weary Night went weeping,
Moaning long and low,
Till dim Dawn, awaking,

Found them so—
The heart that bled,
And his dim dead.

IV.

"*Measure him for his coffin*,"
He heard a stranger say;
And then he broke to laughing,
"*God! measure my poor clay,*
And shut me in my coffin,
A soul gone grey!
For hope lies dead,
Life is fled."

EARLY PRIMROSE.

THERE was a paly primrose,
Budding very early
In the little garden,
When he lay so ill.
"Do you think I may be
Well enough to go there
When the flower opens,
Papa?" he asked of me.
But only a day after
Our little Sunshine left us,
And the primrose opened
The very day he died.
I wonder if he saw it,
Saw the flower open,
Went to pay the visit
Yonder after all!
I know we laid the flower
On a stilly bosom
Of an ivory image;
But I want to know
If indeed he wandered
In the little garden,
Or noted on the bosom
Of his fading form
The paly primrose open;
How I want to know!

THE TOY CROSS.

My little boy at Christmas-tide
  Made me a toy cross ;
Two sticks he did, in boyish pride,
  With brazen nail emboss.

Ah me ! how soon, on either side
  His dying bed's true cross,
She and I were crucified,
  Bemoaning our life-loss !

But He, whose arms in death spread wide
  Upon the holy tree,
Were clasped about him when he died—
  Clasped for eternity !

"THAT THEY ALL MAY BE ONE."

WHENE'ER there comes a little child,
My darling comes with him ;
Whene'er I hear a birdie wild
Who sings his merry whim,
Mine sings with him :
If a low strain of music sails
Among melodious hills and dales,
When a white lamb or kitten leaps,
Or star, or vernal flower peeps,
When rainbow dews are pulsing joy,
Or sunny waves, or leaflets toy,
Then he who sleeps
Softly wakes within my heart ;
With a kiss from him I start ;
He lays his head upon my breast,
Tho' I may not see my guest,
Dear bosom-guest !
In all that's pure and fair and good,
I feel the spring-time of thy blood,
Hear thy whispered accents flow
To lighten woe,
Feel them blend,
Although I fail to comprehend.

And if one woundeth with harsh word,
Or deed, a child, or beast, or bird,
It seems to strike weak Innocence
Through him, who hath for his defence
Thunder of the All-loving Sire,
And mine, to whom He gave the fire.

IN LONDON.

THE mighty towers of Westminster
Loom beneath me in murk air,
While a vast expanse of street
Echoes to loud-hurrying feet
Of men and horses, and swift wheels,
Where a clanging steeple peals,
Where he, who with deep feeling cons
The souls of animals, in bronze
Wrought majestic lion forms,
Brooding, slumbering, dark storms,
Symbols of our England's power,
Whose dread lightnings brood and glower,
Like those fulvous eyes ; their claws
Are death, hid sheathed in vasty paws.
On the lion a child gazes ;
Grave brown wondering eyes he raises
To the form : compelled to leave,
With all my sight to him I cleave
In departing ; often since
As from a sickening stroke I wince,
Journeying by the very place
Where I beheld his little face

Pondering on the mighty beast,
More than all to me, though least,
Seeing now through tear-suffusion
Without him all the loud confusion !

Once again the living creatures,
With their weary sullen features,
I behold behind the bars,
Where the den's dull limit mars
All wild splendour of their pride,
Abates the grandeur of their stride
Bondage tames the fervid eyes,
As night doth the torrid skies,
To a lurid sultriness,
Clouded o'er with vague distress ;
Emblems of our human race,
Fallen from their lofty place,
Blind, bewildered, bound within
By the manacles of sin !

With a glad and grave surprise
The terror of their gleaming eyes
He considers, mirthful mime
Of them in a little time.
Again I view the elephant,
Slow-pacing in his wonted haunt,
On whose tall, broad, howdah'd back
The child and I along the track
Three years ago swung, full of glee—
Now the child is not with me !

When our wild praying seemed to stir
God's awful executioner,
Whose blank, set countenance faint quavered,
Whose dull resolve a moment wavered,
And when sweet life appeared to quell
Death's white horror, it befell
That when he would descend the stair,
Patient he paused for one to bear
Him feeble, and I filled the want;
So he named me his elephant.

Passing through the gay arcade,
Where toys for children are displayed,
Anon I pause before a toy,
Dreaming how a little boy
Will lighten mirth from his dear face
If I buy it—for a space
Unremembering my home
Without him is but blind and dumb!
His sacred toys lie idle now;
O'er them the pale anguished brow
Of Love's forlorn despair we bend,
Hoping life's dull pain may end;
Till anon some organ sounds
In the street, but no glad bounds
Of a child's light feet we note
Run to hear the music float,
Climb upon a chair to see
Dancing dolls' bedizened glee,
Or the monkey's mimicry.

What shall I do? . . . Full many others,
Little ones who seem his brothers,
Take delight in things like these !
Do they ail, or doth the breeze
Of pleasure ripple o'er their faces,
I will contemplate their graces ;
I will be a minister
The fountain of their joy to stir,
In such resorts, and by such measures,
As were wont to yield him pleasures ;
Or where little hearts may ail,
Love's yoke-fellow, I will not fail,
Where are tears and visage pale,
To quell the tyranny of Fate,
Or man, that renders desolate :
And I deem he will approve
In the bowers of holy Love,
Near and nearer to me move.

LEAD ME WHERE THE LILY BLOWS.

FRIEND, you tell me of a valley
  Where the pure white lily blows,
In a shadowy woodland alley ;
  Lead me to their summer snows !

      Oh, lead me where the lily blows !
      I would wear it in my life,
      Weary of world-soil and strife,
      Lead me where the lily blows.

Angels planted in my garden,
  A vain pleasance of ill weeds,
One white Lily, and the Warden
  With sweet air from heaven feeds.
Ah ! one night my lily died,
  And I mourned him night and day ;
" For the bosom of My Bride,"
  The Lord saith, " he was borne away."
Then I wandered through the world
  To find the flower-de-luce I lost,
And my wings will ne'er be furled,
  Summer-poised, or tempest-tost,

Till my lily of the valley
   Somewhen, somewhere, my spirit find,
In a sweet celestial alley,
   Far from our lost humankind ;
Ah, my lily of the valley !

      Lead me where the lily blows,
         I would wear it in my life,
         Weary of world-soil and strife,
      Oh, lead me where the lily blows !

I wander till I find my flower
   Breathing a divine perfume ;
IIis white petals are a power
   My lone spirit to illume :
And I will follow where the Lord
   Wills my weary feet should go,
While ever in my soul I hoard
   The glimpse allowed to me below
Of what belonged to Paradise
   Allowed awhile on earth to beam,
Until my weary, wandering eyes,
   With patient use, more native seem
To shadowy regions of dim death ;
   Till I faint behold my blossom,
No more in the outer Court have breath,
   Earth's outer Court of life and death,
      As erst, but in my very Bosom !

NOCTURNE.

THE shadowy portals of dim death
Unfold alluringly,
And all my soul importuneth
Unfathomed worlds for thee!
O ye illimitable realms
Of awful amplitude,
From your immensity that whelms
I crave one only good!
From unimaginable wealth
My soul demands but this,
Nor fame, nor power, nor gold, nor health,
A little child's warm kiss!
If I may feel him when I part,
And if he greets me then,
Unsorrowing will my weary heart
Forsake the haunts of men.
Ah me! engulfed in the wild storm,
That drifts the lost like leaves,
Mine arms may never clasp thy form,
Where a still water heaves,
Where God's own sunlight cleaves to thee,
My holy little child!

Yet through a storm-rent might I see
Thy joy, my undefiled,
I deem that I could bear my fate,
However dark and drear;
But I behold no Heaven's gate
From our confusion here!
I think the love between us twain
May raise me for awhile;
Yet if the shadow of my pain
Would only cloud thy smile,
Ah! move not near me, till my doom
Of whirlwind, ice, and fire
Be all accomplished in the gloom,
And I be lifted higher!
Our Love shall save, whate'er delays,
And thou be fain of all thy dole!
Dear Love hath many secret ways,
Whereby She steals from soul to soul;
Are any hells beyond the rays
Of Her all-healing miracle?
If the Abysses could devour
Thy love and mine, then all were lost:
But where Love breathes, a fadeless flower
May bloom from Death's inveterate frost!
And though the fiends would whelm me low
With mine own sins for ponderous stones,
Child-angels all around me flow;
I loved them; they have heard my moans!

.

MAGIC-LANTERN.

I WAS within a darkened chamber,
    Full of children small ;
Upon my knees I felt him clamber,
    One of the least of all,
    Answering my call.

He was a baby of the people,
    Nor aught of him I knew ;
Only the shadow of one steeple
    Abode upon us two ;
    His arms around me grew.

Quaint figure, battle, bark, snow-mountain,
    The lantern-wizardry,
Arouse joy's hidden silver fountain
    To pretty wondering glee,
    Plashing full merrily.

Albeit nor now, before, nor after,
    Mine eyes beheld the boy,
When he so pealed with innocent laughter,
    Methought my own, my joy,
    Awhile with me did toy.

Athwart the drear unwarmed abysses
Of all the later years,
He leaned awhile from angel blisses,
To calm my foolish fears,
To kiss away my tears.

LOST LAMB.

HE is gone, he is gone,
The beautiful child!
He is gone, he is gone,
And the mother went wild.
Babble all silent,
Warm heart is cold;
All that remains now
The hair's living gold!
Summer hath faded
Out of his eyes,
On his mouth ne'er a ripple
Of melodies!
O where will be joy now,
To-morrow, to-day?
O where is our boy now?
Far, far away!
Light is but darkness,
Unshining from him;
Sound is but silence,
And all the world dim!
Spring's in the air!
I feel him to-day,

Spring's in the air,
He's on his way !
Warmth in the air,
Cold in my heart,
Winter is there,
Never to part!
Snowdrop asleep in the
Loosening mould,
Crocus apeep with thy
Flame-tip of gold,
Lark song who leapest
Aloft, young and bold,
My heart groweth old, for
Joy lieth cold!

TO ERIC FROM THE ALPS.

THE fragrant pines are green, love,
  The pines are fair and tall ;
Dear is the Alpine scene, love,
  Peak, flower, and waterfall ;
But my heart's tendrils lean, love,
  To humbler pines at home,
For there the feet have been, love,
  That never learned to roam.
One day about the wood, dear,
  Thy steps began to go,
And all my stony mood, dear,
  Was moved to happy flow ;
But when they ceased from pleasure
  Upon the woodland floor,
Silence in deeper measure
  Than e'er was known before
Returned for evermore, dear,
  For evermore.

TO MY MOTHER.

I AM weeping, mother, in your empty chamber;
Beyond the pane, a fair familiar scene;
As a far dream only may the man remember
All the mirth of childhood that hath been—
Hath been here about thy young joy, O my mother,
All the mirth and laughter of a child !
Was it I, indeed, and not another,
Whom you folded in your dear arms undefiled ?
Our nursery with snowy-folded curtain !
Here you came to bless the dreaming boy;
All is melted to a memory uncertain,
Evening prayer, the game, and many a toy.
Clad in tender vivid verdure, early summer
Kindles leaf and bloom about the land,
While the nightingale, our passionate early comer,
Overflows in song for one at hand.
Winds the river in the valley by the meadow,
By the old grey bridge, anear the water-mill;
Old elms are on the green lawn with their shadow,
A bloom involves the orchard on the hill.
You were wont to give me orange-petal candied,
From the china bird, laid yonder near the clock. . . . .
Ah ! visionary seasons, are ye banded
To weave illusion round me and to mock ?

In the chestnut grove our nest, where in the leaf-time
We children took our strawberries and tea,
Hath fallen; dove, and cuckoo here renew their brief
    time,
Pale primrose, and the windflower, wood-anemone.
While I recall delightful days of childhood
In the home of our forefathers, when from school
I came to wander with you in the wild wood,
And my happiness ran over, very full.
How I lingered on the hard road in the damp night,
When you left me at my school, until aloof
I beheld no more your lessening line of lamplight,
Nor heard the minished trample of the hoof!
Among German forest-firs you tell the story,
As we go, her hand who died, and mine in yours.
Ah! the bonfire on the hillside, and the glory
Of our rural meal among the bilberry bowers!
Then a cottage o'er a torrent-haunted valley
In the summer-sounding vines was our abode,
Where Morn and Eve upon the mount continually
Wrought a robe of glory, as for God.*
Yearly, later, on an evening of the winter weather,
With our youngest born who died we came to you :
On arrival, what a welcome, at the meal we ate
    together,
You gave to weans, and wife, and me, so tender and
    so true ! . . . .
All our converse in my manhood ! by the healthful
    ocean-margin,

---

* Above the Rhone Valley ; in sight of the Dent du Midi.

Or where we loved to hail the holy morning-glow,
Beyond blue water, on the mountain men have named
    the Virgin,*
On the glory of her heavenward height of pure and
    solemn snow.
In the isle where cloudy, melancholy Blaaven,
Of noble mould, empurpled, rules the heaving sea,
You, enfeebled, I supported from the haven,
To where Coruisk glooms crag-immured in lone
    sublimity. . . .
And the churchyard lieth beautiful to-day, love,
As in yonder dearer, earlier time,
When we wandered hand in hand with you in May, love,
We children, you in all your lovely prime !
Every green grave is a garden gently tended,
And birds sing in the orchard near the dead,
Meet repose for one whose day serenely ended,
Very weary, when the saintly spirit fled !
Joy was yours, and yet your life knew much of anguish,
Disenchantment, weariness, and pain;
In the later years of weakness, when I saw you
    languish,
I felt our aching void would be your gain.
Love unfailing, kindly counsel, all the pleasure
In your mere delightful presence, and your smile !
It is a loss that none may map or measure ;
Life will feel it every weary mile !
O you, who were so kind and so forgiving,
If I grieved you, how my heavy heart hath bled !

* Beutenberg.

Ah ! and though unloyal hours may wrong the living,
We never think unkindly of the dead !
Friend in need, O consolation of the mourner,
Faithful heart, who suffered unremoved !
You leaned upon the Faithful, not a scorner ;
You loved well ; yea, and you were well-beloved.
A little lamb is playing in the orchard,
Faery gleams are fleeting on the hill ;
There is a breadth of lilac in the churchyard,
And the dead are lying very still.
All the vernal loveliness a shadow
Of lovelier havens wherein you abide,
Cooler woodland water, warmer meadow,
In the love of Him, who healed you when you died !
Faded letters, and our pilgrimage in dreaming
Raise the dead, more dear than living men,
For, however we believe it only seeming,
Night brings them warm and real to our arms again !
It may be, mother mine, when you departed,
White and silent, that you did not wholly go,
Never left your children broken-hearted,
Help them more, are nearer than they know.
And your remembered tones are more than music,
More than day the memory of your smile ;
Clear from all the cadences of sorrow,
May I hear them, and behold them in a little while !
Our eldest, and our youngest, are they gone now ?
For a moment I may linger by the grave ;
It may be that my day is nearly done now ;
Lord, I would have them yonder ; heal, and save !

SEVERN, FRIEND OF KEATS.

SEVERN, dear Severn, friend of our boy-bard,
Thy hallowed offices of love for whom
Through that long closing agony in Rome
Outshine bright beams of great verse we would guard
Among the soul's regalia unmarred,
Thy patient loving care in that dark doom
That fell on Keats, the singer, doth illume
Our night of life above the noblest word
Of noblest poet ; yet I love the boy
Who sang and suffered, saw the glorious sight
Behind the poor appearance, child of light,
Told some of his high vision, nursed a joy,
Undreamed by those who stoned him, sons of earth,
Denying, hating, envying his high birth.

TINTAGEL.

TINTAGEL, from thy precipice of rock,
Thou frownest back the vast Atlantic shock !
Yet purple twilight in cathedral caves,
Moulded to the similitude of waves
Tempestuous by awful hands of storm,
Along whose height the formidable form
Of some tall phantom stands on guard, huge boulders
From iron crags reft, toys of ocean shoulders,
And thine own venerable keep that yields
To slow persuasion ancient Nature wields,
Inevitably sure, forebode thy fall ;
For she compels the individual
To merge in the full manifold of Her
His cherished privacy of character.
And therefore Arthur's ancient ramparts range
From human fellowship to Nature, change
To semblance of the fretted weathered stone,
Upreared by mystic elements alone.
That old grey church upon the sheer black crag,
Where generations under the worn flag,
Or in God's acre sleep !   There one dark morn
I worshipped—heights of heaven all forlorn

With drifts confused, wild wind, and the blown rain.
I mused of those who in the lonely fane
Halted world-weary through the centuries,
Kelt, Saxon, Norman, English; on their eyes
The dust of Death; oblivion holds the psalms,
Where now in turn we celebrate the calms,
The Sabbath calms, with hymns and chaunted prayer;
But what indignant wail of wild despair
Storms at the doors and windows, shakes the walls?
Before the void unsouled sound that appals
Our human hymns in that dim sheltered place
Seem to fall low, to cower, and hide the face.
Awhile faint praise wins victory; uproars
On overshadowing vans without the doors
Whirlwind insurgent, as in awful scorn,
To be controlled no longer, nor forborne,
Of poor brief fluttering human hopes and breath,
Played with a moment by the winds of death,
Ere dissolution and dismemberment
In the undivine, dim void where all lie shent,—
A shivering foam-flake, or a timid light
Spat upon by the rains, extinguished quite !
We laugh in fair pavilions of light love,
Or worship in the solemn sacred grove ;
We rest in warm affection built to last :
And all will leave us naked to the blast !

What means the wind ?   Yon ruin's proud decay—
We know not who in far-off years did lay

The strong foundations : Arthur, Guinevere,
And Launcelot, were they indeed once here?
Are all fair shadows of a poet's dream?
Or did they ride in the early morning beam,
Armed and resplendent, radiant within,
Champion redressers, quelling tyrant sin,
Slaying grim dragon Wrongs, who held in ward
The maiden Innocence : from Joyous-guard,
Camelot, or Tintagel, brave and glad,
Did they indeed ride, Launcelot, Galahad?
Have lawless love, and Modred swept to ground
That glorious order of the Table Round?
Who knows? they are but creatures of the brain;
Or if they were, behold our mightiest wane
With all their sounding praise, like dream-shadows,
Storm-rack that drifts, or billowy foam! none knows
Whether they were, or were not; sombre keep,
And chapel crown twin crags, one ruin-heap,
While the sea thunders under, and between,
And cliffs no hand hewed mimic what hath been
In weathered buttress, pinnacle, and tower!
Where now the prancing steed, the ladies' bower?
No clang of arms, no battle-bugle blown,
Only in sounding cave the wild sea clarion!

But then my heart responded to the blast,
I deem that in those clouds of the dim past
Tall god-like forms loom verily; with us
Dwell souls who are not less magnanimous.

They pass, yet only to be self-fulfilled ;
They pass, yet only as the All hath willed,
To enter on their full-earned heritage,
More righteous, and momentous wars to wage ;
And if these heroes were not, then the mind
That holds high visions of our humankind
Is mightier than mighty winds and waves,
And lovelier than emerald floors of caves.
Nature herself is the high utterance
Of holy gods ; we, half awake in trance,
Hear it confused ; through some half-open door
We hear an awful murmur, and no more :
We are under some enchantment ; lift the spell,
What mortal then the wondrous tale may tell ?

Tintagel, 1884.

NOTES.

———◆———

LYRICS.—The Lyrics on pages 3-16 have not till now been published in a volume.

LOVE—TO A.—Reprinted, by permission, from *Lippincott's Magazine.—Page* 17.

WAS IT WELL.—The Lyrics on pages 19-62 are from "The Red Flag," "Songs of the Heights and Deeps," "A Modern Faust," and "The House of Ravensburg, a Drama."

MYSTICAL POEMS OF NATURE.—Some of these poems are from "A Modern Faust," "Songs of the Heights," and "A Little Child's Monument," and some are printed for the first time.

THE SEA, AND THE LIVING CREATURES.—From "A Modern Faust."—*Page* 76.

SIREN BOWERS, AND THE TRIUMPH OF BACCHUS.—From "A Modern Faust.—*Page* 167.

THE NILE, AFRICA, AND EGYPT.—From "Livingstone in Africa," an Epic Poem.—*Page* 177.

REFLECTIVE, PHILOSOPHICAL, AND ALLEGORY.—From "A Little Child's Monument," "The Red Flag," and "Songs of the Heights."—*Page* 285.

ELEGIAC.—These Lyrics are from "A Little Child's Monument," "Songs of the Heights," and "A Modern Faust."—*Page* 337.

24

NOTICES OF THE PRESS.

"With these words I quit what seems to me one of the most remarkable products of poetico-philosophic genius in the literature of our prolific century."—J. A. SYMONDS on the "Modern Faust and other Poems" (*Academy*).

"The poem appears to me to exhibit much power, with high moral aims."—Rt. Hon. W. E. GLADSTONE.

"The exaltation of enthusiasm, which distinguishes Goethe, Wordsworth, Shelley, appears rarely in their contemporaries and successors. Only perhaps in Roden Noel does the cult of nature rise to the fervour-point of philosophical and religious inspiration . . . No one will deny the fact that literature in our age is penetrated through and through with a sympathy for nature which we do not find in the literature of the last century, and which culminates in the poetry of Wordsworth, Shelley, and Roden Noel."—J. A. SYMONDS, in essay on "Landscape" (*Essays Speculative and Suggestive*, vol. ii.).

SONGS OF THE HEIGHTS AND DEEPS.

"He is clearly as natural in his utterance as a modern poet can be. He has something of Byron's impatience of technical restraint, something of his fervent flow of words. He has already won a deserved place among the few who write verse to express emotion stirred by the sufferings of man, and the terrible riddle of his destiny . . . He has words to say, and they are words of cheer . . . 'The City of Dreadful Night' is scarcely more terrible than this awful picture of modern Babylon, 'A Lay of Civilisation, or London.'"—(COSMO MONKHOUSE, in the *Academy*.

"These are signs that Mr. Noel is doing what Wordsworth, and even Tennyson were compelled to do—he is creating his own

audience. This volume contains poetry too monumental and
memorable not to stamp an enduring impression upon the mind
of every reader . . . Mr. Noel has all the notes of a true poet.
. . . He has many of the notes of a great poet. Those qualities
in his verse which we naturally associate with greatness have
been the very qualities which have largely helped to make his
work 'caviare to the general.' . . . The two sea-pieces,
'Thalatta' and 'Suspiria,' which, with the sonorous music
of their buoyant and bounding verse, fill our ears with the
eager onset of the wave, and make us free of the wonder and
mystery of the ocean . . . We could readily forgive even more
serious defects in a volume containing the magnificent 'Temple
of Sorrow.'"—*Manchester Examiner.*

"There is no such thing in it as an empty, aimless phrase.
Thought is packed, sometimes even crowded, into the rich, magnificent lines. Epithet follows image with such tireless haste
that the reader's brain is dazzled with the masses of treasure
that are poured out around him. Now sorrow, desolation, and
doubt, and anon faith, triumph in acquiescence, form the
burden of the song."—*Literary World.*

"Il nous plaît aussi d'entendre se prolonger les chants de
l'ancienne lyre, de celle on si longtemps, de l'Edda à Shakespeare et à Byron, et de Byron à Browning et à M. Roden Noel,
vibrèrent et vibrent encore ces trois cordes alternantes, a notes
profondes on suaves, sentiment du sublime, sentiment du
tragique, sentiment de la nature.
"En ces trois termes tient le nouveau volume de M. Noel.
'A Lay of Civilisation, or London,' est une terrifiante peinture de
la Babylone Anglaise. Plus loin se dresse le 'Temple of Sorrow,'
immense nef symbolique et douloureuse batie des angoissies de
tous les déchirés d'ici-bas. La pièce intitulée 'Beethoven,' une
des plus belles que je sache dans la poésie Anglaise contemporaine, répond comme un chant d'orgue au colossal appel des
symphonies du maître, et les résume en larges vers aériens, et
grandioses."—GABRIEL SARRAZIN, in the *Revue Contemporaine*,
April 1885.

"There is in all M. Roden Noel's work, when fully representative of his powers, peculiar individuality. It is always marked
by great and very obvious earnestness and sincerity, and is
entirely free from any affectation or trick."—*Saturday Review.*

"Whatever may be said of his large utterance—which, in its
breadth of sympathy, its force of satire, its affluence of music,
reminds us of the utterance of Victor Hugo—this, at least,

cannot be said of it, that it is a voice and nothing more. Many are the spells of the singers of the day which are not Mr. Noel's, but he has his own enchantments; and we have endeavoured to draw within his circle those who, with us, are prepared to welcome any poetry that by virtue of its imaginative force, directness, and breadth, stimulates thought, deepens sympathy, and uplifts and upholds aspiration."—*The British Quarterly Review*, October 1883.

A LITTLE CHILD'S MONUMENT.

Fourth Edition, Small Crown 8vo, Cloth, 3s. 6d.

UN POETE PHILOSOPHE EN ANGLETERRE.—"Cette sincerité, cette absence de toute pose dans l'expression de la plus intense douleur on la trouve à un degré peu commun dans 'A Little Child's Monument.' . . . *Lament* qui dans sa simplicité presque sacrée, mais déchirante, est d'une incomparable beauté de forme. . . . La mélodie, la musique du vers est presque toujours d'une grande beauté chez M. Roden Noel. . . . A côté du père et du poète, toutefois, il y a le philosophe. Le chercheur, le savant, a sans doute été conduit par la souffrance à essayer du moins de pénétrer à nouveau le mystère des choses. . . . Il faut lire 'Southern Spring Carol' pour comprendre comment il sait penetrer jusqu'à l'âme même des choses."—From *Le Parlement*, Paris, June 10 1882.

"We do not know where, in all the range of English poetry, to look for so forcible an expression of utter grief as is presented in some of the poems."—*Scotsman*.

"One of the few remarkably gifted poets of our time. . . As a poem of the affections, the 'Child's Monument' has hardly ever been surpassed."—*Daily Review*.

"It may fairly take its place beside 'In Memoriam' as a book of consolation for the bereaved."—*Leeds Mercury*.

THE HOUSE OF RAVENSBURG:

A DRAMA.

"This story is much more powerful than appears in the foregoing narrative, and in its presentation of vague terror recalls the famous verse of Dobell—
'O Keith of Ravelston, the sorrows of thy line.'
Portions of the treatment are fine, we might almost say splendid, from the poetical standpoint."—*Athenæum*.

"Taken as a whole, the picture of Sigismund, both before and after death—Mr. Noel assumes Shakespeare's licence, and brings Sigismund back to us from the other world, and, even bolder than Shakespeare, undertakes to show us his character still undergoing change in that world—seems to us one of very considerable power. The following passage, for instance, spoken by Sigismund the disembodied, and presenting the central idea of the play with great fire, seems to us a noble one."—*Spectator.*

"The scheme of his poems, his line of thought, the rhythm of his verse, are all his own, the direct working out of his own bent."—*Examiner.*

LIVINGSTONE IN AFRICA.

Small 8vo, Limp Cloth Extra, 2s. 6d.

"We should say that if any one wants to imbue himself, as far as the medium of language will enable him to do so, with the moral and physical nature of this great unknown world, he can hardly do better than study Mr. Noel's poem."—*Spectator.*

"Without tumult, but with epic fulness, and definiteness of articulation and relief, and choice of what is most significant in incident or circumstance, the poem moves harmoniously to its close. Certainly the purest, and perhaps the most brilliant of modern poetical colourists, he presents us in these transcripts of polymorphous African life with passages of tropical beauty, of tropical grandeur."—*Scotsman.*

"His qualities as a poet appear to be a passionate and catholic sympathy with human life, a power of seeing the romance of contemporary history, a faculty for describing grandiose effects of tropical scenery, and a peculiar skill in the employment of strange and sonorous local names. . . . Few poets have used scientific guesses or discoveries more felicitously than Mr. Noel in this passage. . . . This is surely stately and admirable verse, and it would be easy to find many passages to match it in the long soliloquy in which Livingstone reviews his life, his hopes, his love of humanity, of mystery, and adventure. . . . Pictures of the greatest originality. The account of a savage execution has the *verve* and colour of Henri Regnault's best known work.'
—ANDREW LANG, in the *Academy.*

BEATRICE,

AND OTHER POEMS.

Foolscap 8vo 7s.

". . . La distinction de votre Muse, soit qu'elle se développe dans des drames touchants, soit qu'elle se complaise à de charmants paysages et à des pièces exquises comme les *June Roses*, vous sentez tendrement la nature et vous la rendez d'une manière bien vive. Il y a dans votre volume un morceau à part et que des amis à qui je l'ai montré préfèrent à tout, c'est ce petit chef-d'œuvre de 'Ganymede.'"—*Sainte-Beuve.*

"The slenderness of the subject conceded, writing more exquisite it would not be easy to find in contemporary poetry. . . . For a companion picture nearly as delicious, and perhaps more compressed, we should have to go back to Coleridge. Out of Coleridge, moreover, it would not be easy to find any philosophical poetry finer than certain portions of Mr. Noel's 'Pan'—a poem very striking and quite original—forming a sort of grandiose pantheistic hymn to Nature. . . . As mere blank verse it is very striking, resonant, grandiose, and full of emotion. Some of the lyrics, all of a very fragile intellectual beauty, are very musical indeed. In moods like these—in a softly tinted sentiment, closely akin to his delicately sensuous feeling for natural colour—Mr. Noel has no rival. . . . 'Ganymede,' an idyl thoroughly Greek, a bit of work which reads like Theocritus in the original. Artistically a finished gem, it remains in the eye like a small Turner."—*Athenæum.*

"Beatrice is in many respects a noble poem : it displays a splendour of landscape painting, a strong definite precision of highly coloured description, which has not often been surpassed. The most intense and tender feelings are realised, and some of the more exquisite and evanescent moments of emotion are seized and represented by the poet with felicity. . . . In 'Ganymede' there is no less faculty of poetic vision than in 'Pan.' So vivid is the representative imagination in this poem that we seem, while reading it, to be looking intently at an old engraving—say of Marc Antonio, after Michael Angelo. In the severity and decision of its outline this picture is classical, but the outline is filled in with modern brillancy of colouring."—*Pall Mall Gazette.*

"The following lines from a poem called 'Summer Clouds and a Swan' are, in their own vein, probably as exquisite as any word-picture in the English language. . . . This really splendid passage, in which the subtle harmonies of sense and thought find a worthy expression in clear transparent words, is characteristic. He excels in delicate colour, floating suggestiveness, and dreamy imaginative beauty."—*Guardian.*

THE RED FLAG,
AND OTHER POEMS.
Small 8vo, 6s.

"There are poetry and power of a high order in the volume before us. There are fine sympathies with the sorrows of London life and wonderful knowledge of them. Perhaps one of the most solemn, awful poems of the present century is ' The Vision of the Desert.' . . . Let his imagination and metaphysical faculty be well yoked and guided by his own cultivated taste, and we must all admit the advent of a great poet."— *British Quarterly Review.*

"It is probably upon the compositions of the third and fourth sections that the reputation of Mr. Noel as a poet of marked originality will ultimately rest. The situation of ' The Red Flag' is finely conceived and powerfully presented. The sincerity of the poet, his intense feeling for the terrible, the realism with which he has wrought every detail of his picture, and his passionate sympathy with the oppressed, make the general effect of this poem very impressive. In 'Palingenesis' and ' Richmond Hill' and the ' Sea Symphony' Mr. Noel exhibits a rarer quality of artistic production. These poems are steeped in thought and feeling: Nature is represented with the most minute and patient accuracy, yet each description is pervaded with a sense of the divine mysterious life that throbs within the world. We need to travel back to the Bhagavadgita or to take Walt Whitman from the shelf if we seek to match the pantheistic enthusiasm of the climax to 'Palingenesis.' The promise of Mr. Noel's earlier poem in this style, ' Pan,' is here fulfilled."—*Academy.*

THE SCOTT LIBRARY.

Cloth, uncut edges, gilt top.   Price 1/6 per volume.

ALREADY ISSUED.

Romance of King Arthur.

Thoreau's Walden.

Thoreau's Week.

Thoreau's Essays.

Confessions of an English Opium-Eater.

Landor's Conversations.

Plutarch's Lives.

Browne's Religio Medici.

Essays and Letters of P. B. Shelley.

Prose Writings of Swift.

My Study Windows.

Lowell's Essays on the English Poets.

The Biglow Papers.

Great English Painters.

Lord Byron's Letters.

Essays by Leigh Hunt.

Longfellow's Prose.

Great Musical Composers

Marcus Aurelius.

Epictetus.

Seneca's Morals.

Whitman's Specimen Days in America.

Whitman's Democratic Vistas.

White's Natural History.

Captain Singleton.

Essays by Mazzini.

Prose Writings of Heine.

Reynolds' Discourses.

The Lover: Papers of Steele and Addison.

Burns's Letters.

Volsunga Saga.

Sartor Resartus.

Writings of Emerson.

Life of Lord Herbert.

THE SCOTT LIBRARY—continued.

English Prose.

The Pillars of Society.

Fairy and Folk Tales.

Essays of Dr. Johnson.

Essays of Wm. Hazlitt.

Landor's Pentameron, &c.

Poe's Tales and Essays.

Vicar of Wakefield.

Political Orations.

Autocrat of the Break-fast-Table.

Poet at the Breakfast-Table.

Professor at the Break-fast-Table.

Chesterfield's Letters.

Stories from Carleton.

Jane Eyre.

Elizabethan England.

Davis's Writings.

Spence's Anecdotes.

More's Utopia.

Sadi's Gulistan.

English Folk Tales.

Northern Studies.

Famous Reviews.

Aristotle's Ethics.

Landor's Aspasia.

Tacitus.

Essays of Elia.

Balzac.

De Musset's Comedies.

Darwin's Coral-Reefs.

Sheridan's Plays.

Our Village.

Humphrey's Clock, &c.

Tales from Wonderland.

Douglas Jerrold.

Rights of Woman.

Athenian Oracle.

Essays of Sainte-Beuve.

Selections from Plato.

Heine's Travel Sketches.

Maid of Orleans.

Sydney Smith.

London: WALTER SCOTT, LIMITED, 24 Warwick Lane.

IBSEN'S PROSE DRAMAS

EDITED BY WILLIAM ARCHER.

IN FIVE VOLUMES.

Crown 8vo, Cloth, Price 3s. 6d. Per Volume.

VOL. I.

"A DOLL'S HOUSE," "THE LEAGUE OF YOUTH," and "THE PILLARS OF SOCIETY."

VOL. II.

"GHOSTS," "AN ENEMY OF THE PEOPLE," and "THE WILD DUCK."

VOL III.

"LADY INGER OF ÖSTRÅT," "THE VIKINGS AT HELGELAND," "THE PRETENDERS."

VOL IV.

"EMPEROR AND GALILEAN." With an Introductory Note by WILLIAM ARCHER.

VOL. V.

"ROSMERSHOLM"; "THE LADY FROM THE SEA"; "HEDDA GABLER." Translated by WILLIAM ARCHER.

London : WALTER SCOTT, 24 Warwick Lane, Paternoster Row.

Foolscap 8vo, Cloth, Price 3s. 6d.

THE INSPECTOR-GENERAL

(Or "REVIZÓR.")

A RUSSIAN COMEDY.

By NIKOLAI VASILIYEVICH GOGOL.

Translated from the original Russian, with Introduction and
Notes, by A. A. SYKES, B.A., Trinity College, Cambridge.

Though one of the most brilliant and characteristic of
Gogol's works, and well known on the Continent, the
present is the first translation of his *Revizór*, or Inspector-
General, which has appeared in English. A satire on
Russian administrative functionaries, the *Revizór* is a
comedy marked by continuous gaiety and invention, full
of "situation," each development of the story accentuating
the satire and emphasising the characterisation, the whole
play being instinct with life and interest. Every here
and there occurs the note of caprice, of naïveté, of un-
expected fancy, characteristically Russian. The present
translation will be found to be admirably fluent, idiomatic,
and effective.

London : WALTER SCOTT, LIMITED, 24 Warwick Lane.

SELECTED THREE-VOLUME SETS

IN NEW BROCADE BINDING.

6s. per Set, in Shell Case to match.

O. W. HOLMES SERIES—

Autocrat of the Breakfast Table.

The Professor at the Breakfast Table.

The Poet at the Breakfast Table.

LANDOR SERIES—

Landor's Imaginary Conversations.

Pentameron.

Pericles and Aspasia.

THREE ENGLISH ESSAYISTS—

Essays of Elia.

Essays of Leigh Hunt.

Essays of William Hazlitt.

THREE CLASSICAL MORALISTS—

Meditations of Marcus Aurelius.

Teaching of Epictetus.

Morals of Seneca.

WALDEN SERIES—

Thoreau's Walden.

Thoreau's Week.

Thoreau's Essays.

FAMOUS LETTERS

Letters of Burns.

Letters of Byron.

Letters of Shelley.

LOWELL SERIES—

My Study Windows.

The English Poets.

The Biglow Papers.

London : WALTER SCOTT, 24 Warwick Lane, Paternoster Row.

www.ingramcontent.com/pod-product-compliance
Lightning Source LLC
Chambersburg PA
CBHW030824110726
47900CB00006B/1739